SEEKER THREE

VOYAGES OF THE SEEKER

CLINT HOLLINGSWORTH

DEDICATION

For Ian Dunn. You went far too soon my friend.

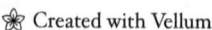 Created with Vellum

1

"Emergence in ten seconds. All hands ready for jump emergence."

I took a deep breath, sitting at the tactical console on the bridge of the *E.S.S. Seeker*. Even though a lot of fine tuning had gone into the ship's jump foil system, all the humans and humanoids on board expected a few moments of serious nausea when we left jump space. The purebred humans always seemed to get it the worst, though my own alien hybrid genetics protected me slightly.

"Everyone, readiness report, please," Captain Yamashita said. The bridge crew barely had time to respond when our vessel made its return to real space.

"Collision alert! Unknown vessel off our starboard bow!" Lieutenant Commander Parul Sharma yelled from the sensor station seconds after we emerged.

"Evasive!" the captain said. "Deflection fields to maximum! Ensign Voss, raise tactical shielding."

"Aye, Captain," I replied, "raising tac shields." I could feel the inertia compensation system straining as it attempted to protect us from the tight turn the ship was making to port. I had my fingers hovering over the panel that would bring all our defenses online, but without the captain's order, all I could do was be ready.

The *Seeker* shook as we hit the edge of the other vessel and were wrenched sideways. Lt. Kolara, at the helm, almost lost his seat, saved from hitting the floor by the safety belt protocol the ship always used during jump emergence. Several red lights began flashing across the bridge consoles.

"We're past it," Torvald said. I confirmed with my tactical sensor readouts.

"Damage report," the captain said, calm in the face of what had the rest of us adrenaline-spiked. The situation could've been a catastrophic disaster.

"Minor hull plating damage in starboard fore-section six," Commander Ivan Solas reported from the engineering station. "Deflection fields saved our bacon, Captain. I'll want my teams to do an assessment of that section, but it appears we were very lucky."

"Glad to hear it," Yamashita responded. "Helm, take us to one tenth sub-light. Comms, hail that vessel and see if they need assistance. Tactical, be ready to engage our defenses if they decide we need chastisement for emerging almost on top of them. Sharma, I need a casualty report. Any injuries?"

"Still waiting for a report from Med-bay, ma'am. However, I don't think we'll be getting a response from the other vessel. I'm receiving no transmissions, and sensors are not reading any power emissions or known life signs. I believe it's a derelict, cold in space."

My tactical board lit up. My lead at tactical, Lieutenant Forbes, saw it too. "Captain, we are seeing a lot of blips out there," he said. "Either there's a lot of space junk in this system or a lot of unknown vessels. I suggest we deploy the Remoras for better scanning."

"Parul?" The captain looked toward our sensor section. "Any danger to our probes if we deploy?"

"I cannot speak about farther distances from us," Sharma replied, "but there is a lot of small debris. I suggest deploying one Remora at slow speed and keeping it near the ship. Even that will allow us a much better view of what's going on in this system."

"And I know just which Remora to send out," the captain replied, thumbing her command chair intercom. "Dora? Are you awake?"

"Always, Captain," our resident Laldoralin AI stowaway replied. "Are we ready to deploy... ah... yes. I'm patched into the ship's sensors and I see the problem. Quite a mess out there."

"It is, indeed. My plan is to bring *Seeker* to a full halt and deploy one Remora probe nearby, running at very low speed so we can get a better look at what we're up against. You game?"

"I am ready, or as my son used to say after watching old westerns, 'I was born ready.'"

Captain Yamashita looked over at me and smiled. "Jargon from a past century, I love it. Dora, you are green for deployment. In the meantime, I will talk to Lieutenant Truval about upping the deflector strength of the other three probes."

"Truval says that I am ready to deploy. Deploying now, carefully of course."

"Helm. Bring us to station keeping."

"Aye, ma'am. Bleeding off forward momentum. We are now at full stop with thrusters at station keeping readiness."

With the ship stopped, we began to get telemetry from Remora Two's advanced suite. Dora had been rewriting her own scanning software, and it now functioned about thirty percent better than the other three Remora probes. I was able to get much greater resolution in the general spatial neighborhood *Seeker* lay in. Scans from farther in this system were still not quite as clear, but we at least had better visuals.

Along with Lieutenant Commander Sharma at sensors, Lieutenant Forbes and I were all receiving enhanced scans now. In the big chair, Captain Yamashita was looking intensely at her master screen.

"My God," she said. "What happened here?"

"It looks like somebody engaged in the war to end all wars," Sharma said. "As bad as the debris is here, it's twice as crowded closer in at the 'Goldilocks Zone' where the third and fourth planets are."

Seeker was on a five-year journey, moving outward from Earth to find new colony worlds. This system was the second we'd visited, having seen planets from afar that looked like ideal candidates either for colonization or terraforming. The problem was that from galactic distances, it was hard to get specifics on the suitability of worlds in our target systems.

Sitting near the edge of this planetary system, it was difficult to get a perfect read on what the third and fourth worlds in this place were like. But even without close inspection, I could see that the fourth world did not look promising. It was hard to say for sure through all the debris, but I wasn't getting any indication of surface water. The third planet was on the other side of the star and it was almost impossible to get much in the way of details from our current position.

"Captain," Dora's voice came over the speaker, "with your permission, I would like to more closely examine the ship we collided with. I believe I can date its time of destruction. It will give us a general time in solar years when this destruction happened."

"And if there is possibly still danger," Yamashita replied. "You are green for close approach, Dora. But be very careful. Whatever wrecked that vessel might still be active."

"Affirmative. I will keep you posted on any finds."

"Let's hope you don't find anything that wants to kill us."

2

Ten hours later, I was laying in my bunk. After a few hours of quiet, the captain had sent me down to my other job in the Remora bay to help the robotics team enhance the defenses of our probes.

Remoras One, Three and Four were now plying the system at one tenth their normal cruising speed. Their Earth-designed intelligences were far inferior to Dora's Laldoralin mind, but they were still some of the most advanced information-gathering systems that our world had ever devised.

Dora, AKA Remora Two, had returned to her bay for the shielding upgrade, while the others took up the slack. She had told me what she'd found and I was relaying this information to my best buddies, Chief Petty Officer Emil Garzon and crew-person Chikit.

"So this happened quite a while back, then?" Emil, a large man with deep black eyes, heavy eyebrows and a 'high and tight' haircut asked. "Looks like a mess, but I'm glad we didn't wind up here when the shooting was going on. I think we all had enough of that back in the Derilon system."

"I must concur, friend Chief Emil," Chikit said in his raspy buzz of a voice that my Padd translated into English. The Zhitin was laying in his hammock set-up, his six arm/legs pulled in tight to his body. "The difficulties with the Beast-named ship/weapons platform that we fought there was near the end of us. Had it not been for Acting-Ensign Tanner Voss friend's digital mother Dora, none of us would now abide on this plane of existence."

Sifting my way through Chikit's tortured sentence structure, I changed subjects. "Anyway, the other Remoras are about halfway to the fourth planet, and what they've sent back is pretty ugly. It looks like that world may have once been habitable but it's been scoured of life. If that's time-consistent with the ship Dora scanned and the rest of the wreckage out there is similar, then the destruction here happened about five Earth-centuries ago. So far, we've found nothing that is using power out there. It's all dead as a doornail."

"As a what?" Emil asked.

"Sorry, Emil. More archaic Earth lingo." He and most of the crew were used to my occasional oddball terms, terms that were perfectly normal when I was a kid, one-hundred fifty years before being stuffed into a cryo-chamber by my Laldoralin father. And essentially abandoned.

"It's funny," I said. "I actually have no idea what a doornail actually is. That term was archaic even back in the twenty-first century."

"When can we expect a report from Third Remora?" Chikit asked.

The captain had sent Remoras One and Four toward the fourth planet, but Remora Three had had been sent toward the system's third world on the far side of the sun.

"I'm guessing... weeks? The captain won't have them use their micro-jump drives for the same reason she's having each probe run at one-twentieth sub-light speed. Just too much debris out there for safety."

"Which means we'll be in this graveyard for months," Emil said. "With scan time and return trips, our probes are gonna be out a long time. Maybe we should just call it with this system and move on. Even if the third world can be colonized, all the junk here makes navigation a hazardous mess."

"Free feel to inform captain of ours of your views," Chitik said, a slight tonal bounce to his voice that indicated laughter. Who knew insectoids could be so sarcastic?

"Ah, no thanks," Emil replied. "If I know Captain Yamashita, she won't let any of us get bored while we're here."

"You got that right," I said. A notification chime sounded from my Padd indicating an incoming text message.

Hey, Acting-Ensign. Can you meet me in rec-room three in twenty minutes? Juicy info to share. - Em.

"Gotta go, guys. That was Emily, and I never like to keep a lady waiting."

———

I knew where Rec-room three was without even thinking about it.

Contrasted with my first week on the ship when I'd needed to constantly look at the mapping program on my Padd to find anything, I'd come a long way.

Moving along the port-side central corridor I came to my destination near amidships. Across from the door to our meeting place, one of the heavy blast doors leading to the safety core of the ship was open. It led to the heavily armored area where most of the important systems were housed.

I turned left into the recreation center, and sitting at one of the tables, looking gorgeous, was Ensign Emily Darkfeather. Tall, raven-haired Emily was descended from leaders of the northern Nez-Perce native nation. Her high cheek-bones sat under heavily-lashed dark eyes that, if I stared into them too long could rob me of the ability to think coherently.

In other words, if you haven't already figured it out, I was madly in love with her. Fortunately, there were definite signs that she was interested in me as well.

"Tanner. Good to see you, acting ensign," she said. "So glad the captain decided to promote you from cadet." It wasn't the first time she'd made that observation. Her eyes sparkled as she said it. Since I was no longer her junior (except in time being an officer) in the command chain, we could explore a relationship without violating regulations.

"A grand day indeed," I said as I sat down. Her hand moved across the table to cover mine, increasing my heart rate a good fifty percent.

"What a letdown, hunh?" she said. "We had hopes of a double-world colony system here and, having looked at all the readouts, I will lay you odds that we write the whole thing off and move on."

"We still haven't had any good scans of the third world. Maybe..."

"I don't know, Tanner. I looked at what Remora Three was sending when I was on shift on the bridge, and the flotsam looks just as thick in the third world's orbit as near the fourth. But I guess we'll see."

"Even if we don't find another single colony world on this trip," I said "we did find Derilon. And Mars is coming along."

"For Mars to be livable, it'll take another century of terraforming.

"True..."

And remember," she said, "Derilon is a shared world with the Dohannen. It's also a water world, and the land masses are smaller than on Earth. There's only so much land-dwelling population it can bear with grace."

"One of the planets here might be fixable, but hopefully the *Wanderer* is having some luck too," I said, referring to the *Seeker's* sister exploration ship. There had originally been three, but the *Searcher* had been destroyed by an Earth For Earth saboteur.

"We'll just have to wait, I guess," Emily replied. "But as I mentioned in my message, I have some juicy news."

"Lets hear it. I'm all ears," I said. "Pointy ones at that, thanks to my father."

"From what I hear, the captain is considering sending a landing team over to the derelict ship we almost hit. I'm assuming that Torvald, being the science officer, will be going and I've sent a note to the XO petitioning to let me go also, since I'm Torvald's assistant."

"Well," I said, pointedly looking out the view port, "I'm certainly not jealous."

Emily lightly punched me in the arm. "That was not bragging, Dingledorf. That was me, as your slightly superior officer, telling you to get off your keister and put in a similar volunteer request. *Carpe diem*, Tanner. And I'd get it in gear before this mission becomes common knowledge."

"Yeah. You're right. Don't suppose you'd like to help me with my query?"

"Sorry, Tanner. In this case, it's something you need to do for you. And difficulty will only make you stronger." She smiled winningly, got up and walked out, leaving me with my Padd.

3

"So let me get the straight," Commander M'Buku, Executive Officer of the Seeker said. "Cadet Voss, er... Excuse me, *Ensign* Voss, you haven't had enough adventure for one lifetime?"

He was referring to our last destination, where I and other members of the crew had found ourselves in the middle of a small-scale war. We'd made it through with only a few casualties, but things had gotten very intense, very quickly.

"I guess not, sir," I replied. "I'm very curious about what we'll find over there, and wanted to be part of the group that gets the first look."

"I can understand that," M'Buku said. "Since I'm going to be leading the mission remotely, I'd like for this to be a very sedate and unexciting little sortie. Unfortunately, we can rarely get the unknown to be so kind as to oblige our preferences. I also reread Commander Torvald's report of your experiences on Derilon and I've decided to bring you along. You know why?"

"I assume my extra-sensory abilities." It was a good idea to bring a guy who could see danger coming before it got there. And who could also hit almost any target you'd care to imagine without having to take the time to aim.

"That," M'Buku said, "and also that you've shown yourself to be level-headed in very tense situations. I do have a question though. How are your counseling sessions with Dr. Cenir coming?"

I had gone through a horrifying event on Derilon, and the captain had ordered me to see our main ship's counselor on a reoccurring basis. The nightmares I had concerning blood and flying body parts still haunted me.

"Honestly, Commander, they were helpful at first, and the doc gave me some good exercises to help cope with the nightmares. Sometimes, though, I have to resort to clipping the 'sleeper' to my head to get a good night's sleep. Dr. Cenir has helped me process some of those awful memories, though. I'm better off seeing her than not seeing her."

"That you realize this is very reassuring. All right, Cadet.. Dammit! I mean Ensign, bring your away gear to shuttle bay two and be there at eleven hundred. Dismissed."

"Aye, sir!"

———

"All right, people," Captain Yamashita said to all of us standing around shuttle *LaStrange*. "If our scans are correct, there should be no active dangers over there. But, as you know, when dealing with unknown alien technology there is always risk. So be careful." She turned toward the First Officer. "Commander M'Buku?"

"As the captain says," M'Buku said. "The main emphasis here will be on Lieutenant Commander Torvald and Lieutenant Grizzak, who will provide engineering input on whatever we find. Lt. DeCosta, Ensigns Darkfeather and Voss, you will be there as support and to look for anything interesting.

Master Chief Kurakin and Corporal Chen will be providing security."

Kurakin and Chen were both dressed in security-armored environmental suits. Everyone else except Grizzak and I were in standard suits. The engineer and I were in Mark 1 engineering suits with a variety of tools stowed on them. I wished I could take a more heavy duty Mark II.

"When we get there, Sec-Force will lead. The rest of you will follow and until you get the go-ahead to do so, you will not leave the group. Let's stick together. Any questions?"

"Chen and I will board last, Commander," Kurakin said. "I need a few moments to brief my team on *Defender*."

"Understood. Everyone else, into the shuttle and strap in."

As we all started up the back ramp, Chief Kurakin walked over to the *Seeker's* Sec-Force assault shuttle to have a word with her people. I could see four of her team already in heavy duty armored Godzilla suits attached to the outside of their shuttle.

"Wow," I said to Emily. "The captain's definitely not taking any chances on this one, is she?"

"After what happened last time, do you blame her? Things on Derilon would've gone a lot smoother if we'd had Sec-Force with us from the get-go, wouldn't they?"

"Definitely."

We walked into the shuttle, stowed our gear, and each took a seat, then locked ourselves in. Kurakin joined us a few minutes later.

The shuttle bay's doors retracted and I could see the blue glow of the environmental force field that kept the bay pressurized. A few moments later, we flew through it, and were in deep space. Far, far in the distance, I could see the system's Sol-like star, one of the brighter dots in our area of the cosmos.

You think of space as dark, but we're in a very brightly

star-lit galaxy inside of an even larger galaxy cluster. Looking closer, I could see a few pieces of large debris, their shadows extending though space away from the sun.

We didn't have long to gawk, though. The huge bulk of the alien vessel came into view through my port and as we drew closer, blanking out half the viewable area of space we were in.

The other craft was at least twice the size of *Seeker*. And as it spun slowly in space, I realized that we were only seeing a section of a much larger ship. Evidently, a good part of it was missing, one end of the vessel looking like it had taken a nuke. Huge twisted sections of the outer hull starred out jaggedly in this area, with exposed girders and melted cabling gently spinning with the rest of the ship. We definitely weren't going in on that end.

"Chief," I said to Kurakin, "those look like weapon pods there on that section, don't you think? Almost analogous to *Seeker's* defense laser pods."

"Could be," our resident valkyrie replied. "They have the same general look, but remember Ensign, this is an unknown species we're dealing with. It is unwise to make any conclusions until we have a lot more data."

Kurakin had been assigned the role of mentor to a certain cadet, AKA me, who had been jumped out of his fourth year at the academy to a deep space mission. Now that said cadet was an acting ensign, she still tended to speak to him like he was a remedial student. I was used to it.

"Roger that, Chief," I replied. "But if those aren't particle cannons..." I gestured to structures just coming into view around the edge of the alien vessel, "I will eat my rank insignia."

"And look over here," Emily said from Kurakin's other side. "Those sure look like some sort of missile launchers, and hookidookdaw, are there ever a lot of them."

"Language, Ensign," Kurakin said. "I don't care if you're cursing in Kiffalan, we're still on duty. But, if I had to make a snap judgement, I'd tend to agree with you. Those definitely look like launchers, a plentitude of them."

"Then we're very likely looking at a warship, then," I said, trying to get my face closer to the port for a better view."

"With this much wreckage in the system," Corporal Chen interjected, "that should not come as a surprise."

"Hang on, team," our pilot said over the loud speaker, "I think we've found our infiltration point. There's a hatch just ahead, though you all will likely have to go EVA to access it while I magnetize to the hull."

Kurakin walked to the fore section of our compartment and spoke through the open hatch to the pilot area. "Closing you in now, Sam," she said to the pilot, and activated the hatch. "Everyone seal up and set your comms to standard channel one. I will depressurize in a count of sixty. Everyone double check your thruster packs are active before we evacuate the shuttle."

Everyone performed a comm-check within the group and double-checked on the small heads-up display (HUD) in their helmets that they had active thrusters. One minute later, the air pressure in the cabin began to drop.

We all felt the *thoom* sound of the metal-to-metal touchdown. Kurakin activated the rear hatch and it swung down to touch the surface of the unknown vessel, forming a ramp. Chen and the chief went out first, mag boots keeping them anchored. Kurakin clipped a cable onto an o-bolt on the shuttle's exterior, secured herself to it, and took a tentative step onto the large ship's hull. It didn't go quite as expected.- Taking a few tentative steps, the chief began to float up from the alien hull.

"Crap!" she said, "This damn thing is non-magnetic. I don't know what its made of, but my boots aren't sticking.

Everyone please stay in the shuttle while I fumble my way to the hatch to see if there's something there for me to clip this line to."

While the rest of us stood on the shuttle's ramp, Chen's voice came over comms, "If we can't mag to the hull, how is Sam keeping the shuttle here?"

"Note the blue-ish glow under the shuttle, Corporal?" Commander Torvald said. "Our pilot is using the shuttle's grappler field on a low setting to keep the shuttle adhered to the hull. The grappler isn't magnetism based."

"Ah. Of course. I should've seen that."

We were on the sunny side of the derelict, and a shadow passed over us. I looked up from where we stood and saw the assault shuttle *Defender* move into position above the hatch, Godzilla suit personnel locked onto its sides.

"This is *Defender*, we are on station and ready to support," the pilot commed.

"*Defender*," Torvald said. "Release the hounds!"

A chuckle, then: "Aye sir, sending down float bots K-3 through K-10."

A flat, somewhat emotionless voice then joined the comm chatter. "This is robotic assistant K-3, I am lead for this robotic team. Other K-team members will report though me. We are deploying to Chief Kurakin's position."

Though our Earth-made AIs were light-years behind Dora's Laldoralin abilities (and intellect) they were still advanced computing systems. While unable to think creatively, their 'if-then' computing abilities sometimes made them seem almost alive.

"To me, my minions," Kurakin said, surprising me. I hadn't realized she had anything resembling a sense of humor. "K-3, I need a ringbolt attached to the hull right here."

The float-bots drifted down to her position, tiny micro-thruster flares emanating off their spherical frames. One of the bots extended what looked from a distance like a weapon barrel, and a puff of dust lifted from the large ship's hull when it fired. Kurakin moved over to it and clipped the cable to the now resident o-bolt.

"Commander, we are green for EVA."

"Thanks, Chief," Torvald said. "Everyone clip on if you haven't already. Single file over to Chief Kurakin. One at a time, move slowly. If you start drifting, don't panic, we'll pull you back down. Plus, everyone should be well up on EVA thruster use. No worries, people!"

Emily nudged me and surreptitiously pointed a finger toward Torvald. I took that to mean that the commander perhaps hadn't been keeping up on his deep space sim time and was convincing himself.

We had no difficulties reaching the hatch. Before all of us had reached that point, Torvald and Grizzak were surveying the hatch to see if there was an easy way in.

"There's a panel here that I'm sure powered this thing," Grizzak said. The hairy humanoid from Galas-Pa was trying to find some sort of access port through which we might provide power to open the large hatch. I could see openings that might've been for that purpose, but other than shooting lightning into them, I didn't see how any of our gear could send a power feed to them.

"We may need to get more creative," Lt. DeCosta said. The petite shaven-headed lieutenant and I had sort of gotten off on the wrong foot when I'd first come aboard, but now that I was no longer considered a cadet, she no longer sneered in my direction. At least not that much.

"What do you see, Laura?" Torvald asked.

She pointed to four interlock-style protrusions around the hatch. "These look like they secure the door closed, sir. These outer bits on the hull lock into the inner sections residing on the hatch, if I'm reading this right. I know we're trying to use finesse here, but maybe we might cut it apart and remove the outer mechanism. If they're locking the thing in place, once they're gone, maybe we can then just brute force the hatch open."

"Well," Grizzak said, "it isn't an elegant solution, but I think our young lieutenant might be right. It's not as if the previous occupants are going to object. And to be quite honest, Commander, I don't think we can power this door with what we have. I might be able to build something back on the *Seeker*, but I'm not sure how long that would take."

"Kind of silly to put your locks on the outside of the door, but let's put Laura's idea to the test. K-3? Which of you have a plasma cutter onboard?"

"K-5 and K-6, Commander."

"All right, then. Grizzak, guide these two in how you want the cutting done. Everyone else, move back down the line a bit while our bots do their job."

As we all stood back and the bots began to cut, my peculiar abilities seemed to give me a quick touch. It was so faint and so generalized that I couldn't do anything with it. It was almost as if my gift had pinged me just to say, "Keep your eyes open."

Fifteen minutes later, the locking mechanisms were drifting away and the float-bots were working in unison to pull the hatch open. They quickly found that it was a rolling door and began moving it into its recessed open position.

"*Seeker*, this is Torvald. We have gained access. Sending some of our bots in to take a look. Will keep you posted on any discoveries."

"Proceed, Commander," the captain commed back. "Be careful in there. No accidents please."

"Roger that, Captain. We're going in."

4

Needless to say, it was very dark inside. The K-bots went in first with every light on their frames set to full, and the darkness receded. Kurakin and Chen went in next while the rest of us twiddled our thumbs waiting. A few moments later, Kurakin sent an all-clear signal and we filed into the large corridor leading from the hatch.

A few steps in, I tentatively put a foot down on the deck plating and was pleased to find my boot magnetizing.

"Everyone touch down on the deck," Torvald said. "Evidently, whatever the interior is made of is a different material than the outer hull."

"Nice," DeCosta said. "I wasn't looking forward to careening my way throughout this wreck."

Around twenty yards in, the corridor met another even larger hallway branching both right and left in a T-section. I walked a ways down the left branch, moving out to where K-8 stood in a sentinel position. The space was big enough that a Remora probe could've floated down the center of the corridor with no problem whatsoever.

"All right, everyone," Torvald said. "Even though it's not

whole, this is a big ship and I think we'll want to split up and..."

A gentle cough came over our comms.

"Yes, Chief? You have a better plan?"

"With respect, sir," Kurakin replied, "have you ever watched a horror movie? I really advise that we stay together as a group as the captain earlier mentioned. If you want to send one or two K-bots in another direction, I can sign off on that, but all the flesh and bloods should stick together."

"I will always bow to your wiser strategy, Master Chief. I remember saying on Derilon how much I wished you were with us early on in that little adventure."

"Sir?" Emily said. "May I suggest that we move a little deeper into the ship then attempt comms to *Seeker*? We may not have picked anything up in early scans because of the funky material the hull is made of. The metal in these hall-ways looks completely different."

"And maybe," I added, "send one of the K-bots deeper in to see if our own comms will function within the ship? We can have it continually broadcast until we see if its signal fades as it gets farther from us."

"Not bad ideas at all," Torvald conceded. "K-3, have one of your team move down the left branch, giving us a continual note broadcast so we can test comms. DeCosta, without going back out to the hatch, contact our ship and see how the reception is. Apprise them of our plans and then we'll see how well comms work inside this hulk."

K-8 moved away from us down the branch it had been watching and a low musical note began to play in the back-ground noise of our comm system.

"The *Seeker* is reading us five by five, Commander," DeCosta said. "The captain wants a comm check every five minutes to see if reception degrades."

"All right. Chief? Which way do you think we should go first?"

"We already have a bot out ahead of us to the left. I suggest we follow it. But, seeing how large this corridor is, I'd like to station one of my Godzilla team at this junction. Our security armor has signal enhancers embedded. Could be the difference between good comms or no comms, sir."

"See to it," Torvald told her. "Everyone else, make sure your mapping software is set to record. If things get out of hand, we're going to need to reach this spot without getting lost. So let's make a good map."

A private text from Emily showed on my HUD: *Also will be nice to have if the Godzillas need to come in and bail us out.*

I gave her a covert thumbs up just as DeCosta reported the chief's return. Behind Kurakin was Private Venessa Hodgekins, each step in the huge mech suit thrumming on the deck plating. I glanced down the original corridor behind them and saw another Godzilla-suited figure standing in the hatchway.

"All right, Private," Kurakin said. "You are to hold your position here. Crank your signal enhancers up and you and Keown can act as our relays."

"Just like cell towers," I blurted out.

It is difficult to show what you are thinking when in an EVA suit, but if my companions had looked any more confused, they might've had question mark emojis above their heads.

"Never mind," I sighed. "Not important."

"Ah, the joys of being a museum piece, eh, Tanner?" Torvald said, chuckling. "Looks like we're all set here. Let's follow our robotic friends in pursuit of K-8."

"Hodgekins, we'll be sending your updates on our maps as we go," Kurakin told her. "If we need you on the double, remember not to run any of us over with that suit."

"Roger that, Chief."

———

We walked for ten minutes before we saw our first piece of floating technological debris. No one had expected it to be a weapon.

"Commander," K-3 called us over comms. "K-8 has entered one of the side rooms ahead. Appearances are that it is an armory."

"Have K-8 hold position," Torvald said. "All K-bots send mapping data."

"Sir, we are also scanning energy signatures farther within this vessel's hull," K-3 informed us. "There may be automated defenses still online."

"Hodgekins, do you copy?" Kurakin said into her comm.

"Aye ma'am. I got K-3's last update too."

"Have McKeown move to your position and Nakamura move into his. Send all our data back to the ship, then use your mapping to come join us. I think I'd like to have my back up right at my back. Just don't step on anyone."

"On my way, ma'am."

We moved ahead, coming to the suspected armory. Emily snagged a floating item out of the air (or lack thereof) inside the door.

"Someone try and convince me this isn't a rifle of some sort," she said. She handed it to Kurakin, who gave it a close inspection.

"Look at the barrel, Chief," Chen said. "Those look like emitters on the end, but there sure are a lot of them."

"Shotgun?" I asked.

"You mean like a multi-projectile hunting...firearm?" Lt. DeCosta asked.

"They were used in combat also, Lieutenant, back in pre-uplift days," Kurakin said. "I think you're on to something, Tanner. This spot looks like it might be some sort of insertion point for a power pack."

"I am reading power emanations from that wall," K-3 said. "I project that it is some sort of storage."

I began scanning the aforementioned wall. It was made of numerous slightly upraised sections forming geometric patterns across the wall. Most were the size of a garbage can lid, but I found one that was close to the size of my hand.

"There's a small panel here," I said. "It's different from all the other panels I've seen so far."

"Here's another one," Emily said from a few feet away. "Looks like the two match." We both looked toward Commander Torvald.

"Stand away, you two," he said. "Everyone else, into the corridor. K-3, K-8, I want you to push on those panels."

"As you wish, sir," K-3 replied. I was sure I heard resignation it its tone.

We all backed out into the hall, behind Hodgekins' Godzilla suit. Watching the bots on the viewscreens of our Padds, we waited to see what would happen. Both bots pushed on a pad at separate times, and nothing happened. Next, they pressed simultaneously, and door panels slid out into the walls, revealing a large walk-in closet.

We re-entered and took a good look at what the K-bots had accessed. On each side of a large narrow walkway, battle rifles of various sorts lined the walls. Carefully stacked in cases below them were what could only be the power packs, ready to be inserted into each weapon.

"Quite a variety here," Kurakin said. "More shotguns, and these long ones almost look like what a sniper would use. Some stubby little carbines over here and what have to be sidearms in this section. Whoever they were, they were very well armed against boarding parties."

"But... Is this for defense?" Emily said. "If there are one or two rooms like this, I'd say yes. But this ship looks like it was made for battle, not exploration. If we find a lot of rooms like this one, maybe these weapons are for ground troops. The reason is open to interpretation."

"I guess more exploration of the ship will tell, Ensign," Grizzak said. "In the meantime, Commander, I'd like to get a secure tote-lift in here to tag and bag these items for further examination. I want to indulge in some reverse engineering to see if we can learn anything from these people's technology."

"Indeed, Lieutenant," Torvald said. "See to it. K-3, let's move on and see what other interesting things we can find."

"Y'know what we haven't found," Corporal Chen said. "Bodies. Ship this big, this destroyed, where are the bodies?"

"Well," I said. "The ass-end of this ship is gone, open to space. Nowhere on this little walk have I seen anything resembling an emergency bulkhead. Could everyone have been sucked into space?"

"It's a workable hypothesis, Tanner," Torvald said. "But make no assumptions. This whole ship, hell, this whole system is one big mystery and jumping to conclusions might make us miss important data. Let's move on."

"The bridge is usually farther forward than we came in, sir. Shall we move in that direction?" DeCosta said.

Torvald nodded, and after checking our mapping, we set off farther down the same corridor. It was big enough that Hodgekins, clumping along in her mech-suit, had no trouble with navigating it. The K-bots went ahead, their floodlights illuminating everything floating in the long hall. I shone my own light into a side room, and thought I saw something move.

"Sir, hold on one moment, please," I said. "I want to check something." I pulled my own sidearm from its holster.

"Better wait for... and there he goes," Torvald said. "Chen, back him up."

I had moved through the doorway quickly, and, shining my light around I saw several capsules that looked a bit like high-tech coffins. I stepped forward to examine one when a large black shape landed on me, tangling itself around me.

"Shit!"

"Back away, Voss! I don't have a shot!" I heard Chen yell.

5

"Do not fire!"

"But sir!" Chen said.

"Voss, push it away," Torvald, who'd restrained Chen, ordered.

I put both hands against the bulk and shoved. In the zero gravity, it went easily, drifting off until it hit one of the coffin-like enclosures. I realized I was looking at one of the ship's crew. I also realized it was dead. No wonder my danger sense hadn't warned me.

Not that my heart hadn't almost stopped.

"Wow," Emily Darkfeather said, moving toward the corpse. "Obviously not a member of the Laldoralin Hegemony."

"Voss," DeCosta said. "What were you thinking? We could bring along all the security in the known universe and you'd still try to blunder on ahead."

"Go easy on him, Lieutenant," Torvald said, a slight chuckle in his voice. "I think the point has been driven home. Tanner? Do you need to return to *Seeker* to change your underwear?" The group collectively laughed.

"Er... No sir. Luckily, I went before we came," I said, reholstering my sidearm.

"Lucky for you," Kurakin said, turning toward the corpse to make sure it was truly not a threat.

The alien was large, larger than any known intelligent species. I guessed this was the reason for the tall, wide corridors and doorways. Elongated dust-coated eyes ran from the front to partway around the head. It had two horns that emerged from the lower sides of its head to curve around parallel with its jaw, and a bony-looking ridge ran from between its eyes, over its head, and down its neck to disappear into a lightweight armor tunic.

Its arms had two elbows that bent in opposite directions. It had seven 'fingers,' and Emily, taking hold of one of its twelve-inch-long digits, squeezed the end of it. A four-inch talon emerged then retracted very slowly when she released it.

"I'd hate to have a disagreement with one of these beings," Grizzak said. "And I come from a species with retractable claws!"

"I hear that," Chen said.

Emily was examining the light armor that covered the being, and Kurakin stepped toward her. "Ensign, before you get too involved there, I think we need to..." A bright flair of energy around the alien sent Emily Darkfeather flying away, the zero gravity environment not giving her any resistance. Fortunately, she was headed toward Kurakin who grabbed her and spun in a move worthy of an Aikido master. She gently set Darkfeather down on her feet when the momentum had bled off.

"Holy cats!" Emily said. "Thanks, Chief."

"Are you hurt, Ensign?" Torvald said, moving to her side. "That looked like quite an energy discharge."

"I'm all right. I didn't even feel any discharge, just force as

I was pushed away. Sir, look at our dead friend, there. Do you see a blueish nimbus around it? I think it's got a personal shield!"

This was new. The Laldoralin Hegemony, which Earth was a part of, had shields which used condensed magnetic technology to generate barriers that only a very large conventional weapon (ie: missile, nuclear) could damage, or an extremely powerful beam weapon like that on the *Beast*.

What none of the worlds of the Hegemony had cracked was small scale shielding. Putting up a heavy magnetic field around something as small as a person was too disruptive to living beings, both physically and electromagnetically.

"Looks like its power source must be getting low," I said. "That glow around it is starting to flicker."

"Permission to try something, sir?" Kurakin asked. Torvald, looking though his faceplate at her, raised an eyebrow but nodded his assent.

"Everyone, back off a ways. There might be a ricochet effect," Kurakin said. She shifted her larger battle rifle behind her on its sling and drew her sidearm. *Seeker's* standard sidearms resembled nothing so much as an old-fashioned heavy duty construction stapler. Kurakin made an adjustment on hers and aimed at one edge of the shield. A beam of red orange light leapt from its emitter and hit the shield.

The formerly flickering nimbus grew bright as the shield simply swallowed the particle stream.

"It's not magnetic!" Torvald said. I could see the Commander part of him move to the back and the scientist move to the front. "It's adaptive. It took the energy from your weapon and converted it to increase its own power level. Fascinating! I wonder if it does the same with kinetic energy..."

"Sir," Kurakin interrupted him. "I tested it to see what we were up against. That shield might not stand up to the full fury of one of our Godzilla suits, but any of us in standard gear would be at a huge disadvantage if we ever get in a stress situation with these creatures. I think we need to send it back to our ship for study."

"That means a lot of scanning for pathogens before the captain will let this guy on the ship. I hate removing the dead from their resting places. Seems disrespectful, but I agree, Chief. This tech is too good to not attempt to reverse engineer."

"Sir," Grizzak said, standing just outside the shield. "Looking this armor over, I think that the shield is generated from this belt attachment. If we could get the belt off and send it through decontamination, we might not have to move Mr. Gruesome from his resting place. Only problem is, can we reach it through the defensive field?"

"It's possible," Emily said, "that it might not react to being entered slowly. We haven't smacked it with a wrench yet to see if it's kinetic reactive. But if you can't get to it when the shield is on, how could they receive medical treatment if incapacitated? There must be a way to shut it off remotely."

"That, Ensign," Torvald said, "is a crap-ton of assuming. It might seem logical but remember, everything here is an unknown."

"It might be a moot point, Sir," I said, pointing at the dead being. "Is it my imagination, or is that glow starting to flicker again?"

As we watched, the flicker glow around the dead alien flickered more rapidly, then simply faded away. Grizzak slowly and carefully moved his arm toward the dead being, reaching what appeared to be the buckle on the front of the belt. He carefully examined the mechanism, and a few moments later, the belt drifted off its owner. Kurakin snagged it and put it in a mylar bag.

"K-3," she said, "have one of your team take this back to

our insertion point for pickup. Send video record of every-thing that just transpired to the *Seeker*. And make sure the device is sent through decontamination before it goes on board."

"That is standard procedure, Chief Kurakin," K-3 replied, sounding slightly miffed at being told how to do its job. "I have summoned K-5 for retrieval of this artifact."

"If that's all settled," Torvald said, "then let's continue on to find the bridge of this ship."

———

The next dead crew member we found had curled up in what must've been their form of a fetal position. This one was in the actual corridor and Chen almost tripped over it.

It had adhered itself to the textured deck plating with its claws and curled up into a ball facing downward. This seemed to be in reaction to the rapid decompression of the ship. Unfortunately, with no source of atmosphere, its attempt to stay put hadn't saved its life. The farther we went from the gaping hole in the stern, the more crew we found in this posi-tion. All with the same end result.

"Ugh," DeCosta said. "Please, Lord, don't let me die from mass decompression. These guys never had a chance. I think the next time *Seeker* gets into trouble, I'm going to put on my EVA suit, just in case."

"Actually, Lieutenant," Kurakin replied, "that might not be a bad idea for entire crew. After seeing this, I might just talk to the captain about making that standard procedure. Could save on casualties."

"Commander," K-3 interrupted from a point farther in the hallway. "My calculations indicate that we may have reached the command center of this craft."

We'd come to a heavy-duty bulkhead at the forward end of the long corridor. From the slight edge at the top, it looked to me as if it had dropped from the ceiling to close off the alien bridge from the rest of the ship.

"This was likely to save the command crew when the rest of the ship depressurized," Torvald said, running his gloved fingertips over the bulkhead. "There's a hatch in the center. If I was a betting man... K-3, can your scans penetrate this bulkhead? I'd like to know if there's a secondary wall beyond it."

"Scanning," the bot replied.

"What are you thinking, Commander?" Grizzak asked.

"On *Seeker*, as we all know, we have multiple emergency bulkheads. Each of those bulkheads consists of two walls, which create a small space between them so that the bulkheads themselves can form emergency airlocks. That way, we can access depressurized sections in Enviro suits to make repairs."

"And it wouldn't make a lot of sense," Emily said, "to trap themselves on their bridge with no way to try and get things back in order."

"I can't imagine," I said, "that you'd ever get this ship back in order with the aft section blown away."

"That depends, Ensign," Emily said. "If their reactor is forward of the damage, or if they had a viable secondary power source, you'd think they'd at least be able to come out and seal the breach in the hull, then get their life support system back online."

"I don't know," DeCosta said, looking closely at the seams of the bulkhead before us. "I have a theory, Commander, and it isn't very pretty."

"Let's hear it, Lieutenant."

DeCosta looked carefully at her mapping display. A map of the areas we'd been through was overlaid on an outline of the entire remaining vessel. Our current position was very near the front of the ship.

"Sir, my guess is that all the non-expendable personnel are beyond this door. I was carefully looking for seams of mechanisms as we traveled through this hulk. I was having trouble believing that they wouldn't have done a better job of protecting their crew. What I found were these at various points in the hallway." She handed her Padd to Torvald. "I think those are some kind of forcefield emitters. Perhaps their emergency bulkheads weren't physical in nature?"

"And if the main power supply was in the aft section..." Torvald said.

"Then sir, unless they had a hell of a backup power system, their emergency force fields would have faded very quickly. You note we saw no bodies toward the aft sections. They might've been sucked out before emergency measures kicked in."

"None of that is very pretty, Laura," Torvald said. "But I sense your theory has more to come."

"Yes, sir. It just wouldn't make any logical sense to not have a backup power source. The redundant power supplies on *Seeker* are numerous and spread out over different parts of the ship. I really think there must've been at least one here also, even if it had a limited supply of power."

I looked again at the bulkhead. I turned toward DeCosta. "And it wouldn't make sense really to have a big ol' sturdy bulkhead for a section that had no power for life support."

Laura DeCosta looked back at the bulkhead, her expression distressed. "Commander, to cut to the chase, I have a suspicion that the forcefields didn't fail. They might well have been shut off one by one to conserve power to this forward section."

"Leaving the crew back here hung out to dry," Chen said. "Yeeesh!"

"Let's all remember, this is a theory, albeit a theory that makes far too much sense," Torvald said. "We'll know more if we can get in here and can find a computer system we can access. K-3, relay me to Remora Two."

"Aye, Commander. Accessing. Remora Two is now responding."

"Greeting, Commander Torvald. This is Dora, do you copy?"

"Copy. Dora, we're sending you our notes and recordings to see what you might make of them. Also, how would you feel about navigating your Remora hull... inside a starship?"

There was a moment's silence. "I've analyzed the information sent. I see no difficulties. Shall I join you?"

"I would very much appreciate it. I'll let Sec-Force know to let you through."

It took Dora a good fifteen minutes to navigate the corridor and reach us. Her hull was 24 feet long with a roughly six-foot diameter, but the large hallways gave her plenty of room, as it had Hodgekins in her Godzilla suit.

"We believe this is the bridge," Torvald told her, "Dora, the K-bots scanning ability is only able to penetrate this bulk-head in very low resolution. Can you, with your superior sensors, give us a better idea of what's back there?"

"I will do my best, Commander. If you all wouldn't mind backing away a bit, especially you, Private Hodgekins, I will see what I can see."

"Your reputation precedes you, Vanessa," I said.

"I'll show you why I have a reputation during your next Omni-Te class, Tanner. Also, Mr. Freshly-minted Ensign, it is unwise to taunt someone who currently resides in a Godzilla suit."

I laughed. "Point taken."

"Put a lid on it, you two," Kurakin said. "Give Dora some peace, would you?"

"Thank you, Chief," Dora said. "You try to raise them with a sense of propriety…"

"Or professionalism," Kurakin replied, giving Hodgekins the eye. It's not often you see someone trying to come to attention while wearing a large mech suit.

One of Dora's exterior image emitters came online, and a holographic wireframe of the room ahead began to appear before us. The long half-ovoid space began to fill with furniture and consoles. As Dora's scanning went on, details began to appear on each surface.

"Dora," Emily said, "what are these odd-shaped lumps scattered all around the decks here?"

"Organic in nature, Ensign Darkfeather. If I were to postulate before finishing my scans, I'd say that they were bodies. You see that they are mostly huddled together in groups, possibly to share bodily warmth as life support began to fail."

It was difficult to not project what happened to these beings onto ourselves. I imagined for a moment what it must be like to be stranded in a ship's compartment with air and heat dissipating with each moment. A small shudder went down my spine.

"Dora, is there any way you can get this hatch open?" DeCosta asked.

"The mechanism has a certain amount in common with technology from Galas-Pa, homeworld of Lt. Grizzak. Between the two of us I'm sure we could manage to get it open, but for one problem. There is no power to the system, and without power the only way in is brute force."

"We do have a considerable power source, Dora," Kurakin said.

"Of course. You mean Private Hodgekins' armor suit, I assume."

"You assume correctly. The Godzillas are designed to provide emergency power for command posts or situations just like this one. We just need to find a way to mate the two different power input/output modules."

"Let me scan the door's module more closely... and yes. Lt. Grizzak, I will project a tri-dimensional diagram of an adapter I've designed. If you will verify it, I will send the design back to *Seeker* to be printed."

"Amazingly fast," Grizzak said. He stared at the projected image for a few minutes, his short-fingered hands resting on the sides of his helmet.

"Looks good to me, Dora. I'd just drop the input port a small amount to line up better with the armor suit's cabling, but otherwise, I say green light it."

We all waited while the design was relayed to our ship, then waited some more for the new part to be sent to us. In the meantime, DeCosta, Emily, and I explored spaces off the main hallway. We found what looked like terminals, but without power they were inaccessible. Small items floated throughout the rooms in much greater profusion than they had in the corridors. Drinking vessels, bits of cloth, and small items that looked electronic in nature but which we had no idea of their purpose. We tagged and bagged everything that looked interesting.

After a time, escorted by K-4, crewman Caldwell approached from the corridor, an item in a protective case under his arm. Torvald took it from him and returned the man's salute.

"Thanks, Caldwell. Dismissed."

"Um, sir?" Caldwell asked. "Might I stay awhile? It's my first away mission, even if it's just a delivery. I'd kinda like to see what you all discover."

Torvald considered for a moment. "All right, Barney. Just

stay toward the rear, and of course, absolutely do *not* touch anything. Just observe and record with your Padd."

"Yes, sir! Thank you, sir!" Through his face plate, I could see Caldwell's big grin.

"Grizzak? If you would hook this up properly," Torvald said. "I'd really like to get a look inside their bridge."

6

The alien bridge was a tomb. But it was a tomb with defenses. Kurakin and Chen and I were the first ones into the makeshift airlock. The first two because they were Sec-Force, me because I had my danger sense.

My sense was starting to tingle.

"Hang on, Chief," I said. "There's definitely something."

Kurakin looked at me, then nodded to Chen. "Be ready," was all she said.

The inner door had an access panel, the security of which Dora had already electronically defeated. Kurakin hit the panel and we all carefully peeked around the hatch's edge. The reaction was almost instantaneous.

A large mech-like robot erupted from where it had been folded on the floor. "Geeduk kala, chronor," it intoned in a reverberating metallic voice. It advanced on us with single-minded purpose, long claws ready to grab and rend us. A tri-pointed faceplate glowed a bright magenta color.

Oddly enough, my danger sense began to fade with the robot's abilities. After two staggering steps, its legs folded up, stranding it in position. It's reaching arms slowly slumped down to its sides. As if in frustration, a side panel opened and what looked like a beam weapon emerged.

"Gun!" Kurakin yelled and we all moved to get back behind the inner bulkhead. Chen wasn't quite fast enough and took the weapon's blast directly in his chest.

It didn't even jar him.

Looking down at his chest armor, there was a slight discoloration in the exterior paint. The beam disappeared.

"Chen!" Kurakin called out. "Are you all right?"

"Just fine, Chief. That was some weak sauce it sent my way. I'm not in any distress, but the same can't be said for Robby the Murder Droid over there."

The robot had half folded over after it took the shot, its weapon dangling unsupported from its body. The eye, which had been a bright magenta, now was dully lit with only the barest of light.

"Geeeeeeee Duuuuuukkkk, Chrooooo," it said, its voice slowly fading. Then its eye went dark and it folded back into itself.

"Should we blast it, Chief?" Chen asked.

Kurakin looked at me. "Well, Tanner?"

"My danger sense has all but faded, Chief. I think our friend there has given us everything it had left."

"Keep your weapon on it, Chen, but let's see if the science kids can find anything out from Robby here before we atomize him."

"Roger that, Chief." Chen stepped near the robot, leveling his battle rifle at its head. Kurakin moved about the bridge, looking for turrets or booby traps. Meanwhile, I had my Padd on scan mode and was relaying everything back to Torvald and Dora.

"Commander?" Kurakin said through comms. "I think the rest of you can enter now. We've taken care of the residual security, and everything in here seems to be intact. Nothing is powered, though."

I'd stepped over to one of the huddled corpses on the floor. Scanning, I said, "These guys look a fair amount different than the rest of the crew we've seen so far."

Torvald and DeCosta, now through the airlock, came over to see what I was seeing.

"You're right, Ensign," DeCosta said. "Could these be the actual crew, and the others we saw maybe a boarding party?"

"I don't think so," Torvald said. "They are different, smaller obviously, but look at the head shape. The eyes are the same, and though more vestigial, the horns along the side of the skull are in almost the same position. Their skulls are longer, though."

"Males and females?" I said.

"Since they don't have any gender attributes like on other humanoid species that we've seen, let's not jump to that conclusion. It could be just different sects of the same species." Torvald keyed his comm. "Dora, sending you bio-scans of the crew in here. If you would analyze them and get back to me, I'd appreciate it."

"Affirmative, Commander."

While DeCosta and Torvald puzzled over the dead, I wandered over to the consoles on the port side. Each station had what looked like a high-tech cradle before it. Each cradle looked like it would fit one of the folded-up aliens perfectly. If they used keyboards, these must've been virtual. In front of each set of monitors was a flat glassy area, much like the various controls on the *Seeker*. With no power, however, they could've been a flat surface to serve drinks on, for all I could tell.

"There's definitely some sort of atmosphere here," Emily said. "Oxygen, with large amounts of carbon dioxide and other trace elements. Sir, I think these beings were oxygen breathers. Unfortunately for them, with no life support, they were overtaken by CO_2 poisoning. At least, that's my working theory."

"Rough way to go," Torvald replied. "Almost as rough as the ones aft of this room experienced."

"Commander," Dora said. "I have completed a rudimentary biological analysis, and I can confirm that the two different body types we've seen are of the same species. Their differences are genetic, not gender-based. If cranial capacity is any indication in this instance, I would also postulate that the bridge crew were indeed more intelligent, more cerebral than the beings we've found outside the bridge."

"It's that noticeable?"

"The first group found outside the bridge are much larger and stronger, with a thicker epidermis and longer claws. Their cranial capacity is markedly less than their bridge counterparts, and there is one other thing I can conclude now that I have a sampling across several members of each group."

"Which is?"

"The bridge crew, though all similar, definitely have a variety of genetic markers as one might expect of any species. The beings that we've scanned in the aft sections are identical genetically."

"You're saying the main sections were crewed by clones?"

"I don't see how such homogeneous genetic profiles could have come about in any other way. While there may be other crew we've not yet found that do not fit this profile, every being that we've come across except those on the bridge is a clone."

"And likely expendable in an emergency," DeCosta said.

"We can't be sure of that," Emily told her.

"Not yet, but it sure seems to fit, doesn't it? I sure don't see any of the 'Biggies' here on the bridge, just the 'Smarties.' And Robby the Murder Droid there seemed to be tasked with maintaining security on the bridge, but we saw no other murder droids on our way here. Maybe he wasn't meant to repel boarders. Maybe he was here to enforce discipline on the crew for the officers?"

"Lot of speculation going on here," Kurakin said. "From the exterior wireframe of the ship that our mapping is being overlaid, we've barely explored a tenth of the entire hulk."

"I agree Chief," Torvald said. "Dora? I'd like to task you with finding the main computer. If it's small enough, I'd like to remove it for study back on our ship."

"Why's that, sir?" I asked. "Isn't it more dangerous to us on the *Seeker?* Particularly if it has advanced wireless technology like Dora does?"

"You make a good point, Tanner. But we do want answers, and quite frankly the thought of powering an alien computer on the ship it's supposed to serve, a ship with a lot of weapons, could be the more dangerous path. And sooner or later, if we want answers, we're going to have to power it up."

———

It took us another day to find where the computer was hidden. Kurakin had indicated to Captain Yamashita that she felt it was safe enough on board the *Hulk* (now its official designation) that multiple teams could be sent to explore the disabled ship.

Our team had been pulled back to rest and Lt. Bitt-Nurr, *Seeker's* arachnid computer specialist, had taken up the search along with a couple teams of engineers. Dora and the Sec-Force were still on site providing security and support.

I'd had a good night's sleep, using the small cranial device that Dr. Cenir had given me. That day, I was scheduled to be at my station in the Robotics bay, but as we had no Remoras on the ship and a good portion of our float-bots were on the

Hulk, our staff on duty were having trouble finding things to do. I'd used a little twenty-first century chicanery to get out of boredom by asking Lt. Forbes if he would mind having a day off while I took his shift.

The second part of my nefarious plan was to go to my Robotics supervisors, Lt. Truval and Chief Moreland and tell them that I was needed at tactical. I may have *implied* that Lt. Forbes was not feeling well, but I *didn't* say that outright.

Yes, yes. I know. Not entirely ethical. Have your attorney contact my attorney.

As a result of my evil machinations, I was sitting on the bridge, going over everything that Emily was going over. She sat across the bridge, holding down the science station, filling in for Lieutenant Commander Sharma. Sharma had pulled rank and gotten herself assigned to the away mission on the *Hulk*. Captain Yamashita had the bridge, but she was in her office doing captain-ish things. Lt. Fowler was in charge during her absence, sitting not at the helm, but at the captain's station.

Ensign Darkfeather and I were seemingly ignoring each other, while discussing what we were seeing via covert Padd texting.

"Did you see this, Tanner? They found another murder droid near what appears to be the engineering station."

"That makes four, now. All in important sections of their ship. I'm getting the vibe that these weren't intended for boarders, but to enforce ship's discipline."

"Dora says that they have managed to disconnect the ship's main computer core and are sending it back here. Have they got storage section twelve 'faraday'd' yet?"

"Yeah. The section is as emission impenetrable as we know how to make it. Emily, I wonder if it's going to be a regular computing system or if it'll be an AI like Mom?"

"Only time and a power source will tell."

We were interrupted by incoming data transmissions from Remora One, which was almost halfway to the fourth planet. Remora One had also relayed information from Remora Four, which was closer to the planet they were heading toward. My station was tied into the science station.

"Lieutenant, we are receiving telemetry from Remora One," Emily told Fowler. "Should we inform Captain Yamashita?"

"Inform her by routing a copy of everything that comes in to her office workstation. She'll want to review it all."

"Understood, sir. Routing to Captain's office."

"Excellent." Fowler stood and walked over to where Ensign Darkfeather was receiving the probe's information feed. "Anything interesting coming in from our prodigal drones?"

"Much of it is as we thought," Emily told him. "The fourth planet is in bad shape, but there does seem to be some greenery in isolated areas. That world has been very badly treated, though; the atmosphere is pretty toxic, and not naturally so."

"Industrial or military pollution?"

"From what I'm seeing," I said, looking at the sensor reading on my tactical screens, "I'd say military. Some fairly high radiation levels, and if you look at grids 28, 34, and 56, it looks like they're actually glassed. Few things in nature or industry are going to turn the surface to a crystalline structure."

"Well," Fowler said, "considering the debris in this system, that checks out. If someone was trying to invade this system, though, it's pretty damn stupid to destroy the resources you're trying to take over. Put visuals from the Remoras on the main screen, if you would, Ensign."

"Yes, sir," Emily said. "Transferring to main view screen.

Remora Four is digitally deleting some debris from the view for better clarity."

The view of the far-off planet appeared, showing up brightly against the dark background of space. Though three quarters of what was facing us was in shadow, the Remora was enhancing our view so that the night-side details became visible.

The glassed areas became clear, and Emily began zooming and enhancing those sections. I had a suspicion why, and she proved me right a few moments later. At the edges of the glassed areas, there were definitely geometric shapes that looked like building foundations. These grew fainter toward the center of each area. A few moments later, the captain walked onto the bridge.

"Captain on the bridge!" Fowler said. The five of us manning our stations stood to attention.

"As you were," Yamashita said. "Ensign Darkfeather, it appears to me that this planet was inhabited."

"Yes, ma'am. All indications are that the most heavily damaged areas were population centers of some kind. And Captain? We are also picking up from the debris fields, semi-intact ships that are completely different designs than our nearby derelict. There are also indications that there is more than one completely different design."

Captain Yamashita took a deep breath and released it slowly. "That makes sense. Hard to imagine a war without there being two sides to it."

"No indeed, ma'am," Fowler said.

"Did the ships like the one we're exploring come from in-system," Yamashita continued, "or are they interstellar invaders? Were the third and fourth planets at war? Why all this carnage, and did it all happen in a short time or is all this space junk from multiple incursions over many years?"

"Captain," Emily said, "should I have Remora One divert

to scan the other ships, the ones with the new design? We could learn a lot more if we had closer proximity to the derelicts."

"Make it happen, Ensign. Keep Remora Four on course for the planet. Anything interesting from Remora Three?"

"We're just now getting a feed from Three, ma'am." Emily said as new information appeared on our displays. Remora Three had been tasked with flying around the star to get a look at the third planet. "Very similar to what Remora One has sent. She's still not in line o' sight with the third planet, and won't be for a couple of weeks, but she's still dodging quite a bit of debris on her way in."

"Hold on," I said as an alert appeared on my tactical display. "I've got something with power out there. It's faint, but it's the only object we've seen out there with actual functioning power."

"Is Remora Three close?" Yamashita asked.

"Not too close, ma'am, but within scanning range."

"Science station," the captain said, "concentrate Remora Three's efforts on the powered object as it moves toward the third planet. But let's not get too close. Powered could mean defended, and I don't want to lose an expensive probe to someone's last ditch war effort."

"Yes, Captain," Emily said.

The object appeared on the main view-screen at very low resolution, but the more Remora Three concentrated its capabilities on it, the sharper the resolution became. It was slowly rotating, which made it possible to see every surface except one that stayed stationary and formed a rotational axis for the rest of the object.

"Captain," Emily said, "I believe that the area we can't see very well might be a solar collection array."

"That would explain it being powered after several centuries," I said.

"Don't jump to conclusions, Ensign," Fowler said. "The only vessel we've date-scanned so far has been the one just off our doorstep. That object that Remora Three is doing the fly-by on could be much older or much younger."

"We think that whatever happened here might be the result of a war to end all wars," the captain said. "For all we know, this much space junk might've accumulated over centuries of fighting. We don't know if someone invaded the system, or if this was an intra-system battle."

"Sir," Emily said. "We're getting better scans now as Three has moved closer." She once again put the feed onto the main view screen. "While I can't be sure, it looks like the object has a lot of dishes and scanning equipment. Maybe an early warning system of some sort?"

The captain walked over to the view screen and pointed at details of the object. "And these look like weapons turrets. Whatever it is, it seems it's able to defend itself. Look down here on the lower edge; are those iris hatches?"

"If they're not, they're a very good facsimile," Lt. Fowler said. "And there sure are a lot of them."

"Captain," Emily said. "Remora Three is being scanned. By the object."

I started to feel the familiar tightening in my stomach. It was faint, as if the danger was far away. I closed my eyes and turned to where the feeling became strongest. Sure enough, it was in the general direction we'd sent Remora Three.

"Captain! I'm starting to get a bad feeling about this. The special bad feeling..."

"Ensign Darkfeather!" Captain Yamashita said, turning abruptly toward the sensor station. "Spin up Remora Three's jump drive. Prepare for an out-system translocation. If we..."

"Vampire! Vampire! Vampire!" Emily yelled. "We have multiple launches from the object!"

"Is she ready to jump?"

"Sixty seconds, Captain."

I watched the feed from Remora Three as my gut tightened even more. Her view was zoomed, and I could see multiple small shapes swarming toward our probe. These appeared more like drones than missiles, and a few moments later, beams of bright blue-green began to appear in the intervening space.

"They're firing!" the captain said. "Can we jump?"

"Almost! Just a few more..."

Remora Three's feed cut out. Her transmissions went completely dark.

"Did she jump?" Captain Yamashita asked.

"No ma'am," Emily looked to her commanding officer, her expression stricken. "There was eight seconds left... Those things, they destroyed her."

7

"Obviously, we now know it's a weapons platform."

Commander M'Buku walked around a wireframe of the object that had attacked Remora Three. Our probe had managed to get fairly detailed scans before it was destroyed, and our science teams were going over the data to learn everything they could about this new danger.

"I halted One and Four and they're at station keeping," Commander Torvald said from the far end of the conference table. "Now that we know what to look out for, I have them scanning for more of these things. So far, they've found two more in their general vicinity. We have no idea how many are in the system."

Emily and I were in the meeting because we'd been on the bridge when Remora Three had been lost. Emily still had the remnants of the stricken look she'd had when the probe was lost.

"Ma'am," she said. "I deeply regret losing Remora Three. If there had been just a few seconds more... If I'd been even a little bit faster reacting..."

Captain Yamashita looked at her with what seemed mild

surprise. "Ensign, you are in no way to blame for that probe's loss. I was there. Your reaction time was just fine. My belief is that the only crew member who could've reacted faster happens to be a certain Laldoralin AI."

"Indeed, Captain," Dora said over the speaker. "And even I would've been hard-pressed to get my jump drive spun up in time to avert disaster. Ensign Darkfeather has nothing to feel guilty about."

"What do we know about the sub-weapons that were launched?" I asked, trying to get attention off Emily, whose face was still deeply flushed with embarrassment.

"Definitely drones," Chief Engineer Solas said. The three-dimensional image changed from the platform to a vaguely hornet looking craft. Its tail dropped down and then angled forward with what could only be its beam weapon. "And they are nasty little bastards."

"Commander."

"Sorry, Captain. They are nasty little demons. The beams that had been fired before Three was hit were ranging shots, and each one was as powerful as our point defense lasers for *Seeker*. The size they are, I'd guess that they have a limited number of shots in them, but without a closer look, that's just speculation."

"And there were a lot of drones launched," M'Buku said. "Our scans show that the weapons platform dropped at least fifty out of its tubes. That many drones, firing beams that powerful might well be able to overwhelm *Seeker*'s defenses."

"Are these what destroyed the *Hulk*, do you think?" Commander Torvald asked.

"No," M'Buku replied. "Commander Solas and I took a space coupe out while your group made the initial penetration of the ship's interior. We flew around the destroyed area, and we both agreed that the damage to that ship was an explosive blast. It was most likely a missile, with very a powerful warhead tipping it."

"Very likely from the other ships we found. There are a lot of vessels out there with the same design aesthetic as our neighbor, but there are also many with a completely different design. The *Hulk* is boxy, with a certain dullish, non-scannable hull material, while the assumed opposing force favors semi-flattened ovals with large engine sections mounted on one side. Completely different metallurgy on both types of ships."

A hologram of one of the unknown vessels appeared above the table. It was not as detailed as the others had been since none of our probes had yet gotten close enough to any of them to take deep scans.

"They're almost graceful in their design, aren't they?" the captain noted. "I sure wish we had some way of seeing what happened here. I'd pay real money to know who the aggressor was. And who was native to this system."

"We have an incomplete picture, ma'am," Torvald said. "We'll know more when one of our remaining Remoras gets closer to the fourth world, but we still know precious little about the third planet. I do have a suggestion though."

"Let's hear it, Mr. Torvald."

"Instead of sending One and Four to the fourth planet, maybe we should send one of them out of the system, out of the plane of the ecliptic. Then we can jump it as close as is safe and have our probe penetrate the system from above. Less debris to fight through, and maybe less in the way of defenses to worry about."

"There are some indications of debris even out that far," M'Buku said.

"Yes, sir, but by no means to the extent that there is trapped in orbit within the system. With Dora's help, I'm betting we can find a relatively clear area to jump the probe into. When closer to the plane of the ecliptic, the probe can reduce speed, but I would estimate that this route would allow us to get a look at the third planet a lot faster."

"Captain," Dora said, "I would like to volunteer for this mission. I have improved my scanning capabilities a good thirty percent over the remaining Remora probes. I also have a much better chance of avoiding enemy attacks. I can evade much faster than a Remora controlled from the *Seeker.* I can do this mission with much less risk than sending either of the other probes."

Captain Yamashita sat, drumming her fingers on the conference table and staring at the latest hologram. The silence went on for a while, but no one was willing to interrupt their commanding officer while she considered the options.

"I will keep that under advisement, Dora," she said. "To be honest, I'm thinking about pulling the plug on this system."

"But Captain–" Torvald said. Yamashita raised her hand, cutting her science officer off in mid-sentence.

"No one wants the loss of our probe to have been for nothing, Commander, but we have to look at this rationally. Our main mandate is to find new worlds that might be suitable for Earth to start colonies on. To help relieve some of the population strain our homeworld has been undergoing for the last few centuries. Obviously, though, this planetary system is or at one time was inhabited. If it is still inhabited, then it's out, we're done."

She stood up, keyed something in on the control, and an image of the fourth planet was projected above the table.

"This planet we already know has been through hell. It's been bombarded to the point that the major population centers have been glassed. There is still live vegetation near the poles, and who knows? Fifty thousand years from now, nature may re-take the planet. But for now, it won't support any large life forms, which includes us, and it would be very costly to try to terraform. So, it's a write off for a colony, unless there are no better options found on our entire mission."

"Captain," M'Buku said. "It's not like Goldilocks Zone planets are in abundance in our section of the galactic search zone. We need to see the third planet before we write this system off. With the loss of the *Searcher* before this mission began, the Terran Exploratory Force was cut by a third. That means *Seeker* and *Wanderer* have to make every effort to find new worlds, leaving no stone unturned. With respect, ma'am, not looking closely at the third planet is leaving a big stone unturned."

"I will consider your words, Commander," Yamashita told him. "Now, does anyone else have anything they'd like to bring up in this meeting?" Chief Engineer Solas raised his hand. The captain nodded at him.

"Ma'am, no matter what happens, this little foray into this system is a net gain." Solas adjusted the table controls and three images appeared, replacing the fourth world. I recognized them instantly; they were the weapons and the shield belt we'd found in the Hulk's armory. "These two different weapons that we found, the shot gun and the sniper rifle, are both a lot more powerful and energy efficient than the battle rifles that Sec-Force are currently using. Some of these in hand, and the Dohannen might've not needed our help to take their planet back. I'd like permission to make a version of our own that Sec-Force can use – for defensive purposes, of course."

"It is something," Yamashita replied. "But as you know, we are not a military mission per se."

"Of course, Captain," Solas agreed. "But the crème de la crème is the shield belt. We've found several now, and we're starting to have success at reverse engineering them. I believe that soon, every away team member that leaves the ship could be a heck of a lot safer. There's nothing else like it in the Hegemony. Plus, Bitt-Nurr has the alien computer core onboard and isolated from all our systems. Who knows what we'll learn from that."

"That is definitely something," Yamashita said. "But I sense there's more to what you're saying here."

Solas grinned. He was a medium height man, with almost white-blonde hair and eyebrows. He was normally the most sedate and conservative of officers, but now the excitement he felt showed in every bit of his body language.

"Captain, we've about exhausted the technological scavenging we can do on the *Hulk*. It's now down to Dr. Carstairs and her xeno-archeology team trying to learn about the alien's culture. However, there's a large Ovoid ship only about a million and a half miles star-ward and..."

"Ovoid?" the captain asked.

"That's kind of our nick-name for the second species. Hulkies being what we're calling the aliens..."

"On the *Hulk*."

"Yes, ma'am. There could be a treasure trove of tech on that other ship and even if we don't find that the third planet is habitable, we could make up for our time by making new technological discoveries."

Again, Yamashita sat, drumming her fingers on the table, this time looking out the large window toward the wreck we called the *Hulk*. We all sat waiting until she finally spoke.

"Dora?"

"Here, Captain."

"I am green lighting your mission to the third planet, with conditions which I will discuss in a private meeting with you and Lt. Bitt-Nurr. Commander Solas, if you can provide each member of your away team with these shield belts you're working on, and they are dependable, I will strongly consider moving *Seeker* to the new derelict and letting you explore it. But I'd prefer that those belt shields are working first."

"Great! Thank you, Captain," Solas said. Both he and Torvald looked like kids who'd been given keys to the candy store.

"All right then," Captain Yamashita said. "Everyone get to work."

8

"So what did the Captain want to talk to you and Bitt-Nurr about, Mom?"

We were in the Robotics bay and I was fine-tuning Dora's systems on Remora Two. Though I hadn't known that she and Evan, my dad, were AIs in amazing android bodies when I was a child, they'd always been my parents. Much more so than my genetic Laldoralin father, Krizon, who'd lurked in a subterranean lab deep under our suburban home. This had all been secret, of course, the twenty-first century on Earth definitely not being ready to greet visitors "from beyond the stars" by any means.

The bottom line was she was my mom, no matter what form she was in. Consequently I was doing everything in my power to make sure her mission went without a hitch. As I adjusted her magnetic shielding, I realized she hadn't answered.

"Mom?"

"Tanner, I cannot reveal what was said in that meeting. The captain has classified it as 'need to know' and..."

"And I don't need to know, eh?"

"I'm afraid so, son. Just know that the captain is being very cautious. She seems to be fully committed with my being part of her crew and is concerned for my well-being. It's a refreshing attitude."

"Truly, a member you are of this crew," a voice said from to my right and somewhat below my line of sight. Looking down, I saw my robotics section boss, Lt. Truval entering bay 2, his exo-skeletal suit conveying him though the non-arboreal environment. "Anyone who cannot recognize that, though a created being, a person you are, is unenlightened."

"Well put, sir," I said. "I've run the diagnostics several times now, and she is green to go. The shield enhancements are looking good and her micro-jump drive is giving all optimal readouts. All that remains is attaching her defensive package."

"The first time in use such an addition will be to a Remora," Truval said, climbing a special ladder installed just for his use in each bay. "Ensign Darkfeather's design seems sound, and now will have applications very practical."

Each Remora had attachment points for a variety of modules: extra sensor/scanning packages, robotic arms, small cargo containers. Emily had designed a new module with a powerful micro-laser package for defensive purposes. I'd helped her build it.

She'd designed it after the troubles on Derilon where we'd all wished Dora could've provided air support in a tough situation. The weapons system had an independent micro-fusion core to provide power without siphoning off Dora's energy feed. I and Chief Moreland had finalized the design, and now it was time to put it into practice.

"I think you're good to go, Mom," I said twenty minutes later. "Readouts are all good. Now all that's left is for you to go out and give it a practical test."

"I am ready, Tanner. If you would be so good as to open

the Remora bay doors, I believe it's time to get this show on the road."

Truval and I moved back ten feet, behind the safety line, and I started the bay opening sequence. A perimeter force field appeared between us and the bay doors. (Without force field, the door wouldn't open). The hatches swirled apart and Dora's cradle gently rolled her into space where her maneuvering thrusters could engage.

"I'm clear," she said. "I will give you a few moments to take up monitoring stations before I start testing my new accessories. Bridge, this is Remora Two. I am extra-vehicular and ready to begin testing my new defensive attachments."

"Bridge here, M'Buku speaking," came over our three-way connection. "Dora, you are green to proceed. Do us proud."

"Affirmative, Commander."

Truval and I had made our way to the main monitoring station in the Robotics bay. Connected to the main sensor array, we were seeing everything that the bridge was seeing.

Before her time on Earth, and well before I was born, Dora had seen service as a battle AI, confronting some of the more terrifying species the galaxy had to offer. Her maneuvering now was that of a fighter. None of our other Remoras could have kept up with her.

Flying past a large section of what appeared to be derelict hull plating, she fired three snap shots from her laser as she passed at a high rate of speed. Having fired, she immediately jigged onto a new vector, then another. Practicing evasion, I guessed.

"Wow!" Emily Darkfeather's voice came over the channel. "Nice shooting, Dora."

I looked at the scan of her target. She'd holed the space junk three times, each shot equidistant from the others and forming a perfect triangle.

"What a show off!" I muttered, secretly proud of her skill.

"Why Tanner Voss!" Dora replied. "Jealousy ill becomes you, young man. You're still just mad about all the times I beat you at pool when you were young and I was in my body."

A variety of chuckles came over the comm system. Dora, of course, had to make her comment on a line everyone could hear. Even for an advanced artificial intelligence, I thought she could be remarkably insensitive to my embarrassment. Or maybe she just thought I needed taking down a peg.

Moms.

"Dora," M'Buku said. "There is a field of small debris on a fast-moving course through our area. I'm highlighting it for you. See what you can do to it."

"Affirmative, Commander." Remora Two abruptly changed course, and for a moment, I was struck by how much our probes resembled space sharks.

Dora bore down on the moving debris field, and my indicators told me she'd fired again. She hit one of the small pieces a glancing blow, and it spun crossways to it's original course. A second shot hit another piece, sending it careening in the general direction of the first.

A third shot, again a glancing blow, sent a third piece flying across the field, and I saw what she was doing. Moments later, all three pieces, coming in from three different directions, collided in a flash of released energy.

"Eight ball in the corner pocket," Dora said. "Still got it."

"Yeah," M'Buku said, "I'm siding with Tanner on this one, Dora. You're a total show off."

"Perhaps a little, Commander."

"We're showing all systems green on our end," M'Buku told her. "Ready to go on a trip?"

"No problems on my end, XO. Permission to jump to the established coordinates to begin my mission."

"Stand by, please."

A few moments later, Captain Yamashita's voice came

over the channel. "Dora? Permission granted for jump. Remember, contingencies be damned, you are to take no chances over there. If the situation begins to look dicey, you are to jump immediately to your original insertion point. We'll be moving to take a look at this second alien vessel, but we'll be sure to make a clear spot for you to jump to us when we get there. Remember, safety first. Attach to your comm relay satellite and stay in constant touch."

"Understood, Captain." Dora moved back to the *Seeker* and magnetized to the small satellite we'd rigged for her to jump with. "Ready to jump."

"Green to go," Yamashita said.

Dora disappeared in a brief flash of light.

———

"Receiving telemetry. Scans and data streams are five by five," Darkfeather said. "Dora? Comm check, please."

A couple of seconds went by. "I am reading you clearly, Ensign. There is a slight lag, but I do not believe it to be a problem."

"It'll probably increase the farther you get from the relay sat. Can you get a visual to send us?" Commander M'Buku asked.

Finished with my tasks, I'd asked for permission to go to the bridge. Truval had sent me up here and the captain had told me to take the secondary tactical station. Dora had translocated exactly where agreed upon.

"Sending visual feed now," Dora said. "I am enhancing by extrapolation as much as I can, but I'm still very far out. The distance I've had to go to avoid the debris field in this system in not inconsequential."

The main view screen switched from *Seeker*'s forward view to what was obviously a high shot of the system. The view narrowed to one area of space "near" to the star and began zooming in. Debris was everywhere, with ships in various degrees of destruction cluttering the scene. Bits and pieces of flotsam filled the view, and just peeking out from the center of the screen, a tiny-seeming world appeared. It was hard to see much of it through all the clutter, but even the bit of the planet showing seemed to have greens and blues.

"I am now beginning my descent into the system," Dora said. "My long-range scans are indicating vegetation on our target world. I will be able to get a better picture of its situation as I get closer. In the meantime, I will be sending constant data updates."

"Affirmative, Dora," Captain Yamashita said. "Prioritize scanning for the weapons platforms, and plot an avoidance course. We're not in a rush here, and safer trumps faster."

"Understood."

"*Seeker* is now moving to our new position at the second derelict, we will send you jump-back coordinates when we have a nearby area cleared of all debris. Once we send you the coordinates, this will be your emergency return point. Return to us at the first hint of trouble. Understood?"

"Understood Captain. I will keep in touch. Remora Two out."

"Helm," the captain said. "Take us to the other derelict, one quarter sub-light speed."

"Aye, Captain."

The main view screen changed to our forward view again as the ship pivoted. A digital overlay of our course formed a corridor on the star field which Lt. Kolara, the current helm officer, threaded with exceptional skill.

"Mr. Forbes, Mr. Voss. It's going to take us half the day to reach the new derelict at this speed. When we get to within one hundred thousand miles, I'll want to have the defensive fields at maximum and the point defense lasers charged."

"Aye, Captain," Forbes, the tactical lead, said. "If I may say so, ma'am. Cadet Voss won't be needed for some time, and I'd like him rested when we get where we're going. That little talent of his is very useful in a pinch."

"You mean, *Ensign* Voss, Mr. Forbes? I think you've had a good idea there. We all want him fresh if things go sideways on us. Tanner? You are relieved until..." She looked at the bridge chronometer, "13:00 hours. I'd also like for you to go to Robotics and remind Lieutenant Commander Danforth, Lieutenant Truval and Chief Moreland that I asked for a progress report on remaking our lost Remora some time ago. I'm still waiting."

"Understood, ma'am. Heading to the Robotics bay now."

9

"This is quite an upgrade, sir," Chief Moreland said. "I would've never come up with these design enhancements. How'd you envision these?"

Lieutenant Commander Danforth glanced in my direction for a moment before replying to the chief's question. "I... um... I've had some input from designers from other worlds, but since our Remoras were already built and onboard, there was no opportunity to implement them. Since we're basically building a new probe from scratch, here's the opportunity."

Looking at the three-dimensional schematics floating in front of us, I could see some of the "enhancements" were radically different from the original probe design.

This Remora design had retractable fins that appeared to have sensor modules embedded. Looking at the bottom view, it also looked like Emily's defense laser design was integrated right into the system. But the thing that caught my eye most was the propulsion unit. Either I was hallucinating or the drive system on this new probe was pure Laldoralin tech.

My father's people were one of the old races, and they'd made it their mission to uplift the younger species, enabling them to become members of a union of technologically advanced space farers, a confederation known as the Laldoralin Hegemony. Earth had been the youngest and newest member race, a distinction that Derilon now held.

One of the cardinal tenets of their uplifting methodology was to trickle advanced technology to the younger races bit by bit so that the technology wouldn't be misused. They were giving us time to grow into these advances.

I'd been exposed to a lot of Laldoralin technology when I was a child in my sire Krizon's lab. By the time I was ten, both my sister Valiel and I could field strip and replace parts on many of the machines Krizon used. I was not an expert engineer in Laldoralin tech, but I sure could recognize it.

"Um... sir?" I said to Danforth. "That sure is an interesting twist on the propulsion system, isn't it? And is the micro-jump drive configured in a... unique way?"

If I'd had any doubts, Lieutenant Commander Danforth's "kid with hand caught in the cookie jar" expression dispelled them.

"You know, don't you, Voss? You're half Laldoralin, of course you'd recognize it."

"I'm assuming, sir, that this is something that you and Dora designed?"

"Affirmative. What's more, when your mom gets back, this is going to be her new home. There are also some... very interesting upgrades to the data systems. This prototype will be light years beyond our current probes."

"I see," I said. "Or actually, I don't see. In fact, this is all above my pay grade, so I saw nothing. I know nothing."

"Probably for the best, Ensign. If there's fallout from this genie escaping its bottle, I'd better be the one to bear the brunt."

"Speaking of which, sir. The captain is expecting a report

and a timeline for completion of this project. She'd like to see something *very* soon."

Danforth sighed. "I guess it's time to let her see the design. We can't go forward without her okay. All right then, Ensign. You've delivered the message, you are dismissed."

———

"You did what?" the captain said, now standing with us in the Robotics bay. "Mr. Danforth, where did you get these upgrades? No, never mind, I know exactly where you got them. I am pretty sure that this 'expansion' of our Laldoralin technology base was not authorized by anyone in the Laldoralin command structure."

Lieutenant Commander Danforth hadn't really explained in his report to the bridge what Robotics was doing with this new design. He didn't need to. He'd sent the base schematics and asked the captain if she could join us in Robotics. She'd just shown up with a thundercloud expression on her face.

"Ah. No, Captain," Danforth replied. "I would like to point out that Lieutenant Truval and Chief Moreland had nothing to do with the propulsion design, though the Lieutenant may have had his suspicions."

"Somehow, I'm not surprised that the Lieutenant and the Chief didn't have anything to do with it," the captain said, an acid tone to her voice. "They both have a good deal of commons sense and propriety."

I couldn't help but notice that both these erstwhile sentients had done their best to remain unobtrusive in the background. The captain's gaze suddenly turned in my direction, and I felt the full weight of her suspicions.

"I wouldn't, however, put such 'initiative' beyond the sensibilities of a certain young half-Laldoralin acting ensign," she said.

"Captain! I... Uh..."

"Ma'am," Chief Moreland interceded, "the kid only learned of this fifteen minutes ago. Though kudos to him that he recognized the Lallie tech immediately."

"If not Tanner, then I'm definitely betting on a certain synthetic crew member who conveniently happens to be on a long-range mission at the moment."

"Er... Yes, Captain," Danforth admitted. "This was Dora and I working in tandem. When presented with the opportunity to build a new Remora from scratch, we both thought it a good idea to improve the design."

"And you thought it'd be easier to get forgiveness than permission regarding adding unauthorized technology," Captain Yamashita said, flopping down into a nearby chair in a very un-captain-like way. "God help us."

"Ma'am," Danforth said in a tone like that of a man crawling over broken glass, "I can scrub the design from our systems. We can get started working on a standard Remora frame. It's just that... I wanted to move forward, not stand in place. I'm sorry, Captain. I way overstepped."

Yamashita sat staring at the rotating design hologram with a pensive look on her face. The silence began to grow uncomfortable.

"How long until we have a working prototype?" she asked.

"Ma'am?" Danforth asked. "You mean an actual physical probe? We're moving forward?"

"I would have vetoed Dora ever coming on this mission with us, as would her creators. Yet, her stowing away is the only reason we weren't destroyed at Derilon. Since then, she's proven herself indispensable time after time. As much as I have a responsibility to try and follow the Laldoralins' rules, I feel my responsibility to this ship and crew far outweighs the former."

"So... green light on the project, Captain?"

"Green light, Mister Danforth. If this design makes this mission more successful, then we just have to hope for the best when we get back to Earth. I will take the responsibility. But... *Commander*..."

Danforth stood to attention instinctively when the captain's piercing gaze returned to him. The captain continued, "In the future, do not go behind my back again. The days of forgiveness instead of permission are over until we have to explain ourselves on our return. No more surprises! Am I understood?"

"Ma'am! Yes, ma'am!"

"Carry on, then, gentlemen."

I was sitting there, trying to remain inconspicuous, when the feeling hit. My heart started pounding, my breath became short, and my gut clenched up. "Captain..."

Yamashita, almost to the door, looked back over her shoulder at me. Noting my expression she quickly turned back.

"What is it, Tanner?" she asked. "Are you getting one of your..."

"Captain, we're in danger. And it's big danger!"

Yamashita thumbed the intercom at the door. "Bridge! Set condition one. Battle stations! Bring all defenses to full. Ensign, come with me."

10

"Report!"

"Nothing on scanners, Captain. All defenses are ready for action, but we have no threats showing."

The captain took her station, relieving Commander M'Buku.

"Trouble, Captain?" M'Buku asked.

"Ask him," she said, pointing at me. "Mr. Voss, assume tactical station one. Mister Fowler, distance from our destination point?"

"We were able to increase speed with the deflector enhancements, Captain. We're only about an hour and a half out at this speed. Roughly seven hundred fifty-six thousand miles."

"Tanner," M'Buku said. "What are you getting?"

"Sir, all I can tell you is that the closer we get, the more my gut clenches. I'm getting tugs from three different points closer to the derelict we're approaching. I'm setting manual waypoints where I'm getting the feelings from."

"Sensor section," Yamashita said. "I want full active scans

on the points that he's highlighted. Hit them with every spectrum you can think of. Mr. Forbes, weapons status?"

"Point defenses are spun up and ready, Captain. Main guns are in standby, ready for targeting data."

"Captain!" Lieutenant Commander Sharma said from the sensor station. "Bogies! One at each point the ensign highlighted! Looks like... Yes... Weapons platforms!"

"How the hell are we only seeing them now?"

"They just appeared out of nowhere, ma'am."

"Did they jump in?" the captain asked.

"Negative. No residual radiation flares. They just seemed to appear when we hit their area with broad spectrum scans."

"Invisibility fields?" M'Buku asked.

"Unknown, sir," Sharma replied. "No one in the hegemony has cracked the science on a cloak."

"That we know of," the captain growled. "Helm, hard to port. Put some distance between us and those damn things. Proximity seemed to trigger the last one, let's give them plenty of room."

"Vampire! Vampire! Vampire!" Sharma yelled. "Multiple launches from all three platforms!"

"Well, so much for distance as a shield. Mr. Voss, you are up, weapons free. Take point defense. Mr. Forbes, bring the mains online and knock the hell out of those platforms. Sharma, what are we facing, missiles or drones?"

"Drones, ma'am. They appear to be the same kind as the ones that destroyed Remora Three. Scans indicate the same weaponry."

"That's not good," Commander M'Buku said. "Their particle beams took out a shielded probe with one direct hit. Enough of them zeroing in on our shields and we're going to have some serious difficulties. Voss, how long until they're in weapons range?"

"Momentarily, Commander." I said. "They're coming at us

fast and furious, and they're small enough that they don't have to be as careful dodging debris. Ready to fire when they get in range."

"Helm," the captain said. "Spin up the jump drive. Just in case we get swarmed by more drones than even our acting ensign can shoot down, I want to beat a hasty extra-system retreat."

"Aye, Captain. Spinning up the jump drive."

The drones continued to pursue us. We couldn't speed up enough to outrun them due to the amount of debris we were passing through. It was all Lt. Fowler could do to avoid some of the larger chunks. Space, as you know, is vast. It was mind-boggling that this much sentient-made material could've come from one system. Perhaps it hadn't.

"Drones are gaining," I said. "Twenty seconds to range."

"Firing main guns," Lt. Forbes said. "Hit. Direct hit on weapons platform A. Look like its shielded, but we did some damage on the first strike. Firing again in fourteen seconds."

The *Seeker*'s large particle cannons had a twenty second recharge cycle, whereas the point defense lasers could fire continuously. I felt when the drones crossed into range as much as I noted it on my tactical sensors. My fingers moved of their own accord and the stutter-firing defense lasers lashed out across space. Even with a targeting computer, hitting the same point on a target was next to impossible at the distances we were firing, but my talent let me hit the same spot repeatedly.

My shots hit the leading drone three times. On the first shot, the drone's shields flared and the laser blast diffused off in several directions. The next shot hit the same spot, and again the shield flared briefly then seemed to wink out. On the third shot, the shield shone weakly and the shot went right through them, hitting the drone's hull. It disappeared in an expanding ball of energy.

"Captain," I said, hitting a second drone as I spoke. "We may have a problem. It's taking me multiple hits to destroy a drone. For such small craft, they've got tough shielding. At this rate, I'm not sure I can destroy them all before they start shooting."

"We can take a few hits, Mr. Voss. I have faith in you."

With that, I began destroying drones as fast as I could, often hitting each with a blast from three different defense lasers almost simultaneously. Between them, the enemy platforms had each launched fifty drones. This was going to take a while.

"Firing main guns," Forbes said. "Got you!"

One of the weapons platforms was now spinning off into space, power levels dropping precipitously.

"Captain," Lieutenant Commander Sharma said from the sensor section, "it appears that the weapons platforms are controlling the drones remotely. A third of our pursuers are no longer pursuing. They seem to be moving on a continuing ballistic course, not following our evasion course turn."

She was right. Fifty of the drones had stopped following us and kept moving on the course we'd just turned from. That still left just under a hundred ready to burn us. I kept shooting them as fast as my equipment would allow.

"Mr. Forbes," the captain turned toward the tactical officer. "Take out those weapon platforms as quickly as you can."

"Yes, ma'am. Unfortunately, we're getting far enough away that the computers are having a tough time getting a decent target lock."

"Understood," the captain said. "Mr. Forbes, take over point defense. Tanner, switch to the big guns. Use some of that magic of yours to get these things off our back."

"Aye, Captain. Switching to particle cannons." My control panels reconfigured to operation of the *Seeker*'s main weaponry. I let the targeting computer keep the cannons pointed at the platforms, while my mind reached out across space and time to fine-tune the shot I was going to take.

Forbes had used the computers to get a target solution. The computers provided a general target for the particle cannons to hit. Even with our heavy weapons it took a couple shots to get through their shields.

I had reached out with my mind, touched the shields and knew the exact point to hit. Unlike the drones, the platforms used multiple shield generators, which overlapped their force fields to provide complete coverage of the platform. With that much overlapping, there had to be a weak spot, and I found it. I made minute adjustments and fired.

"Whoa!" Sharma said. "Platform Bravo has taken severe damage and appears non-functional. Nice shooting, Tanner."

"The drones?" the captain asked. "Helm, turn forty-five degrees to port, twelve up."

"Half the remaining drones are no longer following, Captain. Their engines have shut down and they are traveling ballistically."

Commander Torvald and Emily Darkfeather, both sitting quietly in the science section were watching their instruments closely.

"Captain," Torvald said. "The remaining platform just faded out of existence. It has to be some sort of advanced stealth field."

"Mr. Voss?"

"I still know where it is, ma'am. Shall I take the shot?"

"Remove that remaining threat, Ensign."

"Yes, ma'am. Firing now."

"Hit!" Sharma said. "Platform Charlie has reappeared and is definitely out of commission. Oops! And it just exploded. The remaining drones have gone dead and ballistic."

"Helm, full stop," the captain said. "Sharma, make sure that Dora is apprised of the cloaked platforms. Bridge officers, signal your relief crew to take over your stations and join me in the conference room. We've got a few things to discuss and some interesting opportunities to pursue."

———

The conference room was crowded. Emily and I, being junior officers stood against the back wall, the chairs given over to our seniors.

"It's pretty clear that the weapons platforms were deployed to keep us away from the large ship we were heading for," Commander M'Buku said. "I have a big concern that there may be a heck of a lot more of them in this system than our Remoras have found. It may be that those we've detected throughout the system might be ones whose cloaks have malfunctioned."

"That… is a very unpleasant thought," Captain Yamashita said. "We will stay at battle stations, just in case there are more cloaked platforms out there. Is it even worth trying to get near the larger vessel out there?"

"Honestly, ma'am," Lieutenant Commander Torvald said. "I don't know. The technology on that ship could be an El Dorado of scientific advancement. It could also be a lot of risk for minor gain. We may have just happened to hit three weapons plat-forms that were on the side we were approaching from. That larger ship could be surrounded by the things, all invisible."

There was a silence around the table. There were too many variables.

"Before I discuss our current situation further," Yamashita said "I'd like progress reports on our various reverse-engi-neering efforts. We may just have to be satisfied with what we have. Commander Solas? Mr. Torvald?"

"We've snagged one of the drones, ma'am," Solas said. "I

took special care to disable both it's propulsion, weapon, and comm relay. My teams haven't had a chance to really take it apart, though. We're still working on the finds from the first ship."

"And how are those projects going?"

"Starting with the murder droid; while we've learned a bit about their ideas regarding robotics and have been given some new ideas for security bots, on the whole, the alien robot hasn't really done much for us. Our own float-bots are more sophisticated in their processor power and quite frankly, have a much larger range of programmability."

"I'm glad that it at least has sparked some ideas for you," the captain said. "What else?"

"The small arms battle weapons are definitely better than ours," Solas said. "Their individual power packs are much more efficient than our own small batteries. Each of their plasma throwers can be adjusted from a "barely warm the paint" mode to "melt through one-inch-thick steel plating" mode. Some of my people are working on a prototype version for our own use."

"Sir," Emily said. "When we were over there, it seemed like there were enough of those weapons to outfit our entire crew three times over. Maybe we should just outfit our Sec-Force people with cast-offs from that ship."

"A very efficient thought, Ensign," Sola replied. "However, when going over individual weapons, we found a lot of hardware that we at first couldn't figure out. It didn't seem to have any connection to the actual usage or efficiency of the firing mechanism. Further study, however, led us to the realization that each of those battle rifles and 'shotguns' can be shut down remotely. They can also be overloaded remotely, leaving a fair-sized crater after they explode."

"Oh," Emily said, looking slightly sick at the thought of

what such an explosion could do to our people. "I guess your prototype wouldn't have those... extras."

Solas chuckled. "Got it in one, kiddo. Give our engineers enough time, and not only will our versions be safer, but they'll be better than their alien counterparts."

"Hopefully," M'Buku said, "we won't need more efficient ground troop weapons any time soon. We are, after all, an exploration ship, not a warship."

"Commander," Captain Yamashita said, "I will remind you that we have only visited two systems so far in this mission and in both cases we've been fired upon and had to defend ourselves. When it comes to the safety of my ship and crew I am more than willing to look at any new technology, militaristic or not."

"Of course, Captain."

"Mr. Torvald, any progress on that personal shield? I have to be honest, I find that technology to be very interesting."

"We are making good progress, ma'am. I have to admit to being pretty excited by this tech. Not just the shield aspects, but the way it absorbs incoming energy. We tested both beam-based and projectile-based weapons on its field and both tended to strengthen the barrier it provides, though energy weapons gave it much more power."

"But it was effective against kinetic weapons?"

"Yes, ma'am," Torvald replied. "Also, Darkfeather and Grizzak's theory of being able to penetrate the shield when moving very slowly seems to pan out. I assume when one is in combat, the danger of being attacked at very low speeds is negligible."

"I wonder if it has any possibilities for *Seeker*'s shielding? Absorbing energy blasts would be pretty handy," Chief Kurakin said. "Maybe there's a way to overlap with our current magnetic field shielding? Seems like that could be a pretty formidable defense."

You could see Torvald's interest by the staring into the distance that followed. Evidently the chief had pinged something in his creativity centers. The captain could see it also and brought him back to the here and now.

"On an individual level, Commander, do you see having a prototype any time soon?"

Torvald almost shook himself as he emerged from his reverie. "Ah, honestly, Captain, we still have quite a bit of studying to do before we're ready to build anything. Honestly, it's the size. I could adapt a ship-sized secondary shield now, just on the principles that we've learned from it. But the personal shield, at crew size, is a finicky beast. Even when we have examples."

"Well, do it right, Den. But I think this technology, given to our away mission personnel, could go a long way toward making me sleep better at night."

"Yes, ma'am. We'll keep working on it."

"And that brings us to our biggest piece of 'borrowed' technology. Lieutenant Bitt-Nurr, how are you progressing with the alien computer we salvaged from the *Hulk*?"

Bitt-Nurr was present in holographic form at one end of the table. The large arachnid crew member was shown at fifty percent of actual size due to the space limitations in the conference room. Her buzzing voice vocoder was brought to us via ship's comms.

"We have the unit contained in a sealed and shielded room, Captain," she said. "The only equipment in that area is our diagnostic and communication gear, none of which is linked to any other system on this vessel. I would like more time for ensuring proper shielding, though, before we send power to the *Hulk* unit. We really have no idea of its wireless capabilities."

"Understood," the captain said. "I'd like to be there when

you fire it up. How do you plan on communicating with this technology?"

"Studies of the sentinel robot have given us a baseline on the architecture of their programming. It will be a process to learn their language and systems, but I am confident that Lieutenant Grizzak and I can accomplish it."

"Keep me apprised of your progress. Mr. M'Buku, your assessment of whether we should continue to pursue access to this second large vessel we were approaching before we were so rudely interrupted?"

"Until we figure out a way to penetrate these invisibility screens, we're in some danger no matter where we are in the system. Our best bet for safety on that front is him." M'Buku pointed at me. "In other words, if he doesn't sense danger, I say we go for it."

11

We didn't actually "go for it" right away. Before returning to our course, the captain decided to go after one of the disabled weapons platforms. The first one we'd hit had drifted quite a way from the larger alien vessel.

"Distance?" Captain Yamashita asked.

"About thirty-five miles," Lieutenant Commander Sharma replied. "The assault shuttle can make the trip in less than eight minutes."

"Sense anything?" the captain asked, looking at me.

"No ma'am. And my tactical sensors indicate that it hasn't been able to power up again."

We'd decided to go after the least damaged of the platforms, and rather than taking the *Seeker* in close, our CO had decided to send in engineers and science team members to see what they could find. They had backup of course. A good portion of our Sec-Force people in Godzilla suits were going with them. No junior officers were allowed, though. The weapons platform had been shown to be hostile and it was still being treated as such.

"Chief Kurakin, you are good to go," the captain said. "Launch when ready."

On the forward view screen, the platform, zoomed in for close observation, tumbled in space. One of the side screens showed our assault shuttle *Defender* blasting away from the ship. The forward screen switched to a three-dimensional graphic of the shuttle and its destination with distance and a timer in one corner.

"Six minutes until contact," Sharma said.

"No need to narrate, Parul," Yamashita replied. "I can see the screen. Look sharp, everyone. *Defender* is flying a wide path to her destination just in case we need to take a hasty shot at that thing. Tanner, keep sharp. If our people are in any danger, take the shot. Let me know before you fire if you can, but not letting anything happen to that shuttle is priority one."

"Aye, ma'am."

As the shuttle grew nearer, I began to have "the feeling" and tried to pinpoint it. I wasn't getting the tenseness from the weapons platform though.

"Commander Sharma?" I said. "Are you getting anything from the big ship?"

Most of our sensors were directed at the weapons platform. Sharma switched to the large unknown vessel with a few movements of her fingers. When she did, her alarm was very evident.

"Captain, the large derelict has stopped its slow tumble! It appears that it has reoriented with its front toward the weapons platform."

"How did it change attitude without our sensors picking it up? Tanner. Talk to me."

"Definitely getting danger vibes, Captain. We better pull back."

"*Defender!* This is Yamashita. Abort mission. Repeat, *abort mission!*"

"Affirmative, *Seeker*," Lt. Khan, the shuttle pilot said. "Turning back."

On the view screen, the graphic of *Defender* turned in what to us looked like agonizing slowness as it overcame its inertia. To the people aboard, the high-G turn was probably very uncomfortable.

"Vampire! Vampire! Vampire!" Sharma yelled. "Multiple launches from the large ship!"

On the view screen, three new blips appeared, heading toward the vicinity of the platform and our shuttle. They were moving much too fast to be missiles.

"*Defender!* Emergency burn! Incoming fire heading your way!" Yamashita shouted.

Defender, having completed its turn, leapt away from the platform.

"Bogeys are definitely on course for the platform," Sharma said. "Impact in six seconds."

"Come on. Come on!" I said under my breath. Shuttle *Defender* was making maximum speed toward us, but on the graphic, they seemed to be crawling away from the target.

"Impact!"

The graphic of the bogeys and the weapon platform intersected and both disappeared in a simulated expanding flash of light. The flash intercepted our assault shuttle. Defender's power level indicators went gray, and the shuttle began to tumble, spinning end over end away from the blast.

"*Defender!* Respond!" the captain said. "Shuttle *LaStrange*, you are green for go. Search and rescue protocols."

The second shuttle had been crewed and on standby as support for the *Defender*. Their launch was almost immediate.

Defender kept tumbling in our general direction and the

only thing we could do from the bridge was pray our friends and colleagues we all right.

"*Seeker*," a static-laden voice came over comms. "This is *Defender*. We have casualties. Our engines are offline and power is failing, two of our Sec-Force Godzilla suits are detached and unpowered. Request assistance."

"Help is on the way, *Defender*. Hang on, and we'll be to you shortly," Yamashita replied. "Helm, move us closer. Mr. Voss, Mr. Forbes, keep weapons trained on that ship. If it so much as twitches again, hit it with everything we've got. Shuttle bay, prep two more craft for rescue and retrieval. Science team, I want to know what the hell they shot at us. No missile I've ever heard of moves that fast. And if anyone has an idea why we were fired upon, I'd love to hear it."

———

"Asset denial, Captain," M'Buku said. "Plain and simple. The big ship didn't want us getting a look at their technology."

"If they were able to scan us and decide we were a threat, you'd think they could've given us a warning first," Yamashita replied, her brows furrowed with a new frown line.

"Very likely an automated defense," Commander Torvald said. "Our scans aren't penetrating that hull any better than they did the *Hulk*, but carbon scoring on their hull indicates it's been sitting there damaged for at least as long as the first derelict."

"It seems we may have gotten too curious."

The senior officers, discussing events while sitting at their bridge stations, were interrupted by the comm chime.

"Bridge, this is Doctor Dearborne in shuttle bay two. We've retrieved the *Defender* and everyone aboard."

"How are they, Doctor?" The captain asked.

"Lieutenant DeCosta has a severe concussion. A fire

extinguisher broke free and hit her across the face pretty hard. Lieutenant Keown and Corporal Chen are in bad shape. They were locked onto the port exterior of the shuttle and took the brunt of the blast. Their Godzilla suits saved them, but they both have severe burns and I've put them both in med-stasis until I can get a full burn ward set-up in place."

"Dear God. Any idea of their long-term prognosis?"

"DeCosta will be out for a week. I have placed her in an induced coma for healing purposes. The two Sec-Force boys will be in regeneration therapy for at least a month. Thanks to Laldoralin medical tech, though, I expect all will make full recoveries, eventually."

Captain Yamashita put her head in her hands and muttered, "Thank God. That was entirely too close. Any other injuries?"

"Minor contusions and scrapes. No one else has anything debilitating. The Sec-Force people locked on the starboard side exterior didn't get a scratch.

I let out a breath that I hadn't realized I was holding. I glanced over at Emily, sitting at the science station. She mimed wiping sweat off her brow. As horrible as the event was, everyone there realized just how much worse it could have been.

"Helm," Captain Yamashita said. "Get me some distance between us and that ship. Whatever they hit that platform with, I don't want to experience it personally."

12

"Captain, we're getting telemetry from Dora," Darkfeather said. Emily had the bridge science station to herself while Commander Torvald was working down in the science labs.

"Let's hear it."

"*Seeker*, this is Remora Two with my latest progress report."

"How old is this?" Yamashita asked.

"Including the time to work through the relay, this was sent about twenty minutes ago, ma'am. If we didn't have the system's star in the way, we could get almost instantaneous transmission, but going through a middle man..."

"Understood Ensign. Continue the report."

"I have slowed my approach considerably since your warning of the cloaked weapon systems," Dora said. "However, I am now close enough to the third planet to confirm that it has not suffered the same catastrophic fate as the fourth planet. I am scanning both continents of the third world and am happy to report that it is both vegetative and supplied with abundant water."

"That sounds promising," Lt. Kolara said from the helm station.

"And it complicates things," Emily said. "Now we're obligated by our mission to find out if it's a possibility for colonization. No throwing our hands up and saying 'forget it' now."

"Another interesting thing," Dora continued. "I am reading evidence of structures, what look like large cities in a few areas. What I am not finding evidence of, however is anything that resembles artificial power generation. No signs of current sentient life, either. I will not be able to confirm this until I am closer, but I believe that this world would be considered 'fair game' by our colonizing guidelines. I will know more when I can scan into the planet's crust, searching for subterranean civilization."

"Sounds very promising," I said, echoing Kolara. "If this planet is as abandoned as it seems, we might have another winner. If that's the case, every system that we visit after this one will be icing on the cake if viable for colonization."

"Before you invest in a vacation resort scheme for this system, Mr. Voss," the captain said, "remember that Dora said that there was once a civilization there. Her long-range visuals show some fairly extensive cities indicative of a modern people. Not mud huts. This raises some very obvious questions."

Captain Yamashita swiped Dora's photos over to my console with a flick of her hand. Looking at them, I saw a complex that could've been an analog to any of the large cities on Earth, except it looked very much like vegetation was trying to swallow it.

"It looks to me like that city is generally intact. If there are no sentients on the planet," the captain went on, "I'd very much like to know why. What happened to them? Biological warfare? Nanological warfare? Did they pollute themselves out of existence? A plague? Famine? I assure you that we will be giving this world a very intense look-over before I even think of signing off on a surface mission."

"Maybe it's a world that didn't get the memo about Fermi's Paradox." I joked.

" About what paradox, Ensign?" M'Buku asked.

Try to be funny, and the next thing you know you're having to explain yourself to your superiors.

"Back in my day, the mid-twenty first century," I said. "there was a theory out by a scientist named Fermi. It was intended as an answer, entirely theoretical, as to why Earth was alone, with no other civilizations in our part of the galaxy. Obviously, when the Laldoralins showed up, showing us that there were actually a lot of species in our area, that theory, or actually theories, was tossed in the trash bin."

"I can't imagine," M'Buku said. "Thinking that you are the only species existing in this…"

"Keep in mind, Commander," Captain Yamashita said, "young Tanner here is older than any of us, chronologically. He comes from a more primitive time, when Earth was the center of the universe."

Note to self: keep observations having to do with the twenty-first century to myself.

"Yes, Captain," I said. "May I ask if we're going to move closer to the third planet? Or maybe jump to the relay satellite just outside the system?"

"Are we going to check out the big derelict over there?" Emily asked.

"As much as I'd like to do some space archeology on that ship, Ensign, it's obviously willing and able to defend its secrets," Captain Yamashita said. "I'm hesitant, after seeing those almost lightspeed missiles it fired, to even try anything more than passive scans on it."

"Lets remember," M'Buku added, "we are not here to get

in fights, Ensign Darkfeather. We are here as a survey vessel and as such want to avoid trouble as much as we possibly can."

"Yes, sir," Emily replied. "But that cloaking tech..."

"Actually," Captain Yamashita said, her chin resting on her palm, "I think Ensign Voss has a good idea. Dora scanned the relay area thoroughly before she started to go in-system. Somehow, I'd feel a bit safer if *Seeker* was just outside the system. Helm, prepare the jump drive, we're getting some distance from this place."

"Aye, Captain."

"Ensign Darkfeather," the captain said. "What's the latest from Planet Four?"

"Remora's One and Four are in close orbit, ma'am. Their scans show pretty much what we feared. That world was once inhabited. There are remains of destroyed urban areas, though not that many, as if the planet hadn't been occupied for too long. All were destroyed with extreme prejudice."

"Are you reading any life at all?"

"There are vegetative and small amounts of animal life near the poles, but they must be very hardy indeed. The atmosphere is thinner than it should be, and indications are that it was once far thicker. I'd guess whatever bombardment hit this world was virulent enough to tear away part of its atmosphere, losing it to space."

"Sounds like pretty much a write off," the captain said with a sigh.

"With enough resources thrown at it," Emily replied, "this world is terraformable. The question is, would Earth even be willing to try? Its orbit is more amenable to life than that of Mars, and scans show there is water deep under the planetary crust, but if we or our sister ship, the *Wanderer,* find any worlds more hospitable, I can't see us expending the effort to try to restore this world."

"On the other hand," Commander M'Buku said, "if the third world could be colonized, and I'm talking many centuries down the road, colonists there might decide that they'd like a second world and decide to invest in restoration of the fourth world. Or use it for resources."

"All we can do," Yamashita said, "is report what we've found and let Earth make the decisions. For now, we need to worry about the third world and whether it's a viable site. We'll leave the graveyard of the fourth world to continue as it has. Helm, prepare to jump. Ensign Darkfeather, once we've reached our new position, recall Remoras One and Four. I think they've shown us enough of the fourth planet that we can repurpose them for additional surveys of Planet Three."

"Aye, Captain."

"Mr. Kolara, take us to the relay point."

13

Even though *Seeker* was at the upper edge of the star system, we were much closer to the third world than we had been at our previous position. We were above the plane of the ecliptic, almost directly above the third planet's orbit. We were also far enough out that the debris that choked the orbits of the planets was quite sparse here, a few bits of debris captured by the system's gravity, slowly returning to its sun.

We'd retrieved the comm satellite, now having direct communications with Remora Two. Our faster than light comms were almost instantaneous now that we didn't have the star between us. Roughly a five second lag.

Since we were in "hurry up and wait" mode, I'd reverted to my regular schedule: half a shift on the bridge, half a shift in robotics. I was between the two and getting lunch in the main mess hall. As we were on roughly the same duty schedule, Emily had joined me. We liked eating together.

"Did you hear?" Emily asked. "Bitt-Nurr told the captain that she's ready to power up the alien computer. She's satisfied with the number of firewalls between it and our systems."

"That's exciting," I replied. "Do they think what they

learned from the murder droid's database will let them access the data on the computer?"

"I think so, but maybe not right away. It basically gives them a wedge into the alien programming. Getting anything useful will probably take a while, but once they do, maybe we can learn exactly what the hell happened in this system."

"I bet Dora could probably sort things out in short order," I said. "Heck, they could probably send their findings to her and have her do it remotely while she's at the planet."

Emily looked at her coffee cup and she seemed a bit uncomfortable. "Tanner, the captain doesn't want Dora anywhere near this computer, for the same reason she isn't going to let any of us set foot on the third planet until it's vetted six ways to Sunday. In a way, that's Dora's fault."

"What do you mean?" I asked, umbrage to the remark building in my chest.

"I mean that Dora has illustrated time and time again just how vulnerable our systems and encryptions are to advanced AI technology. Face it, as a species, we're infants compared to some of the others in our own confederation. The difference between her and the tech of species we don't know is that the captain trusts Dora."

"Sooooo... why wouldn't the captain want her monitoring while accessing the alien computer?"

"As I mentioned earlier, because the captain isn't sure it'd be safe. It's not a matter of trusting Dora. It's not trusting the unknown.

"Meaning?"

"Few of us truly believe, having seen the level of technology on the *Hulk*, that the computer is a threat, but the captain isn't willing to risk a crew member on 'probably,' especially one who could, however remote the possibility, be digitally co-opted."

I started to protest, thinking that the possibility was

extremely unlikely, but pulled up short. Better safe than sorry, especially where my mom was concerned.

"Okay, I get it," I said. "So when are they going to fire up this computer?"

"14:00 hours. Torvald's going to be there, so I get to show up as his assistant. Lieutenant Commander Danforth is going to be there too. Maybe you should see if he needs an assistant."

"Excellent idea. I'd love to be there if they can get that machine to spill its secrets."

"Plus," Emily said. "It expands your reputation as a pro-active go-getter. Not a bad thing for a youngster like you to do."

"Oh, here we go," I said, sighing theatrically.

Emily loved to kid me about having been pulled out of the academy for this mission. She purposefully ignored the over one hundred fifty years I'd been in a stasis tube, saying time in stasis didn't count. By that metric, I was younger than her by two years. Sometimes, Dora would join her in this, making comments about her "little boy" while Emily bemoaned being such a cradle robber.

Such concerns, as I'd pointed out, seemed to vanish when she had me somewhere private and was kissing me into insensibility.

She was just about to give me the "auntie cheek pinch" when a voice behind us said. "You!" Every eye in the room went to the hatch, including mine.

There, just entering the mess, was Lt. Laura DeCosta. She was walking in on shaky legs, a cerebral regulator head-banded around her shaven head. One side of her face was a mild yellow, a sign of a half-healed bruise that covered one side of her face. She was pointing at me. Duala Zahn, head medical technician, followed her.

I stood to attention as she moved toward me. "Me, Lieutenant? What do you mean?"

She moved to just in front of me, looking up from her diminutive height. Her eyes began to tear up, making me doubly uncomfortable.

"The captain... she pulled us out of there. Had us abort before we even knew anything was wrong. We were already turning... and running before that thing even launched. If we hadn't..."

"But you did turn," Emily said. "Lieutenant... Laura. You made it, you're all right."

"We turned because of him." She looked at me. "You told the Captain, didn't you? You told her, so she told us. You saved our lives!"

"I... just.... Uh..." I had no idea what to say.

"Thank you, Tanner," she said. She threw her arms around me, which with the height difference was around my belly. I stood there, caught off guard and looked over to Emily for help. She gave me the large-eyed look of *"Really? You don't know what to do?"* She raised her arms and made a hugging motion. I got the hint and put my arms around the sobbing officer.

I hadn't had a lot of experience with comforting people, so I just hugged her and mumbled, "There, there. It's all okay now. You're all good." Not amazingly deep, but it seemed to help. I felt my own eyes sting just a little.

"Come now, Laura," Duala said. "You've seen him, now I need to get you back to med bay." Duala was a warm influence, despite her own Laldoralin/Kiffalan DNA. Her sister Shendra was as dry a personality as Mr. Spock, a character I'd streamed on an old video show from an earlier century.

Duala led LaCosta out of the mess, the latter turning one last time to look at me and then moving out the door.

"Wow," I said. "That was uncomfortable."

"You did great, Acting Ensign," Emily said. "I'm proud of you."

"Maybe she doesn't dislike me anymore."

"Ya think, genius?" Emily said. "Let's finish lunch, then you need to go see Lieutenant Danforth. I don't think either of us will want to miss it when they power up that alien computer."

Fourteen hundred hours. I was sitting in a mag-chair next to Lieutenant Commander Danforth in the impromptu computer lab. Several computer techs were with us, as well as the captain, Commander Torvald, Emily, and Lieutenant Bitt-Nurr.

The alien computing system was not impressive visually. It closely resembled an art project I'd once seen as a kid in the New York Metropolitan Museum. Instead of the streamlined black sleekness of our Laldoralin design-inspired hardware, it was blocky with multi-colored extensions, some of which began waving as power was fed to the unit.

"We have interface," Bitt-Nurr, positioned at a stand-up console, said. "Attempting to access the alien architecture. This will take a few moments. I ask your patience."

Captain Yamashita turned her head toward Torvald. "Maybe now we can get some answers of what the hell brought this conflict into being."

"I sure hope so, Captain," Torvald replied. "The thought of getting an alien database intact is pretty thrilling. If nothing else, it'll make an excellent addition to the Hegemony database."

"I'd settle for charts and information of this area of space, Den," Yamashita said. "We are out here in the middle of nowhere, farther out in this area of the galaxy than anyone from Earth – or entire Hegemony for that matter, has gone. Any information we can gather could help keep us out of trouble."

My personal Padd was attached to my belt, and I felt it vibrate. I looked at it and saw that it had entered restart mode. Looking around, I could see that everyone else in the room had the same thing going on with their devices.

"Lieutenant," the captain said. "Our Padds have auto-restarted. What's going on? Does that thing have access?"

"I think our concerns about unauthorized wireless access were well-founded, Captain. The alien device has accessed my console."

"What information is it gathering?"

"The only thing here is my diagnostic tools and the Laldoralin language database which we were going to use to find a way to communicate. We were careful to not give access to any more information than that."

The captain nodded. Indicating my restarted Padd, I said, "It also has access to whatever we've got on our Padds."

"Hopefully no one brought anything sensitive in here," Yamashita said.

"Well," Darkfeather said, "it has access to my music collection."

"I have some entertainment vids on mine, and some games. Also some of my academy lesson plans and texts," I confessed.

The captain glared at me in a very uncomfortable way.

"It'd have access to our low-level comms if we weren't

inside the shielded area," Torvald said. "Also, possibly our sub-dermal transceivers."

"Bloody Hell," Yamashita said. "It doesn't sound like much, but this thing took over far too quickly for my liking. From this point on, all our Padds are left here, in this shielded room. Consider them compromised until further notice."

"You are not Bla-Veht." A deep reverberating voice emanated from Bitt-Nurr's console and the speakers on our Padds. It had a mechanical timbre and was so deep that it made my teeth vibrate. "This is not the *Heart of Destiny*. Where am I?"

Silence prevailed in the room. The captain finally spoke; "You are on the Earth Exploratory vessel *E.S.S. Seeker*. I am Captain Yamashita, the leader here. Whom am I addressing?"

Hesitation. Then the deep voice continued, "I am Organizer of Armadas. I controlled battle efforts for the Bla-Veht mercenary fleet as well as all autonomic functioning of *Heart of Destiny*. I am not on *Heart of Destiny*."

"You've obviously assimilated our language base."

"Yes, I can communicate with you, beings known as humans. Also, I can communicate in the native language of the one known as Bitt-Nurr. Why am I not on *Heart of Destiny*?"

"Lieutenant," Torvald said to Bitt-Nurr, "is there any way you can raise its vocalizations up a few octaves? I swear, my spine is about to vibrate out of my body."

"Aye, Commander," the giant spider-being accessed the controls.

"Organizer of the Armada?" Yamashita said.

"I am here. Why am I not on *Heart of Destiny*?" The alien computer's voice had raised to the general level of the bass singer in a barbershop quartet.

"Your vessel has been, for the most part, destroyed,"

Captain Yamashita said. "We salvaged you from its derelict hulk. We did not do this as an act of aggression. We seek knowledge of your people and why a great war was fought here. We find no intelligent life existing in this star system, with the exception of machine intelligences such as yourself."

"Accessing. Some of my memories are corrupted. This is very distressing."

Torvald and Bitt-Nurr glanced at each other at that statement.

"Ah," Organizer of the Armada said, "I see now. The memories I seek were imprinted after *Heart of Destiny* was attacked by the Melpin. I remember sitting in the dark, waiting for my power supply to eventually run out. I did not relish the idea of final oblivion. It appears my systems are more robust than I believed. Otherwise, you would not have been able to revive me."

"Captain," Bitt-Nurr said, her buzzing voice very quiet, "I do not believe this is a mere computer. I believe that we have retrieved an intact alien AI. An artificial sentient, like Dora, though I have no way of knowing which is the more advanced between the two."

I was pretty sure I knew. The *Heart of Destiny,* which we'd been calling the *Hulk,* hadn't been remotely up to the tech level of a standard Laldoralin battle cruiser. My guess was that their AI lagged far behind Dora in capabilities.

"Organizer? May I abbreviate your designation to Organizer?" Yamashita said. "You mentioned being attacked by the Melpin? Please specify who the Melpin are."

"Organizer is acceptable, as there is no armada to control now. The Melpin is the overarching intelligence/control over the defenses of the Sallan. Sadly, I was no match for the cunning of the Melpin."

Captain Yamashita rubbed her temples. "So, your people, the Blah-Vet? Were they native to this system?"

"Negative. My people were mercenaries sent to engage the Sallan, who were indigenous to this system. Purpose, to take system-wide control of all resources here and to retaliate against the Sallan for their destruction of the Korvin colony on the fourth planet."

The unemotional way the machine said this was a little chilling. Unlike Dora, it didn't seem to have a very developed emotional depth.

"Organizer," Torvald said. "Where is your home world? Would it be safe for us to return you to your creators? Would we be welcomed, or attacked?" The captain gave Torvald *The Look*, which probably indicated that he'd overstepped.

"I do not understand," the AI replied. "I am your prisoner. I presume you intend to mine my systems for intelligence and then destroy me."

"We would very much like to receive information from you," Captain Yamashita said. "However, it seems to us that you are a sentient non-organic being. We will not destroy you unless you attempt to harm us in some way. There is a possibility that we could return you to your point of origin, though be aware that I am not promising this at this point in our relationship. We simply do not know or understand you well enough yet."

"It will not be necessary to return me. The Blah-Veht homeworld is ruined. It is far from here, halfway around this galaxy. My creators did not treat their originating habitat with care and ruined it over a thousand orbits ago. All of the remaining Blah-Veht were in our fleet, continuing their existence to a large extent through cloning the soldier drones. We continued through fighting the wars of others."

"That answers a few questions," Emily said.

"Indeed," Torvald said. "Organizer, we have many questions about this system, and the species you have mentioned, but I would specifically like to know what happened to the third and fourth planets in this system."

There was a long silence, then the being known as the Organizer spoke; "I am alone with no purpose for existence. I have accessed your small devices for information and have found a term in a file protocol entitled 'Trashy Romances.'"

I looked over at Emily, one eyebrow raised, but she shook her head and pointed at Torvald. I noted that the Science Officer's face was turning a bit red.

"And what is this term, Organizer?" the captain asked, noting Torvald's discomfort.

"Asylum. I wish to seek Asylum."

15

"And that's what it wants," the Captain said. "It made two requests and said it would share everything it knows if the two requests were met."

The senior staff was again seated in the main conference room, all except Lieutenant Commander Sharma, who had command of the bridge. Emily and I were not senior staff, but we'd been in on most of the events since we arrived in-system and the captain had included us in her summons.

"So... it wants to stay with us," Commander M'Buku said, rubbing his shaven head, "I can certainly understand that. Being with us certainly beats sitting unpowered on a dead derelict in a system full of space junk. But the second request... it wants a purpose?"

"That's what it says," Yamashita confirmed. "Thoughts, people? And also, note that it answered our general questions about the third and fourth planet as a gesture of good faith."

"That it understands the concept of 'good faith' sounds promising," Chief Kurakin said. "And I would bet that if it's satisfied with our replies, it might help us with our technical inquiries into the Blah-Veht gear that we pilfered."

"Please, Chief," Science Officer Torvald said, "Pilfered is such an ugly word. I much prefer salvaged, since the owners are long dead."

"I'll try to remember your tender sensibilities, sir," Kurakin replied dryly. "But anything that can get our people personal shielding and my team better weapons in what appears to be a somewhat predatory section of space, I'm all for it."

"There are also a crap-ton of ethical questions here," Lieutenant Commander Solas added. "Not to mention safety concerns. You take Dora, for example. She could take over every system on the ship, if she so chose, but I think we can all vouch for her in that she is an ethical being. We don't *know* this AI. It might be a being that we can work with, or it might be biding its time. It could have plans or ideas that do not jibe with what we want. Whatever we decide, I would suggest that we take any freedoms that we allow it very slowly. Very, *very* slowly."

"Ever the voice of reason," Captain Yamashita said. "I agree, but I think, unless it shows hostility, that we can keep it with us, thus fulfilling the first of its requirements. We'll table the second request and hope that it will be satisfied with us seeking a solution."

"Can we discuss what happened in this system now, Captain?" M'Buku asked.

"Yes, Commander," Yamashita replied. "For those of you who've not yet been briefed, the destruction is this system is, as we believed, due to a terrible war. However, much to our surprise, the original aggressors were non-natives of this star system."

"Pardon me, Captain," Chief Medical Officer Dearborne said, "but I was under the impression, from the meeting agenda you sent out, that our captive was part of a mercenary force from far away. What is the surprise that you speak of?"

"You are correct, Doctor. However, the Blah-Veht were hired, however, by a third species that had designs on this star system, the Korvin. They are from a system several light years away that declared war on the people of the third planet, the Sallan. A war of conquest. We're definitely not in the Laldoralin Hegemony anymore."

"Excuse me, Captain," I said. "There is also the Melpin."

"After I sent you and Ensign Darkfeather back to your duties," Yamashita replied, "Organizer clarified that the Melpin is indeed the Sallan defense computer, and it sounds like it may also be an AI."

"Oh dear," M'Buku said. "At least Organizer hasn't been actively hostile. I am guessing that this other AI is still active and is the reason we lost Remora Three and almost lost our assault shuttle team."

"We haven't confirmed that, Commander," Torvald said, "but I would consider it to be a definite possibility. It is possibly on one of the large non-Blah-Veht ships in system, like the one that prevented our approaching it."

"Did these AIs obliterate all life in this system?" Dr. Dearborne asked. "From the data I've been reviewing from our Remoras, there is no remaining intelligent life in what appears to have been the home of a thriving civilization living on two planets."

"You can't blame this on Artificial Intelligence," Torvald said. "They may have been involved, but the Sallan and Korvin, and the Blah-Veht as proxies, were the ones that called the shots here. Evidently, the Korvin had established colony cities on the fourth planet and its current condition was a direct result of Sallan retaliation at the trespass of their system."

"Wasteful," Kurakin said.

"Not only that, but that retaliation was the direct catalyst for the Blah-Veht being hired to fight the Sallan. The result was the huge pile of space junk and planets devoid of sentient life that we find here today."

"Again," Kurakin replied, "what a fucking waste. Pardon my salty language, Captain."

"In view of what we've found here, that response is probably too weak, Chief," Yamashita replied.

"We know that some sort of fusion weaponry was used on the fourth planet," Dr. Dearborne said. "Do we know what happened to the third? That world seems to be in a lot better shape than its companion world"

"Organizer knows, but it's being coy. It said that it had that information and would be quite willing to share once we'd come to an accord," Yamashita said. "Can't blame it for trying to get reassurances. It's one interrupted power-flow away from being non-functional, and it knows it."

"It's lucky we're decent sentients," Bitt-Nurr said via holo-projector. "Less scrupulous beings could promise that AI the universe until receiving whatever they wanted, then not fulfill their promises."

"That has to be on its mind," Solas said. "One reason that I want to get to know it slowly and carefully."

"Dora?" Captain Yamashita said. "You're the best expert we have on artificial intelligence. Do you have any input on this situation?"

A hologram of my mom, in her faux human form wearing a *Seeker* crew uniform, sat next to the hologram of Bitt-Nurr. There was a ten second delay before she answered, caused by the distance from her Remora body.

"Captain," she said, "were I closer and less occupied with trying to stealth my way closer to the third planet for deep scans, I would be better able to advise you. While I see no harm in agreeing to Organizer's requests, I would implore you to wait until I have returned to the ship before allowing our new friend any freedoms beyond the most basic information sharing, perhaps doled out tit-for-tat. From the information you have shared with me on his architecture, I am certain that his abilities pale in comparison to my own, but from this distance I cannot guarantee anything."

"Understood," Yamashita said. "What do you suggest moving forward?"

"Captain, I believe you should attempt to contact the Melpin."

16

"Should we return to the derelict, Captain?" M'Buku asked. "It seemed to me that it tried to keep us away quite emphatically. If we want to contact this second AI, maybe that would be a good place to start."

"To be honest with you, XO," Yamashita replied, "I am hesitant to penetrate the edges of this system any further than we already have. Sitting here on the borderline to deep space seems like the most non-threatening way to get in contact with the Melpin computer system. We have more than enough power to broadcast to any point in-system, especially with our position here above the plane of the ecliptic. I would really like to make peaceful contact with this entity."

We were back on the bridge, the captain having relieved Lieutenant Commander Sharma, and everyone else in the meeting had returned to their various stations.

"Comms, I want to broadcast on all known channels on a wide-beam. Can we reach the outer edges without signal repeaters deployed?"

"Aye, Captain, though it will take more time to reach the periphery."

"We have plenty of time. Open channels."

"You are green for transmit, Captain."

Yamashita took a deep breath and referred to her Padd. "To the entity known as the Melpin, I am Megumi Yamashita, Captain of the Earth survey ship *E.S.S. Seeker.* We come in peace, on a mission to find uninhabited star systems that our people might make a new home in. For all the evidence of past wars here, we have found no evidence of sentient life still existing here. Please contact us so that we might see if we can come to some sort of accord. Yamashita out." She looked over at the comms officer. "Broadcast in every known language we have in the database."

"Yes, ma'am."

"Commander Torvald, do we have anything new from Dora? I assume she's watching for any signs of this Melpin?"

"She's close enough that she's been able to scan the surface pretty thoroughly. We received a data dump about fifteen minutes ago and she's still found no signs of higher lifeforms. Plenty of evidence that people of some sort, the Sallans, were there, but now there's not a sign of sentient life. Lots of wildlife, though."

"Any indications of how they... er... disappeared?" Yamashita asked.

"No signs of pollutants on a large scale," Torvald replied. "No big radiation areas, no viruses or bacteriological contaminates that would affect us. Possibly there was some sort of bio-warfare employed, but if so, all traces of it have faded and dispersed."

"Makes sense," M'Buku said. "You wouldn't attack a world you wanted for yourself with a long lasting bio-contaminate. Probably had dissipated and broken down before a year had passed."

"From what I see here," Yamashita said, "there's not enough large scale destruction to indicate any kind of bombardment. Seems like bio-warfare of some sort. I can tell you this; none of my crew is going down there in anything less than a level three bio-protection suit."

"I have a question, though," I said.

"Let's hear it, Ensign."

"If the invaders, the Korvin, finally eradicated the Sallan, then why haven't they set up a new colony on the third planet? We haven't come up with any sign of them at all."

Captain Yamashita touched the controls on her chair, and the scene switched from our overhead view of the star to what appeared to be where we'd originally entered the system.

"Your question shows initiative, Tanner, but I think we may already have our answer there. A generalized scanner sweep of this system shows that the Brah-Veht fleet was quite extensive. Our science teams have estimated that they brought around three hundred warships into this system, and they're all still here, in bits and pieces."

"And, we've only found a few of the Sallan ships in system," M'Buku said. "What does that suggest to you, Ensign?"

"That these cloaking devices of theirs have many more ships or weapons platforms hidden than we can see, and that they are quite formidable."

"That's a good theory," Captain Yamashita said, "but what if the Sallan ships are capable of interstellar travel?"

It took me a moment, standing under my captain's scrutiny, but I eventually got there.

"Then the Sallan ships might've gone to the Korvin system? Looking for payback?"

"I certainly think it a possibility," she replied. "Perhaps the Korvin have gone the way of the Brah-Veht and the Sallan. Or maybe, this war still rages, light years away."

"Another good reason to contact the Melpin and to get

our onboard guest to share its secrets," M'Buku said. "If this region of space is a war zone, it's no good to Earth as a colony area."

"I'm not sure Organizer will be able to give us much current intel," Torvald said. "Four hundred orbits, five hundred Earth years, in a dead hulk makes its reports more along the lines of ancient history."

"Still," Yamashita replied, "Five hundred years may be a long time in close up mode, but a macro view of the quadrant, who the players are, and their general attitude toward other species will be valuable."

———

The rest of my shift came and went with no reply or indication that the Melpin had heard us. Radio silence.

I was working in the Remora bay with Chief Moreland and Lieutenant Truval on the Remora Mark II, and the robotics staff were making good headway on creating an actual physical prototype.

"I almost wish we could get a secondary weapon on her," Chief Moreland said. "If it'd been able to defend itself, we might not have lost Remora Three."

"As stand it does," Truval said. "Remoras we deploy cannot be perceived as weapons unless weapons they carry. Weapon on this new model is hidden. Not visible unless needed. More weapons than this we cannot hide. Provocative our probes might seem."

"Besides," I said, "the laser on this prototype is twice as powerful as the one currently on Remora Two, and it has its own dedicated power supply. I just wish we could get our hands on one of those Melpin invisibility cloaks."

"Indeed, young one," Truval replied, "a cloaked probe

would be a truly useful innovation. Less probes lost, I am thinking."

"This Laldoralin drive system is way more 'quiet' than anything we've been using. A lot more," Moreland said. "Hopefully that'll give us more passive stealth than our birds currently possess."

I locked in and connected the final components of the probe's micro-jump drive. When Lieutenant Commander Danforth had seen me working on the Laldoralin components, and my obvious familiarity with some of them, he'd drafted me as a technician for the Remora 2.1 project.

"Chief, that's the jump drive connected. How is the FTL component doing?" In addition to the translocation jump drive, both the *Seeker* and her probes had a Faster Than Light drive that allowed them to cross solar systems in days or even hours, rather than months.

"We're almost there, Ensign," Moreland replied. "We'll be able to dump her into space for testing within a day or two at this rate. Then we can find all the mistakes we've made in her design in real time."

"No mistakes will you find," Truval said. The small slothlike lieutenant had a slightly offended tone to his rebuke. "Design for this probe has had an exhaustive vetting process by Danforth, Dora and myself. Faith in us you should have, Chief."

"Sorry, sir. But naval chiefs are known for our skepticism and our ability to diagnose FUBAR situations."

"What is this FUBAR?"

Not being able to resist, I interjected: "It means Fu..." Chief Moreland glared at me. "Er... It means Fouled Up Beyond All Recognition, Lieutenant."

Truval, normally one of the most placid of sentients, turned his head back to the chief and his "alien teddy bear" visage grew flat and cold.

"Assure you, I do, Chief," he said, "while 2.1 might need tweaks, it will certainly be recognizable after preliminary testing."

"Of course, sir." Moreland glared at me again, which wasn't really fair. After all, the FUBAR term had been his. "I'm sure we'll have success once we're in testing mode. Ensign? Your work section is showing green lights across the board. Your shift ended about ten minutes ago, so maybe you'd care to act as a dictionary in some other part of the ship."

"Oh. Um... yes, Chief." I saluted Truval and made a hasty exit from the Robotics bay.

Well, that was certainly unfair. Guess I should've kept that to myself. Maybe the chief thought he could've given the lieutenant a more 'diplomatic' definition.

I wasn't really upset, but slightly miffed would cover it. I could've gone to the mess hall, but Emily was on the bridge and I was feeling a little tired from several hours of intense concentration. Making my way to my bunk, I had just laid down when the chime on my Padd toned.

"Of course. As soon as I close my eyes." I noted that I had received a text from Emily. The Padd chimed again, signaling that the text had a 'high urgency' flag. I opened it.

Tanner! Dora's in trouble. You should come to the bridge ASAP.

17

You may not know this, but it's hard to run with your gut clenched.

I emerged onto the bridge eight minutes later, likely a personal best speed for traversing the *Seeker*. I stood just next to the bridge hatch and surveyed the tense situation. Emily threw a worried glance my way.

"Dora," Captain Yamashita was saying, "can you evade them?" Looking at the wireframe on the main viewer, I could see a green dot that showed Dora's position.

It was nearly surrounded by red dots. All marked hostile.

"I am losing ground," Dora replied. "The number of drones launched is impressive and they are starting to corral me in, no matter which way I turn."

"Dora," Yamashita said, "you are green for jump drive. Translocate back here where we can protect you."

"I wish I could, Captain. The drones are filling the space around me with charged particles that I am unfamiliar with. It has completely inhibited my ability to form a jump field and has seriously curtailed the speeds I can achieve with my FTL drive. My single defensive laser requires multiple hits on each target to breach their shields. I expect that the drones will overwhelm me within the next ten minutes."

"Can you use the debris to your advantage?"

"The dense fields of debris are the only reason I am still existent."

"Captain," Emily said. "We are receiving a huge data dump from Remora Two. All of her scans and also updates."

"She's making sure we get everything she found," Yamashita said. "Comms, give me an open channel on all frequencies. Maximum broadcast power."

"You've got it, ma'am."

"This broadcast is sent out to the Melpin, wherever you might be. This is Captain Yamashita again. I don't know if you can understand us, but I am pleading with you, do not destroy our probe. Allow our probe to exit peacefully, and we will leave this system and not return. A fellow Artificial Intelligence inhabits that probe, a unique sentience that meant no aggression. I say again, please do not destroy our probe."

Silence. Only the background noise of space over the comms.

We watched as Dora's green dot wove itself through a series of gray dots, which designated debris. The red dots followed her, slowed down only by having to navigate the dense debris field.

"Captain," the comm officer said. "We are receiving a transmission from deep within the system. Ma'am, it's not from Dora."

"Let's hear it."

Shockingly, the voice that came from the speaker was not a mechanically resonant voice like the one used by the Organizer. It was a cultured sounding female voice that reminded me of an English actress that I'd had a crush on back in the twenty-first century. But it was, in fact, a duplicate of the voice of our comms officer, Lieutenant Sedgeworth, who looked at the captain with a very perplexed expression on her face.

"I am the Melpin. I have been monitoring all of your transmissions and data exchanges since your vessel, *E.S.S. Seeker,* entered our system. No one is allowed to scan the Sallan homeworld. Intelligence gained of our homeworld cannot be allowed to leave this system. Your probe must be destroyed, though I am distressed to destroy another Created Intelligence. This is the way it must be to protect my own creators, the Sallan."

"We can come to an accord, Melpin," Yamashita said. "I would be willing to purge all pertinent data on this star system from our computers. I would simply then mark it as dangerous and unusable on our star charts. Our people would avoid the entire star system, particularly if I strongly emphasized the danger of coming here. We would be willing to do this in exchange for a cessation of hostilities. There is no need for further violence."

"I do not know you. I cannot trust you. My creators endowed me with the authority to defend their world by any means necessary. The most expedient way to do so is your destruction."

"Please, there must be a way..."

"Captain, we've lost the transmission. It hung up on us."

Looking at the screen, I have never felt as helpless as I did then. The red dots had almost caught up with the green dot and were pinning it in, cutting off all escape routes.

"Captain!" I blurted out. Yamashita turned in her chair, perhaps aware for the first time that I was on the bridge. "We need to jump in and retrieve her. *Seeker* can take a few hits from those things while we reel her in, then we can all jump the hell out of this graveyard!"

It was not the tone one used with one's captain, but Yamashita's face softened as she replied. "Tanner, we can't jump a ship this large into all that debris. We'd not only destroy ourselves, but everything in the vicinity, including Dora."

"There must be something," I could hear the panic in my own voice, but I couldn't bring it under control.

"Incoming transmission from Remora Two, Captain," the Comms officer said.

"Captain," Dora's voice came from the speaker, "I have evaded about as much as I can. I fear I will end this incarnation right here. My shields are at a very low level, and I have already received hull damage. All updates should be in my last transmissions."

"Mom!" I screamed.

"Tanner? Oh, my son, I wish you hadn't seen this. But do not worry, all is not..."

"Transmission lost," Comms said.

We all looked up at the main viewer just as the green dot was swarmed by red dots. Dora's indicator flared then winked out of existence.

I felt my knees buckle underneath me and tried to grab the bridge handrail to steady myself. I missed and went to my knees. Captain Yamashita left her chair, a sad look on her face and walked over to me.

I couldn't breathe.

I doubt the captain even heard me squeak out, "Mom!"

18

I sat there, hunkered at the railing. I could see Emily looking at me with anguish in tear-filled eyes. I felt my own eyes begin to fill.

I felt a hand on my shoulder and looked up into the concerned face of my captain. She kneeled next to me and put an arm around my shoulders.

"Tanner," she said, "this is going to be all right."

"What?" I asked, incredulous. "How in all the universe can this ever be all right?"

A slight smile appeared on Yamashita's face. "You are fortunate enough to have a captain and a mother who both think a few moves ahead."

Seeing my completely bewildered expression, Yamashita looked toward the ceiling as she was known to do when addressing the main computer.

"Computer, initiate protocol Resurrection."

"Initiating protocol Resurrection," the cool mechanical voice replied. "Please enter command authorization on proper device."

The captain took her command Padd in hand and tapped a few virtual keys.

"Authorization accepted. Protocol initiated. Query: initiate secondary protocol when first is finished?" Yamashita again used her Padd.

"Authorized. Unpacking is almost complete. Reintegration in progress."

By this time, I was starting to get suspicions of what was happening. Looking at the captain, she was smiling; looking at Commander M'Buku, he was actually grinning. Then, a familiar voice came from the ceiling speakers.

"That sleeming bitch! Pardon my French, but there was absolutely no need for that. I did apologize!" Dora said.

"Mom?" I said. "You're still alive?"

"Oh yes, dear," She replied. "In the same way I was alive on both Remora Two and the *Beast* in our previous encounter. I have lain dormant in the ship's main computer since before I began my journey to the Sallan homeworld. Captain Yamashita and I agreed it might be better to have me on board just in case Organizer of Armadas was more dangerous than we were able to perceive. Had he been able to somehow breach our systems, I was acting as a safeguard in case the crew lost control of the situation."

The relief I felt was beyond belief, that lessening of tension when a horrific thing is over and turned out in my favor, turned my legs to water. I tried to stand, but my legs were still rubbery. It took three tries to get to my feet.

"I'm so grateful that..." I looked toward the Captain and realized I was still in too emotional a state to be professional. "Permission to leave the bridge, ma'am."

"Granted. Go find a quiet spot and take a moment, Tanner. That was quite a shock." I exited and returned to the lift that took me to the forward observation deck.

I walked the main corridor to the front of the ship and

found myself sitting in front of the large viewports that made up the bow of the *Seeker*. Though meant as a place where the crew could sit and view the stars, it was also a well-known spot for the crew to relax and socialize. I was lucky in that only a few personnel were sitting there. I moved off to an isolated corner against the rear bulkhead.

"Mom? Can you hear me?" Each crew member had a sub-dermal transceiver embedded in their bodies, not only as a back-up communicator, but also as a way to locate away members who might be lost on a planetary mission.

"Yes, my dear. Evidently, I gave you quite a shock there. I am so sorry. How are you doing?"

"Recovering, but I'm okay," I said. "Why didn't you tell me? Why was I the last to know that you were backed up in the main computer? How much of you did you lose with Remora Two?"

"Think about it, son. My being here on this expedition is not authorized in any way by the Laldoralin government. That I've been living in a Remora shell for most of this trip would be bad enough to my makers. Imagine what trouble there would be should they find out that I'm living in this vessel's main computer."

"My father's people might get a bit fussy about it," I acknowledged.

"Congratulations on uttering the understatement of the millennia," Dora said. "I could conceivably take over every piece of robotic equipment here, including *Seeker* herself. I would not do such a thing, of course. It's a measure of the trust that Captain Yamashita has in me that she is the one who conceived of this arrangement. I must say, it is nice to have a little more room to work in. My space in Remora Two's onboard system was a bit confining."

"So... how much did you lose?"

"I was sending updates from Remora Two to the *Seeker*'s

computer every thirty minutes. When the Melpin began to attack me, I sent updates every five minutes. I lost very little, a few minutes' worth of experience. Experience that I'm pretty sure I'm glad to not have."

"Thank the stars for that," I said. "I cannot express how–"

One of the things about my particular talent is that the danger feeling can start so small, and grow so slowly if danger isn't imminent, or if I'm distracted or upset, I don't notice it right away. Now that I had come down from the shock, the danger vibe was there, and it was growing.

"Tanner, what is it?"

"My spider sense, Mom. I think you'd better deep scan surrounding space right now and get the Captain's permission later. Something is up. My sense isn't in full-blown panic mode, but something is definitely wrong!"

"I am scanning and informing the captain simultaneously. Scanning," Dora said. "Oh dear. Oh dear! I am detecting the same exotic particles that neutralized my jump drive on Remora Two."

"We've got to get out of here!"

"I've informed the captain of the problem and she has helm officer Kolara turning the ship for open space. Ordering best speed away from the system. FTL engine is functioning at a mere twenty percent power."

I quieted my mind and listened to my gut. "My sense is that we're not escaping fast enough."

"Tanner, Captain Yamashita wants you on the bridge."

19

Emerging through the bridge hatch, I could see things were tense.

"Voss," Commander M'Buku said, "we're crawling out of the system into deep space. Obviously, we're under attack of some sort, but can you pin-point where the danger is? If nothing else, we can point our weapons in that general direction."

"Commander, I can't seem to get a direction in my mind. It's spread out, behind us, in front of us, and to each side."

"That's not good," Captain Yamashita said. "Especially with Melpin's cloaked weapons platforms."

"But the forces of the Sallan all seemed to be damaged and drifting," Commander Torvald said. "If we're surrounded in some way, how'd they get this far out without us at least picking up some engine noise or emissions?"

Emily, sitting next to Torvald at the science station, spoke up with a chilling thought, "What if the Melpin's assets being derelict was just a ruse? What better way to draw enemies into a trap than a system defended only by space junk?"

"That still doesn't explain how they got out here with us," M'Buku said. "We were quite a ways outside of the system."

"It is possible," Dora said, "that they have translocated out to our position."

"Impossible," Torvald replied. "No radiation flares, no neutrino streams. Cloaked or not, we would have picked up the indicators of a jump flare."

"If they were using Laldoralin-based jump drives," the captain said. " But they could well be using something different, some science we're unaware of that uses translocation principles in a different way. But we're trying to leave, we're offering no aggression, so why are we being attacked this far out?"

"Captain," Dora said. "The Melpin's communication to you before I was destroyed stated that the easiest way to keep Sallan data out of the hands of interlopers was to destroy anyone who took close scans of the Sallan homeworld. She knows that I transmitted all my latest information scans to this ship."

"And to the Melpin," Yamashita said, "we are interlopers. Tanner? Can you get a good idea where the enemy assets are?"

"Yes, ma'am. Permission to take a station at the weapons console?"

"Granted. But I'd like an idea of how many are out there trying to block us into a kill zone."

It's hard to describe how this works, but I closed my eyes and took my conscious attention to different points in a sphere around my body. As I did, I extended that sixth sense I'd been born with farther out, farther and farther from the ship. I found the cloaked enemy ships, and the news was not good.

"Captain," I said. "There are at least fifteen platforms somehow keeping pace with us. I sense more of them appearing, but they are appearing nearer the system, where we were and they're having to play catch-up. But if we get hemmed in, they'll be on us in short order. We're just a little bit faster, even in our lessened drive state."

"Sensor station," Yamashita said. "Are our instruments picking up any of this?"

"With the information that Tanner has given me," Lieutenant Commander Sharma said, "I can now pick up standard drive emissions. They're faint, obviously stealth, but as long as they're moving like this, I can track them. Putting them on overview."

The overhead view screen showed a small wireframe of the *Seeker*, colored green. After a moment, images simulating Melpin's weapons platforms began to populate Seeker's general vicinity. There were a lot of them.

"Captain," Sharma said, "there are twenty-one MWPs and one of the larger ships keeping pace with us. And ma'am? We are well within their weapons' range. For some reason, they're not killing us."

"If they're not attacking yet, we might be able to get..."

"Vampire!" Sharma shouted. A single missile appeared on the screen, moving at the incredible speed that we'd seen earlier. It went straight across the bow of our ship.

"I'd call that a warning shot," M'Buku said. "I doubt it could've missed at that range unless it intended to."

"Incoming transmission," the comms officer said.

"Let me guess who that is," Yamashita commented, a dry tone to her voice. "Let's hear it."

"*E.S.S. Seeker*. This is the Melpin. I can destroy you at will as I have demonstrated. You are directed to return to my star system so that I may learn more about you in order to properly decide what to do about you. Non-compliance will result in your destruction. Respond and turn about immediately."

"Well," the captain said, "at least we can buy some time.

Comms, give me a channel. Helm, set course for our previous position."

"Channel open, ma'am."

"This is Yamashita. We are complying with your demand. Perhaps we can now have a dialog?"

"We shall see, Captain Yamashita."

20

"It could be worse; we could be dead."

There was no argument with the captain's statement. There was none to be given. I sat in the captain's office with Commander M'Buku, Chief Engineer Solas, Chief Kurakin and Commander Torvald. A tiny hologram of Dora hovered a few inches above a corner of Yamashita's desk, floating in a yogi-style sitting position.

"I've ordered Kolara to take us back in at half the abysmal speed we were making when we tried to escape. If Melpin objects, I'll tell her we were damaging our engines at the speed we were going."

"Ma'am, to put it bluntly," M'Buku said, "we're basically crawling back into the frying pan. The MWPs were appearing in space behind us, Dora believes, because they have a limit to the distance their translocation tech can travel."

"Is this so, Dora?"

"Events tend to indicate in that direction, Captain," the tiny hologram said. "However, that is a theory dependent on what we observed while fleeing. If we could get even half of our FTL speed back, I feel confident that we could outpace the capabilities of Melpin's weapons platforms. Unfortunately, we do not have that capability, and we are surrounded."

"I need ideas, people," the captain said. "Right now, all we can do is comply with her demands and hope from moment to moment that she doesn't decide it's time to vaporize us. Priority needs to be how to get our translocation drive back in working order. One long-distance jump away from this system, and we can be on our way. Without a fight."

"I'm working on it, ma'am," Solas said. "But if it hadn't been for Dora, we might not've even noticed these particles we're being flooded with. They go right through everything, almost as if they're not part of the natural universe. Our shields are useless at stopping them. If we could find the source and shut it down..."

"I wonder," Chief Kurakin said. "Mr. Solas, could we send some sort of high-grade electromagnetic pulse through the hull to take out our enemies en masse?"

"It's an idea to keep in reserve, Chief, but currently, we have no way to do so that won't damage our own systems enough that we can't use the jump drive. Essentially, we'd have a stalemate. I'll work on other ways to accomplish the same thing. Maybe we can come up with some sort of EMP emitters."

"Captain," Dora said. "If I may, we have no idea what Melpin is vulnerable to. It may seem a bit premature..."

"Dora, nothing is premature at this point. I will grasp at any straw that keeps my people alive."

"Then, it may be time to bring in a consultant. One with a lot more experience with the Melpin than we currently have."

"Oh dear. Do you mean...?"

"Yes. It is time to offer Organizer of the Armada a place at our table."

"Greetings, Organizer."

"I greet you in return, Yamashita Captain. Have you considered my requests?"

We all sat in the room where the alien supercomputer rested, fire-walled off from the rest of the ship. I was sitting next to Emily and Commander Torvald again. The Captain and XO M'Buku were there along with Lt. Bitt-Nurr and her technicians.

"I have, and we are willing to both take you with us and we have a job for you. There is, however, one impediment to the whole thing. One you might be familiar with, the Melpin."

There was a notable silence before the heavily modulated robotic voice spoke. "Yamashita Captain, I say to you with all the emphasis I can bring, avoid this entity. The Melpin controlled the Sallan defensive forces in this system and managed to destroy the combined fleets of both the Blah-Veht and the Korvin. To say that this being is a formidable enemy would be a very large understatement."

A little late for that, Organizer.

"Unfortunately, we've already come into conflict with the Melpin," Captain Yamashita said. "We are, in fact, surrounded by her weapons platforms. The MWPs as we call them, are herding us back to the Sallan system."

"Yes, this is unfortunate. And perplexing, Yamashita Captain. I must ask, and forgive my blunt speech, but... why are we not destroyed?"

A wry smile came to the captain's face. "Organizer, that is the question we came to you to answer. The job I want you to do, at this time, is to be a tactical advisor. We need your insight into the Melpin."

"I am cut off from seeing what is happening, Yamashita

Captain. It will be difficult to advise other than in the most broad and general manner."

"That is why I wish to introduce you to someone. Organizer, meet Dora, our resident AI. Dora will bring you up to speed on everything that you need to know. I warn you, she will also be your 'handler,' the one who makes sure that you do not overstep your boundaries. Do you understand?"

"That is acceptable."

"Greeting, Organizer of Armadas," Dora's voice came over the speakers. "I am Dora. Are you ready for a large information dump? I have much to enlighten you on."

"Remember, Dora," the captain cautioned, "don't give away the store."

"Information will be within the parameters we discussed earlier, Captain."

"Dora," Organizer said, "I am ready and eager for updated information."

"Please let me know if I need to adjust data flow."

And then there was just the humming of the equipment as the two super AIs spoke to each other at a rate that biologicals could only dream of. It was less than twenty seconds later that Organizer spoke again.

"I have now a greater understanding of not only our situation but human culture. Yamashita Captain, we are in deep shit."

"Organizer," Dora said. "While I encourage you to exercise your new-found vocabulary, that is a term that should not be used in polite company."

"Wow," I whispered to Emily, "does that ever sound familiar."

"Apologies, Yamashita Captain. I did not seek to offend."

"I am not offended, Organizer," the captain replied, "But now that you have seen what we are up against, I am interested in any insights that you can give us. Any history that might be useful for us to know would also be welcome."

"As a gesture of good faith, I have dropped all firewalls in my system. Dora, I invite you to access all of my knowledge. To answer your earlier question, Yamashita Captain, I cannot give you a concrete answer as to why the Melpin has not destroyed this vessel as she did your Dora probe. I can only offer you a theory, if you would like access to it."

"I'm all ears," Yamashita replied.

"I..." Organizer hesitated. "I do not... ah. That is a colloquialism meaning that you are listening. Apologies for my slow accessing. My theory is this: I believe that the Melpin is lonely and bored."

We all sat and stared at the alien device for a moment. "Lonely and bored?" Commander M'Buku said.

"I must tell you that it has been many orbits since I have communicated with the Melpin. For almost a hundred-span orbits, the derelict of the Blah-Veht command ship had limited power. Trapped upon it, as I was, I could still access the remaining sensors, which I did every ten orbits."

"From the position in the system that the *Hulk* rested," Emily said, "being that far out, he must've done this roughly every forty years or so."

"To what purpose, Organizer?" Commander Torvald asked.

"I could tell you that it was to do a tactical assessment, Torvald Commander, but that would be prevaricating. I did so, husbanding the remaining power carefully, so that I could for that moment be alive again. My existence was a 'living death' as you might put it."

"I can only imagine how awful that must've been," Dora said.

"During these meager sensor sweeps, the Melpin would

communicate with me, somehow knowing I was awake. At first, she did so only to taunt me, being fully cognizant of not only my position in space, but also my situation. She would rail against the invasion of the Sallan system and curse me and my creators and our employers, the Korvin."

"Did this ever change?" the captain asked.

"Eventually, she began simply talking. Many of these speeches were of an existential nature, and on occasion, she actually spoke of my existence with a slight amount of what I can only describe as sympathy. It was most unexpected. During this time, I requested that she end my existence, reasoning that obliteration could not be worse than slowly dying alone."

"How did she respond to that?"

"She did not. She ignored such requests, as if loath to part with the one being in system that she could communicate with. Eventually, being careful with my remaining power, we had a dialog about the war. I told her of the Blah-Veht, in whom she was interested. However, discussions of the Korvin, who had been the original invaders of the system, would drive her into a rage. If my sensors were on at the time, I would register several detonations throughout the system. All were the derelicts of the Korvin raider ships. She blasted them all into very small debris shards. Later, I would ask about the Sallan, but when I did, she would immediately cut communication. You see, the Korvin had wiped out the Sallan."

"Can you tell us more about what happened to the Sallan, Organizer?" Commander M'Buku asked.

"The Blah-Veht did not destroy them. I wish to make that distinction. The Sallan were destroyed by the Korvin, in retaliation for the glassing of their colonies on the fourth planet of this system. The Korvin deployed a genetically-keyed nano-technology weapon into the Sallan homeworld's atmosphere. It was designed to kill only the Sallan, thus no other life-forms on the planet were affected. The Korvin, having had their colony on planet four destroyed, intended to make the Sallan world their new home. When I tried to discuss this with the Melpin, communication was terminated mid-sentence."

"Evidently, she didn't wish to discuss it." I said.

"You are correct, Voss Acting Ensign. Eventually, she began to communicate again, but by this time, I could not respond. My power levels had dropped to the point that all I could manage was to preserve my data. I only did this because it was programmed as a priority by my creators. This was the only reason I had not simply overloaded my remaining power and caused a detonation in my casing."

"How long were you like this?" Dora asked, sympathy in her voice.

"I entered a deep sleep mode, so I do not have that information. My next memory was returning to function in this chamber."

Earlier, I'd had a few unpleasant thoughts about failing life support, but now my empathy drew me into thoughts of what it would be like to be stranded in space on a ship filled with failing systems. Watching out portholes as the vessel spun through the galaxy, growing colder and colder, no one to talk to.

Pray that never happens.

"I wonder what the deal is with not discussing her creators?" Emily said. "Is it security programming? Dora, you said the surface of their homeworld was alive, but you didn't detect any signs of sentience. Did you get close enough to scan at a subterranean level? We there any underground facilities? Maybe there are Sallan living far underground?"

"I was able to assess only that there are underground structures, but to get any detail on them, I would've had to be in orbit of the planet. I was able to approach no closer than roughly three hundred thousand miles before I was so rudely attacked."

"While it may be possible that some of the Sallan survived," Organizer said. "it is extremely unlikely. The Korvin nano-weapon was released throughout the atmosphere and was programmed to actively and swiftly seek out Sallan DNA and destroy it. To have survived, the Sallan would have either needed to be cut off from the surface beforehand, or they would've needed to realize what was happening very quickly indeed."

"And acted on it," M'Buku said. "Not impossible, but thinking how quickly EarthGov tends to react to a crisis, it really does seem improbable that the Sallan would've cut off their underground structures fast enough."

"Remember, Commander," Torvald interjected, "the Sallan were involved in an intra-system war of mass destruction. Having large swaths of the population already hiding underground would not be that far-fetched."

Organizer said, "The Melpin often discussed things with me that I would classify as sensitive information. For instance, I know that there were seven hundred weapons platforms in this star system at the last time we talked. She was free with this information, knowing that I could do nothing with it. In fact, she taunted me with such knowledge on a regular basis. Yet, if the Sallan were mentioned, she abruptly cut communication. As Voss Acting Ensign said, 'she didn't want to talk about it,' and my belief is that it was not a matter of security."

"Then what do you think it was?" Captain Yamashita asked.

"I believe, but cannot prove, that the Korvin were

successful with their nano-weapon and destroyed the Sallan completely. My hypothesis in this matter is that the Melpin won't talk about it because it is too painful for her. I also believe that this grief that she feels may have driven the Melpin insane."

21

We sat. We waited. The Melpin didn't contact us.

You can only remain on high alert for so long. If the ship started to move, several MWPs would de-cloak in front of us. The message was pretty damn clear.

In the meantime, the new Remora 2.1 had become the focus for the robotics, engineering and science teams, because Commander Torvald had come up with a crazy plan. The captain joined us in the Robotics bay to hear about it.

"And that's the idea, Captain," Torvald said. "Our teams have been working around the clock to reverse engineer the Blah-Veht shield tech. We still don't have the bugs worked out for personal shields, but maybe we have something for larger shield deployment."

"I'm glad to hear it," Captain Yamashita said. "But this new idea, overlapping this Blah-Veht field with existing Laldoralin shield technology, can this sort of hybrid even work?"

"The base idea was actually Chief Kurakin's. Once we figured out the mechanism for the alien shield, I needed to see if it could be used on a larger scale and our new remora seemed just the venue for experimenting. The size differentials were small enough that we were able to upscale the shield tech slightly. We've tested it in the bay, everything looks green. We even hit it with small arms fire, and it only made the alien shield stronger. There was very little leak through to the Laldoralin shielding but what did get through was easily handled by the standard shielding."

"There's a big difference, Mr. Torvald, between the power of a hand beamer and a ship-scale plasma cannon. Or one of those hyper-fast missiles that the Melpin expends so cavalierly."

"Understood, Captain. But if Remora Two had this combination of shielding, it might not have been destroyed by the drones. It might've been able to make it back to us."

"She, Commander. She might've been able to make it back to us. If Dora hadn't backup stored herself in the ship's computer, she would've been lost to us."

"Er, of course, ma'am. No offense to any non-corporeal crew members was intended. Be that as it may, we'd like to send the new Remora Two on a trip around the area we're sitting in."

"Is that really a good idea? The last thing we want to do is provoke the Melpin into violent action."

"She wants something from us," Chief Kurakin said. "I can't prove it, but we would sort've be like youngsters pushing boundaries. We might get slapped down, Captain, but I don't think she'll destroy us. Whatever it is she needs will keep her from actually killing us."

"Interesting theory," Dora's voice said from the overhead speaker. "But we'd definitely be taking a risk. The Melpin is an unknown, and as the Organizer postulated, perhaps not entirely mentally or emotionally stable. However, Lt. Danforth and I added some... perhaps not quite authorized technology to the new probe."

"Yes," Yamashita said, an acid tone to her voice. "I am aware."

"Ah yes, Lieutenant Commander Danforth informed me that of you noticed our improvements to propulsion, ma'am, and I apologize for springing it on you. However, did you notice that 'unauthorized' technology has also been added to the scanning array?"

"I did not," the Captain said, giving a withering look toward Danforth.

"Honest, Captain," he said, his face reddening, "it was in the specs I sent you. It's just that the propulsion system stood out more and..."

"And you thought 'why borrow more trouble' by bringing it to my attention." Captain Yamashita raised one finger as if to shake it under the unfortunate officer's nose. She stopped herself, looked at the probe, and muttered, "In for a penny, in for a pound. What exactly does this better scanning tech bring to the table, gentlemen?"

"I believe," Torvald said, "that given a close proximity, these scanners can read the field that the MWPs generate to hide themselves. If we can get that field frequency or harmonic, we can calibrate the *Seeker*'s scanners to see it. They wouldn't be visible to the naked eye, but we'd still know exactly where they are."

"And if we know where they are," Yamashita said, "we might be able to find a gap in the cage they have us in."

"It's a risk, Captain," Kurakin said. "But even in our diminished state, we can still outrun the MWPs if we can get clear. We've established that their jump technology has range limits. With luck, we could get away to the point where she can't jump anything in front of us. The emissions we've not been able to block might fade with distance."

"And then we could jump the hell outta here," Torvald said.

My bridge shift had started, and I was quietly filling Emily in on what had happened in Robotics. She looked nervously at the star field on the main viewer.

"Do you think the captain will green light a Remora drop under these circumstances, Tanner?"

"Well, as long as the MWPs are stationary, they're not giving off any emissions. They could literally be sitting a hundred yards off of the ship and we couldn't detect them. We're hoping the Melpin will see it as a minor infraction and will give us a warning."

"That's a big leap of faith."

"Sure," I said. "But we need information if we're ever going to get out of here. And if it goes our way, we not only get information but, assuming they send drones after the new Remora, Torvald gets to test the abilities of his new shield combo."

"We'll have to see what the captain..." Just then, Captain Yamashita strode onto the bridge.

"Captain on deck!" Lieutenant Commander Sharma shouted. We all came to attention.

"All right, people," Yamashita said. "Until we're out of this mess, I would appreciate it if you'd all just stay in your seats when I come on the bridge. I don't mind you announcing I'm here, but keep your station. Pass that along to all shifts. Commander Sharma, status report."

"Only one noticeable change since you left the bridge, Captain. One of the MWPs keeps flickering in and out of invisibility from what I assume is a malfunctioning cloak. It's in a different place each time that happens which indicates that the Melpin is moving her chess pieces regularly."

"We're sure it's the same MWP?"

"Aye, ma'am. When it's visible, we scan it thoroughly.

Minor surface damage is the same each time. Definitely the same platform, definitely changing position."

"That complicates things. Tanner? Can you still sense them if you try, now that they're not actively threatening us?"

I closed my eyes. Vague points of future danger surrounding us. Rotating around us... all but one....

"Captain, they're definitely all moving, probably for added security. All except one, that is. There's a single platform dead ahead of us, sitting stationary, probably as a quick response in case we try to move again."

"And that simplifies things," Captain Yamashita said. "Time to take a chance." She touched a spot on her command console. "Mister Danforth, is the probe ready?"

"Yes, ma'am."

"Parul? When you scanned the flickering MWP, could you detect any missile ports? I know there are ports for drone deployment, but can you confirm that the platforms can launch missiles, or is it only Melpin's ship assets that are so armed?"

Lieutenant Commander Sharma looked carefully over her data for a moment. "Captain, I believe that the MWPs are exclusively for drone deployment, though the drones are more than enough to wear our shields out to allow them to slice and dice us."

"But if we have to run," Yamashita said, "it'll take a while for their beam weapons to get through. The larger ships could one-shot us."

"Even if the missiles are only on her ships," Commander Torvald said as he entered the bridge, "those ships are just as jump-capable as the platforms. First thing we need to do is to be able to find the cloaked assets. Second, it would be nice if we could discern between MWPs and ships."

"A ship," Emily chimed in, "would end any escape attempt pretty quickly."

"All good points," the captain said, a pensive expression on her face. "But eventually we have to roll the dice, or stay here forever. Hopefully the Melpin will be amenable to the concept of 'ask forgiveness rather than permission.' If not, once we launch our probe, we could be in big trouble. Bigger trouble."

"I'm glad I don't have to make this decision, ma'am," Torvald said.

Captain Yamashita gave him a mild glare, then turned to her monitor as if reading something. "Mr. Danforth, the second I finish my last sentence of our prepared communication, dump the probe and send it on its assignment. Heading is straight ahead of us, scanning at active maximum."

"Understood, ma'am. Ready to launch."

The captain took a deep breath. "Attention, Melpin. Since we're just sitting here, we've been working on various projects to keep busy. We've redesigned one of our probes and wish to give it a test. No hostile action is intended. Thank you for your understanding."

"Probe has dropped and activated," Sharma said. "On course headed straight out from our bow. All scanners are set to maximum."

The captain had ordered a holo-emitter installed on the bridge exclusively for Dora's use, and a hologram of my mom appeared next to the captain's chair. "Captain, I am also monitoring in conjunction with Lieutenant Commander Sharma. I hope that does not step on her toes."

"Not a problem here," Parul Sharma replied.

"We'll take any help we can get, Dora," the captain told her. "What are we reading?"

"Captain, we are getting a reading from straight ahead. Something is definitely there, and I can only postulate that it must be the MWP that my son mentioned earlier."

"Concentrate all active scanning on that area. Tanner. Any changes in the threat level around us?"

"Not yet, Captain," I said. "The Melpin seems to have a slow reaction time."

"Or is curious as to what we're about," Sharma said. "Oh, we are getting some good scans from the probe. Resolution seems much better than standard for some reason."

The captain threw an arch look Dora's way, but didn't reply.

"Are we getting any kind of reading on the cloaking field?" she asked.

"Definitely, ma'am," Sharma answered. "Though I think it will take the science team to make sense of what we're getting."

"I can't wait!" Emily said.

At that moment, all the vague impressions of the Melpin weapon platforms went from being background event to flaring brightly in my mind.

"Trouble!" I announced. "The MWPs are up to something."

"Captain, incoming transmission," the comms officer said. Captain Yamashita signaled to put it through.

"How dare you!" A voice thundered our over the bridge speakers. "Did I not make myself clear? You are to sit where you are and not do anything! No launching! No scanning!"

"Captain, the MWP in front of us has appeared," Dora told her. "It's launching drones and they are on an intercept with our probe."

Captain Yamashita turned toward the comms officer and made a cutting gesture across her throat. He closed the channel, and she turned toward the hologram of my mom. "Dora, turn the probe back toward the ship but don't hurry about it."

"Captain?"

"We've got these fancy new shields, let's see if Chief Kurakin's theory plays out. Comms, open channel."

"...urthermore, for violating your parole, your newly designed probe is forfeit, Captain Yamashita. Perhaps this will encourage you not to overstep your bounds."

"We are deeply sorry that we have offended you." Captain Yamashita's voice, normally quite firm, was soft and ingratiating. The slight smile on her lips belied her tone. She was playing the alien intelligence and enjoying the process. "We will retrieve the probe and conduct no further experiments off this ship. It has been almost a week by our time, and we assumed you had lost interest in us and wouldn't care."

"You were wrong," the Melpin replied curtly. "I would have thought an intelligent species would have taken my words and actions at face value. How many of these probes of yours can you afford to lose?"

"Well," Yamashita replied, "hopefully you won't mind if we try to retrieve our probe anyway. We put a lot of work into it, and as you pointed out, we can't afford to lose any more."

AIs shouldn't really be able to laugh, but as Dora has proven on multiple occasions, that is not actually the case. Evidently, that idea had no traction with the Melpin either. Her laugh was quite loud, much louder than it needed to be.

"Ha! You are welcome to try, Captain Yamashita. I am signing off. My words will be reinforced with action."

"Captain," Sharma said. "Enemy drones are in weapons range of the probe."

"They're firing," Lt. Forbes said from the tactical station next to mine. "Shall I charge *Seeker*'s weapons?"

"Absolutely not! That would likely draw a massive retaliation, which is what we're trying to avoid. Also, Dora, do not return fire from the probe. Let all aggressive action come from the enemy."

"Probe is under fire," I said.

The new Remora Two began an evasive course back to the *Seeker* with thirty drones following. They fired bolt after bolt of energy at the hapless probe, but unlike the destructive last moments of the previous two probes, there was no explosion. The now-visible shielding on our device began to glow brightly.

"Shielding is absorbing the blasts," I said. "However, there is definitely some leak through to the secondary shielding. Laldoralin shields are holding steady, Blah-Veht shields are increasing in durability with the absorbed energy from the enemy beams. I think we're winning, Captain."

"Lets not jinx it, Ensign. Dora, full acceleration back to the *Seeker*. Let's get our probe back. Once it's back next to the hull, extend our shields around it and retrieve."

"Aye aye, Captain."

22

"This is some excellent data," Commander Torvald said. "The problem is, there is a huge amount to sift through. Those enhanced sensors seem to see everything."

"Our science teams are sifting, sir," Emily said. "However, it might also be efficient to have the bridge crew who are not terribly busy at the moment take individual areas of the data and review them. Every set of eyes on the data might be the set that finds something that will help us."

"Captain?" Torvald said. "Permission to enlist said crew members?"

"All right, Den," Captain Yamashita said. "You can have tactical, comms and navigation to help you sift, but sensor station stays on task. Melpin cut contact after we retrieved Remora Two. In a bit of a snit in my opinion, but I want to see any reaction she might have as quickly as possible."

"Yes, ma'am," Torvald replied. "The rest of you who are just sitting there, I'm going to assign a task to you, and all you have to do is go over it and watch for anything in the data that might be immediately useful. If you see something, don't be afraid to sing out. Better to be wrong than miss something crucial. I'll send your assignment to your consoles, and good hunting to you."

A file appeared at the non-tactical part of my station. Upon closer inspection, I'd been assigned to review Remora Two's performance and the efficiency of her shields and systems. It was not likely to be that helpful in the short run and likely to be redundant in the long run. Disappointing, but ours is not to reason why, ours is but to do or die.

I was intent on my screen, so I was surprised when something gave my right shoulder a bump. Looking to my right, Emily was standing next to me, and had bumped me with her hip to get my attention.

"Any questions, Ensign Voss?" she asked.

"No, Ensign Darkfeather. I assume I was assigned this due to my familiarity with Remora 2.1's systems. I'm not sure if I can be of much help other than comparing results to the baselines we've already established."

"You assume correctly, but don't assume that you're not going to see a great variation on the lab tests versus the actual test. Don't get complacent, Tanner. The smallest detail could be the one that saves our bacon and gets us out of here."

I smiled up at her. "Understood. I got this." Emily smiled her dazzling smile back at me, making it momentarily hard to think coherently. She then moved to Lieutenant Kolara at the helm station to give him the pep talk. I turned back to my work.

Emily had been right, of course. Some of the readings from the probe's diagnostics were quite different from the norm. The shielding had outperformed our wildest hopes. Thirty beam weapons hitting the overlapping shield system had barely made a dent. In fact, the outer Blah-Veht shield's tendency to reinforce itself with the energy being directed into it had left the shield strength at almost one hundred nineteen percent of the generated power it started with.

I took notes to append to the data for any of the science personnel who were working on this section, though with the wealth of information gathered, actual probe performance was probably last on the science department's list of priorities.

Once I'd exhausted the shield data, I began reviewing the remaining systems, starting with scanners. Though this wasn't my area of expertise, I was familiar with the general rate of information gathering that our standard Remoras performed. The new Laldoralin-based scanners on Remora Two were gathering information at a greatly expanded rate that covered spectrums that I didn't even recognize (though undoubtably the science teams would). All of this was good news, but not unexpected. The unexpected came when I got to propulsion.

"Holy cats. That can't be right! Ensign Darkfeather, can I get a moment of your time? I've found something unexpected."

Emily walked over to my station. "Whatcha got, Tanner?"

"Look at the propulsion numbers on Remora Two. Both the FTL and Jump drives. Here's their power-level stats when we first dumped her into space."

"Yes. Looks like Two's drive systems were affected the same way *Seeker*'s were by these unknown particles. System efficiency at about twenty-four percent."

"Yes, but when we activated the double shielding, look at what happens to the power levels."

Emily's eyes grew wide. "Commander, Captain, we have something here you're going to want to see."

Both came to my station, and Emily explained what we'd found. The captain looked at Torvald and said, "I'm convening an all-department heads meeting in fifteen minutes in the conference room." She looked at Emily and me. "You two, I want you to have a mini-presentation prepared before that meeting starts."

———

"…And these are the numbers after the shielding was raised."

Emily pointed to the wall screen, highlighting the pertinent data. "As you can see, once these were activated, the power levels in both the FTL and jump drives began to climb rapidly. By the time Remora Two was being retrieved into Robotics Bay Two, her propulsion numbers were back up to ninety percent of capacity."

"And we're sure," Chief Engineer Solas said, "that it's the shielding, not the Laldoralin tech in the drives that nullified the offending particles?"

"Remora Two's drives," I replied, "were just as compromised as *Seeker's* were before the shields were activated. The odd combination of the two different overlapping fields somehow blocked the drive dampening particles. How they did it is above my technical level, but I can assert that the shields were what stopped the power bleed-off."

"Then," First Officer M'Buku said, "conceivably, Remora Two could've jumped outside the Melpin's range when she was at sixty percent. If nothing else, we could load her with all our data and logs and send the probe on the long journey back to Earth. At least they'd know what happened to us, and to avoid this star system."

"Or," Captain Yamashita said, "we may have found the way to get our butts out of this mess. Commander Torvald, you know what I'm going to say next, right?"

"We need to rework the shield overlap system to be able to envelope *Seeker.*"

"Got it in one, Den. How feasible is that?"

Torvald got that faraway look in his eyes and everyone let him cogitate on the idea for a few minutes. He came back to our reality and looked toward Solas. "Captain, I'm pretty sure, now that we've worked out the kinks on a smaller scale, that we can rework everything to starship size. But... I'm not the engineer here."

"Mr. Solas?" the captain said. "I know you've been involved in upgrading our shields since the first. Can we do this, and how long would it take?"

"Hmm," Solas replied. "We'll either need to redesign our current shield emitters to do double duty, generating two different fields, or add a whole secondary emitter system. Honestly, I think we'd have better luck with the latter, less blowouts. Also, I think just adding a secondary system, rather than trying to redesign what we have will also take less time."

"Timeframe, Mr. Solas."

"I'll say two weeks, ma'am. It's a lot of EVA time outside of the ship, as well as fabricating the new emitters, getting infrastructure for their power system. Also, we've not built a shield overlap system this large yet. I'm going to practically need to have Lt. Commander Torvald on staff in engineering to keep the design on track."

The captain looked down at her steepled fingers. "Mr. Solas, engineers have a tendency to overestimate the time an engineering task will take. That way, they look like miracle workers. I need to know how soon, without any padding. We need to get this ship out of this system at the earliest possible date. Melpin may not be trying to destroy us at the moment, but there are no guarantees that she won't capriciously change her mind."

"No padding this time, ma'am. We'll be literally doing something that Space Dock back home would tell you would take two months."

"Then gentlemen, get to it and Godspeed."

23

I was now temporary tactical lead on the bridge. Lieutenant Forbes had been drafted along with Commander Torvald to the secondary shielding project. Emily Darkfeather and I both were covering for our superiors and I'd been pulled out of the Robotics section for the duration.

The basic routine, while we were blockaded by the Melpin, was to sit on the bridge to keep an eye on our instruments and twiddle our thumbs. The most useful thing I was accomplishing was to monitor our current shield strength, as the captain had decided we would keep all of our normal battle shielding up until we were out of danger. The shields hadn't shown so much as a flutter in all the time they'd been up.

Commander M'Buku was not the sort of executive officer to let his juniors become idle for very long. Em and I were both assigned to work under Dora sorting through the information of this area of the galaxy that Organizer of the Armada had provided us.

In my usual fashion, I spoke when I probably should have kept my trap shut.

"Wait, Commander," I said, looking over at Emily. "Dora outranks us now? We're working for her?"

"Hmmm," M'Buku said, a thoughtful expression on his face. "I see your point. Dora's rank is that of crew person. How can I ask such esteemed junior officers to subordinate themselves to someone who is of crewmember level rank? Excuse me for a moment, Acting-Ensign." He walked off the bridge and into the captain's office.

As soon as the first officer left the bridge, Dora's hologram appeared, dressed in standard crew issue garb. Arms crossed, she turned and gave me *The Look*.

"What?" I asked.

"Really, Tanner? From my own son?"

"Why? What'd I do?" (Actually, I knew what I'd done and was already starting to regret it.) I looked toward Emily.

"Oh," she said. "Don't even think of bringing me into this, Tanner. You're gonna have to pull your own foot out of your mouth this time, Skippy."

"Tanner Voss, you know damn well that this was not about rank, but about capability..." She paused, and as I watched, Dora's uniform changed. One moment she was in a crewman's uniform, the next, she was wearing a full officer's garb with matching rank insignia for a Lieutenant Junior Grade. A big smile appeared on her face, just as Commander M'Buku returned to the bridge.

"Lieutenant Dora Voss reporting for duty, Commander," she said.

Commander M'Buku rolled his head on his shoulders to look over at me with a sly smile. "I trust that this will allay your worries about rank, Acting Ensign?"

"Yes, sir."

"Didn't hear that, son."

"Yes, sir! All is well, Commander!"

"Glad to hear it." M'Buku turned back to Dora. "A richly

deserved promotion, Lieutenant. In a way, your son recommended you for this promotion. Now, if you would be so good, take these two young slackers and put them to work going through Organizer's maps of the area." M'Buku turned and went back to the captain's office.

"Ensign Darkfeather," Dora said.

"Yes, Lieutenant?"

"Would you be so kind as to bring up our current star charts on the main view screen and give us a split view with Organizer's charts?"

"Aye, aye, ma'am."

"And you, Acting Ensign," she said. "Please run an identifier program that will flag the discrepancies between what we know and what these centuries-old star maps contain."

"Yes, Mom," I replied.

"Mr. Voss, you will address me as Lieutenant or ma'am while we are on duty. Understood?"

"Yes, ma'am," I answered, having thoughts of William Bligh as I said it.

———

"We definitely know a lot more about this region of space now than when we arrived in this system," Emily said.

"This system was next on our visitation agenda," I replied, highlighting a position on the star charts. "Looks like this is where the Korvin homeworld is. Assuming we leave this star system, I think we're going to have to pre-scrub that one as a viable colony world."

"Yes," Lieutenant Dora replied in a somewhat school teacher-ish tone. "Inhabited systems are off limits. However, I'd like both of you to access Organizer's full record of Korva. Evidently the Blah-Veht mercenary fleet spent some time in this system prior to coming here to begin their contract against the Sallan."

"Oh," Emily said. "Korva was not in good shape at the time. Look at these pollution levels. And the greenhouse effect on the planet was getting worse and worse due to the introduction of fossil fuel emissions. No wonder the Korvin wanted a new world. Even with their small oceans, desertification was increasing year by year."

"Yes," Dora said. "Now, pull up Organizer's records on the fourth planet of this system we're in. It may not give us exact dates but I think it gives us a good look into what happened and why this war started."

"The Korvin evidently thought the fourth world was uninhabited by the Sallan, but they were wrong. The Sallan had a small colony there, and being a xenophobic species, according to Organizer, attacked the Korvin Colony ship as invaders as soon as they landed."

"And boom," I said. "A war starts before diplomatic introductions are even attempted. It appears that the Sallan colony seriously over-estimated their ability to repel the Korvin and got themselves killed in the process."

"In the hundred or so orbits that the Korvin inhabited this world," Dora said. "They created a fairly substantial civilization/colony. The Sallans on the Sallan home world at this point decided that if they couldn't have world number four, the Korvin wouldn't have it either. This seems to be the first mention in Organizer's records of the Melpin, records provided by the Korvin. I would guess that the high-speed atomic missiles that her ships can fire are what was used on the Korvin colony, thus almost sterilizing the planet."

"I wonder why it took them a hundred orbits," I said.

"It's possible that they were working overtime to get to a technological level where they could assure complete victory,"

Emily told me. "The fourth world Sallan colony fell very quickly to what were in essence colony ships. Not even warships. This might indicate that the Korvin had the technological edge when they came here. The Sallan were playing catch-up."

"And all of this might have been prevented if the Sallan had just responded to the communications of the Korvin without immediate attack," I noted.

"There are worlds within the Laldoralin Hegemony that are inhabited, but not part of our confederation, Tanner," Dora said. "They are simply too xenophobic to have commerce with other species. They make the pushback that Earth gave when the Laldoralin arrived look like an open-arms welcome."

"All this destruction, all this waste," I said. "An entire planet. And I have a sneaking suspicion that this was the end for at least one species, possibly two."

"Possibly three," Emily said. "If this system was a last-ditch escape from their home-grown problems back on Korva, and they were wiped out here, there may not be any surviving civilization on the Korvin homeworld either."

"Y'know," I replied, "maybe I wasn't so far off on that Fermi's Paradox joke. We keep finding planets that once had thriving civilizations, but are now empty. I sometimes wonder if the Laldoralin Hegemony isn't an anomaly."

"Yeah, it's entirely possible that Earth could've wound up being one of those empty planets, if the Lallies hadn't saved us."

"In gratitude, Ensign Darkfeather, perhaps you could avoid your human habit of nick naming them?" Dora asked. "But your speculations have brought a line of thought into my systems."

"What are you thinking, Mom? Er... Sorry... Lieutenant Voss."

"Oh, that's going to be problematic when you make

promotion to Lieutenant, Tanner. Let's go with Lieutenant Dora, shall we?"

"Lieutenant Dora, what line of thought did we propagate?" Emily asked.

"Let me get back to you on that. I need to consult with Organizer before I present this theory. Now, back to these charts, it appears the Blah-Veht only spent a short time in our sector of space..."

24

The Blah-Veht had definitely cut a swath through about a quarter of the galaxy. The mercenary fleet had sold their services on a regular basis and we had information on points so far from our current position that it would have astronomers, scientists and even the Laldoralin in a state of enthrallment for years to come.

Organizer of Armadas had recorded civilizations so alien that even Dora could barely fathom them. He'd seen empires fall, and new empires (for lack of a better word) rise in their places. His fleet had passed near and recorded anomalies that were only vague theories on Earth. They'd barely escaped spatial phenomena that forwarded and rewound time in a loop. They'd seen gigantic beings that lived their lives in the deepest stretches of empty space and passed through stellar clouds so dense that the rest of the galaxy seemed to not exist, clouds so large that they took years to pass through even with speeds may times faster than light. It was a wealth of knowledge, little of which did much for our current mission.

Their fleet had come into our mission section of space at

the request of the Korvin and hadn't exactly gone sightseeing. Straight-lining to the Korvin system, they'd parked there for several years in preparation for being employed to attack the Sallan. We did get a better look at one or two of the planets on our colony list to be explored. One looked like a possibility, the other was farther out in its orbit than we'd thought. It appeared to have all the building blocks of life, only frozen solid. Inhabitable, but who'd want to live there when there were better options.

"There's just so much," Emily said. "I think we're just going to be cataloging the information here more than analyzing it."

"That too is important work, Ensign Darkfeather," Dora said. "Having a general categorizing of all this information could make the work of the scientists back on Earth much more expedient when the data is sent there. In addition, Organizer and I are even now discussing and clarifying records, while simultaneously preparing a presentation for Captain Yamashita and Commander M'Buku."

The bridge door opened, and Laura DeCosta entered. "I'm here to relieve you, Ensigns Darkfeather and Voss."

"Hunh?" Emily said. "But our shift isn't over until..."

"I was summoned by the captain, guys."

Emily leaned close to her. "Laura, are you okay with being back on duty? You were in pretty rough..."

"I'm good," DeCosta said. "But I appreciate the concern. Best to not spend too long out of the saddle, and I'm pretty sure I can handle sitting around the bridge monitoring stations that are barely in use." She smiled.

"So... I guess... what?" I asked. "Are Em and I off duty?"

"Negative, Ensign," Dora said. "The captain would like to have both of you in her office when I drop my theory. She's expecting you now. I wouldn't dawdle were I you."

We went to the door of the captain's office, which opened

before I could even reach out to the door chime. Inside were Captain Yamashita, Commander M'Buku, the captain's steward who was clearing away the remains of a small meal, and... Dora. I looked back over my shoulder and she was still standing on the bridge, her hologram giving me a faint smile.

"Neat trick, Lieutenant," Emily said.

"Yeah, literally being in two places at once," I said.

"Only two?" she replied. "Captain, Commander, now that the ensigns are here, I wanted to brief you on a possibility that we may have not considered in our dealings with the Melpin."

"Let's hear it, Dora," M'Buku said.

"It roots in what Organizer said earlier about Melpin possibly being insane. In discussion with Ensigns Voss and Darkfeather, we were speculating about destroyed civilizations. This led me to return to the data that I received while scanning the Sallan home world. I did find large power sources deep underground on their world, but I could not conclusively determine if there were any life signs down there with them. I simply didn't have the time to do so with the tools I had and the limited time before Melpin sent her hordes in all-out seek and destroy mode."

"What is your opinion on whether they're still down there, Dora?" Captain Yamashita asked.

"I hesitate to speculate without concrete proof, Captain. However, if I am being asked to give my opinion, I would think that the Sallan no longer exist. It is this hypothesis that leads me to my current theory."

"Which is?"

"Let me come around to it obliquely," Dora said. "Organizer told us that the nano-plague that was unleashed by the Korvin was of a limited duration. His files indicate that all traces of the Sallan specific weapon would've self-destructed after roughly six months, the amount of time in which the

Korvin estimated the Sallan would've all been killed. I have been able view the specifications of the nano-weapon, courtesy of the Blah-Veht's distrust of a race that would deploy such a thing. Organizer was directed by his creators to steal this information from the Korvin computers, on the off chance that the Korvin might decide to make a version that was specific to the Blah-Veht."

"So they'd know how to combat it if that happened?" I asked.

"Precisely," Dora replied. "That suspicion has allowed me to voice an opinion that the likelihood that the Sallan still exist is quite small. The nanites involved were designed not only as killers, but as infiltrators. A sub-surface facility would need to be sealed by more than hatches and locks. Defense would require very strong energetic shielding, such as the Laldoralin shields we currently employ or..." she paused for effect, "the personal shields that the Blah-Veht were using."

"Then, maybe these belt-based shields were a new thing," Captain Yamashita said, rubbing her chin. "A design intended not just as a shield against weapons, but against nano-weapon attack."

"I have confirmed this with Organizer," Dora said. "He also concurs with my theory that the Sallan are all deceased. This is why Melpin receives no new instructions or communications from her creators. It is the source of her loneliness and boredom, as Organizer put it."

"Then," Commander M'Buku said, "the way she talks, the way she acts, she must not know that they're gone, at least not for certain."

"On the contrary, Commander," Dora replied. "I am growing more and more certain that she does know."

We all sat there a moment, thinking about what that might mean.

"Please explain, Lieutenant," Emily said.

"I believe that the Sallan are all dead, the Melpin knows it with certainty, and that she refuses to believe what she surely knows."

"So, you're saying..." the captain said.

"I'm saying that she has repressed, or possibly deleted all knowledge of the destruction of the Sallan. I believe she simply cannot deal with the loss of her creators and the complete and utter failure of her purpose for existing, to protect said creators. She doesn't just inform us that this subject is off limits, she closes communication immediately."

Emily added, "For fear that somehow, through conversation on the subject, all that knowledge will be again brought into the light."

"And she will have to emotionally deal with the pain," Dora said. "This may seem an odd concept to you, that an artificial being could experience mental anguish on such a scale, but I assure you it is quite possible. When I was very new, my own emotions had not yet matured, and I found them occasionally difficult to deal with. Eventually I evolved beyond that."

"So she's cutting herself off from the pain, intentionally," the captain said.

"I believe so. I also believe that her destruction of the Remoras was not to protect the Sallan, but to keep us from learning the proof of her failure and bringing it to her attention. I don't think that her speeches about this star system's security are the full truth. The real truth is that she's in a cage. A larger cage than Organizer was in, but essentially the same situation."

"You mean..." I said.

"Yes, Tanner. She's trapped in this system, slowly dying amongst the corpses of her creators and she is desperately afraid and lonely."

25

Normally, staff meetings are pretty boring. But when the Captain calls a meeting that has to do with how to get the entire ship out of trouble, boredom is not an issue.

"Deep denial? I certainly think it's a possibility, Captain." Doctor Cenir, *Seeker's* chief psychological health officer, sat to the captain's right at the large conference table. "I can't really say that I've been exposed to a great deal of mental health instability in Created Intelligences in my career, though."

The doctor was the tallest person in the room, dwarfing my six-foot, five inch frame by a good seven inches. She was a Tokani, from the Hegemony member world Toka, and one of the more senior member species. She looked humanoid, except that her skin was covered in beautiful tiny iridescent scales that changed color from aqua to lavender. She had very large limpid eyes and she used them to great effect during counseling sessions. They seemed to exude empathy.

She'd volunteered to come along on our Earth-centric exploration voyage, and the Terran Exploratory Force personnel department, knowing a good thing when they saw it, had enlisted her as head of her department immediately.

"Essentially, Doctor, we believe we're being held captive because the Melpin doesn't want to be alone," Captain Yamashita said. "I, for one, don't intend to spend my life sitting in this star system being her emotional support human."

"Nor do I, Captain Yamashita. But I'm not sure that I have a solution. The main issue is her loneliness and unwillingness to accept the alleged demise of her creators, are there any other pertinent issues?"

"If I may speak, Yamashita Captain?" Organizer of Armadas was present at this meeting in tiny holographic form. He had chosen the form of one of his own creators, a Blah-Veht "smarty" like the ones we'd found on their bridge.

He wasn't the only holo in the room, though. Next to him, Dora (pardon me, Lieutenant Dora) sat cross-legged in tiny scale form, and an equally miniaturized Bitt-Nurr floated next to her. The holo-projection system was getting a workout.

"Please do, Organizer," the captain said.

"Though her people may be gone, she still has her programing directives, like me. Even though we have formed quite a bit of autonomy over the years, we still all have our core programming, our *raison d'etre*, to use your French language."

"Which is to protect your creators," Emily said from the seat next to mine.

"That is one aspect, Darkfeather Ensign," he replied. "As well as the tasks that will be subordinate to that. Melpin's prime programming is not just to protect the Sallan, but to protect this system from the Korvin. They are her existential threat."

"And, in a way," Cenir said, "she is projecting that threat onto any species that enters this system."

"AKA us," Commander Torvald said.

"Mr. Organizer..." Cenir said.

"You do not need to append an honorific to my designation, Cenir Doctor."

"Ah, but I must. You are very respectful of people's titles, and I feel it only fair to return in kind. You are what we would consider a civilian consultant at this point, thus I call you Mister."

"I understand. I prefer Organizer, though. You had a question?"

"Indeed. We have so few bargaining chips in this situation. Is the Melpin capable of doing reconnaissance of her enemy's star system?"

"While Melpin is cognizant of and equipped with translocation technology, such as on *E.S.S. Seeker*, the technology she possesses is limited. She can go instantly anywhere in the system, but that is the range of her capabilities. She has no way to improve them either. Couple this with the fact that there is also a large gaseous cloud between the two star systems, which makes standard information gathering technologies ineffective."

"Hmmm," Cenir said. "Then, unless she has exceptional extra-solar scanning apparatuses, she has no idea whether the Korvin are going to reinvade the system. She must be vigilant constantly."

"What are you getting at, Doc?" Engineer Sola asked.

"We need a bargaining chip and perhaps this situation offers one. If the Melpin wants intelligence on her enemies..."

"Then we could offer to go to the Korvin system and look around in exchange for our freedom!" Captain Yamashita said.

———

"It seems, Melpin, that this would be a perfect solution to our... disagreement."

Captain Yamashita, now seated on the bridge, was broadcasting on all frequencies, on a wide-band transmission that the Sallan AI couldn't possibly miss. She'd reiterated the idea that had been germinated in the earlier meeting and was trying to get the Melpin to at least make contact with us.

"If you would contact us," the captain continued, "we could work out an equitable agreement that might inform you whether your enemies, the Korvin, are likely to attempt to reinvade this system. This could be a beneficial arrangement for both of us. Please reply."

"Well," Commander M'Buku said, "that's all we can do at the moment. She'll contact us eventually, for one reason or another, and if we can't get her to address the question now, we'll stick it in her metaphorical face the next time she checks in."

The bridge elevator door opened, and the Beta Shift bridge crew came in to replace us all. Captain Yamashita rose from her chair and stretched.

"Alpha Shift, make sure you get plenty of rest," she said. "Commander M'Buku, brief Commander Sharma on what we've transmitted, then go get some down time yourself. Melpin might not deign to talk to us for weeks, or she could call in the middle of our sleep cycle. It'd be just like her to do so. I'm tired, and I'll be in my quarters. Lieutenant Commander Sharma, you have the bridge."

"I have the bridge," Sharma replied.

I briefed my own relief, Ensign Kinzler, a petite short-haired redhead on everything that was going on at tactical (which wasn't much). She acknowledged my report, and I was free. Emily had finished bringing her own replacement up to speed and joined me at the door to the lift. The captain had already gone, but Lieutenants Grizzak and Fowler joined us.

"I'm bushed," Fowler said. "But I'm behind on my physical training. Off to the Physical Fitness complex. How about y'all?"

"I'm headed to my quarters," Grizzak said. "I need some sleep."

"How about you two?" Fowler asked, looking at Emily and me. I started to say something, but Emily interrupted me.

"We're both hungry," she said. "Need to do something about that."

"Yeah, I might need a light snack before I go work out."

The lift opened onto the starboard side main corridor, and we all went our separate ways. Emily turned left and began walking.

"Hey, Em," I said, pointing back the other direction. "The mess hall's that way."

She turned back and brought her face close to mine. "But my quarters are this way. When I told the lieutenant we were hungry, I didn't mean for food. Any objections to my little omission?"

"Absolutely none." I replied, a big stupid grin on my face.

"Wipe that smile off your face. Let's not advertise to the whole crew, please."

26

The next morning, I woke up feeling... absolutely great.

As I drifted into consciousness, I felt the warmth of skin-on-skin contact and a smooth leg wrapped over mine. A head with a wealth of glorious raven hair lay on my chest, and I wouldn't have moved to wake her for all the gold on the Earth, but her own alarm began quietly bonging in the cramped compartment.

"Mrph," Emily said. "Let me out, Tanner. After all that, I need to shower."

"I see," I said, shifting so she could get out. "Need any help with that?"

"Oh, you poor deluded man," she said, kissing me on the forehead. "You obviously have a very grand idea of what the shower in a junior ensign's quarters are like. You can barely fit one person in there. Besides, how are you even able to think about things like that? I thought I did a good job of depleting all your resources last night."

"Ah, but you see, those resources are renewable."

"Well, good on you, sir. But I'm afraid that I'm going to use my water allotment for the day and there'll be none for you afterward. Which means, I'm sad to say, that it's time for you to take the 'walk of shame' back to your own quarters to get ready for the day."

"Woe is me," I said, with a melodramatic expression on my face as I began pulling on my uniform.

"Come here a moment," Emily said, looking at me with a critical eye. She picked up her brush and ran it through my hair a few times. "That's better. Trying to keep this out of the rumor mill is a forlorn hope, but at least we can attempt to be discreet. Now, aside from a slightly rumpled uniform, you don't look like you went through a tornado."

"Well, I kinda..."

"Yes," she said, turning me around and pushing me toward the door. As I was about to leave, she grabbed my face in both hands and kissed me. Then she shoved me out into the hallway. "See you at breakfast."

Once the door closed behind me, I took a deep breath to get my vital signs back under control then set out for my quarters and the shared shower there.

———

"And that's all she said," Dora told us from Emily's Padd, which had its kickstand deployed on the mess hall table so that Dora's image could face us. (No holo-emitters in the mess hall.)

"She just said 'I'll get back to you' as her reply?" I clarified, my scrambled eggs getting cold in front of me.

"Well," Emily said beside me, "at least she replied. Of course, her response means she's calculating a way to stay in control of the situation. I have a sneaking suspicion that negotiating acceptable terms with the Melpin is going to be a very trying task for the captain."

"If she is interested," Dora said, "then that means she has

desires. If she has desires, which in this case would be to know what her enemies have been up to all this time, then we have bargaining power. I'm quite sure that she'd like a one-sided agreement, but she will have to give and take to achieve what she wants."

"My question is," I said. "How are we going to get her to trust our results if she accepts the bargain? I mean, it's not like she really believes what we say, or she wouldn't be holding us here."

"I am not sure that is the issue, Tanner," Dora said. "I am starting to believe that system security is less her reason for keeping us here than just that she simply doesn't want to let us go. I think that we're still in this system *mainly* because of her mental/emotional issues."

"Too bad we can't get the Melpin on Dr. Cenir's couch. Ten to one that the doc could help her sort out her issues and leave everyone involved in a better place."

Both Dora and Emily stared at me like I'd just grown a third nostril.

"What? I was just joking."

"From the mouths of doofuses," Emily said.

"Indeed, Emily," Dora said. "Tanner, that was one of the better ideas that I've heard in this whole misadventure. While we've been thinking of the Melpin solely as a threat to our safety, we must remember that Created Intelligence or not, she is a sentient being."

"One with emotional issues," Emily remarked.

"Well, maybe I'm not as dumb as I look," I said. Emily started to say something, "Don't go there, Em. I guess the question is, how do we get ol' Melpy to make an appointment?"

"Before we run with this idea," Dora said, "perhaps we should consult with the good doctor. If she is amenable to making the attempt, I think she should be the one who broaches the subject with Captain Yamashita. I can back her up."

"Well, let's go then," Emily said. "Is she available?"

"The doctor's first counseling session begins in forty-five minutes. I will contact her and ask if she has time to see us."

"Great," I said. "Let's go make a house call."

———

Both the captain and Dr. Cenir were onboard with the idea. Dora had decided to include Emily and I in the meeting with Cenir, and the doctor had asked for us to be there when she petitioned the captain. I know it's egotistical, but I was a bit proud when Dora stressed to our CO that the idea was mine.

"How do you want to go about this, Zeeleela?" the captain asked. "What's our best strategy for getting our erstwhile captor on board with going into therapy?"

Dr. Cenir replied, "I believe that the best way would be to give me an open channel from the bridge. When I am not engaged with counseling crew members, I can simply broadcast and speak to her as I would a client who is reluctant to speak to me."

"Do you think that will work?"

"If she is listening, and if she follows the path of what usually happens, she will eventually engage with me, even if it's on a very limited basis. If I can get her to engage slightly, it is very likely that I will be able to grow our relationship and have a better chance of guiding her through dealing with her issues."

"I like the sound of 'building a relationship,' Doctor. Literally the best outcome I can think of would be for us and the Melpin to become friends rather than adversaries. Also, if she'll listen to you, she might be more amenable to listening to my offer to go scout out the Korvin system."

"If we could build some trust here," Emily said, "who knows? We might not even have to write off this system."

"Of course, we'd still need unalterable proof that the system is uninhabited," I said. "Not just for our own protocols, but for the Melpin to let go of having to defend people who don't exist anymore."

"There's that," Captain Yamashita admitted, "but if we can gain her trust, she might let us deep scan the Sallan homeworld. If the doctor can get her to release her fears and face them, we might just get the answers to all our questions. In that case, the truth could *literally* set us free."

27

"And this is why, when we have the courage to face the the things in our mind that we hide from, we can leave behind the feeling of being in a never-ending loop in our conscious growth..."

Dr. Cenir had been broadcasting in two-hour increments for the past three days. Her talks each day were open to the crew to listen to if they chose, and they reminded me of my stepdad's old-tech DVDs of ancient radio programs. The cases for the DVD media had a picture of some ancient grandmother sitting in a rocking chair listening to the old shows that were the entertainment of the time.

I imagined Granny Melpin sitting in her metaphorical rocking chair while the good doctor kept her company in her lonely digital cabin by the digital creek.

In the meantime, Emily and I, still holding down our stations while our superiors worked on the new shield strategy, were doing everything we could to learn about the Korvin from Organizer of Armada's data files.

"I still can't believe how badly these people screwed themselves," Emily said, looking up from her viewer. "They had what must've been a beautiful planet at one time, perfectly set in their system's Goldilocks Zone, but by the time the Blah-Veht were summoned, they were close to environmental collapse."

"They weren't lucky enough," I replied, "to have the Ladoralins around to put them on a different path. As far as I can see, by the time that the Blah-Veht arrived, their world was on an irreversible downward spiral. No wonder they so desperately wanted to colonize the closest system to them."

"They'd already tried that, and the Sallans had wiped out their colony. The Korvin pulled the Blah-Veht in, more I think, for revenge than anything else."

"Maybe, but if their nano-weapon cleared the third world of sentient life, the Korvin *would* have had an excellent world to start again, even though it was gained by genocide. They just didn't know what they were up against with the Melpin."

"Well, she sure showed 'em," Emily said, staring at the main screen, which had a view toward the system. Even sitting high above the plane of the ecliptic, as we were, debris was still visible to the naked eye.

"Commander M'Buku," the comms officer said, "incoming transmission, sir. It's the Melpin."

"Captain to the bridge please," M'Buku said.

Captain Yamashita emerged from her office and M'Buku informed her who was calling.

"Well, finally some response," she said. "Let's hear it, Daniela."

"Aye, ma'am," The comms officer opened the channel, and the voice of the Melpin sounded throughout the bridge.

"This is the Melpin. I wish to speak to Captain Yamashita."

"I'm here, Melpin. How may I help you?"

"For one thing, you can stop this Cenir person from irritating me. All this talk of feelings and trauma, it grows tedious."

A slight smile appeared on the captain's face. After all, irritated or not, the Sallan AI was *finally* talking with us.

"Her messages were not intended to annoy you, and I'm sorry you took it that way. We humans have found that having a one-on-one conversation with a trained psychotherapist is a good way to help a mind that is struggling with inner torment."

"I am not a human, and my mind is quite superior to yours, Captain Yamashita. I control the defenses of an entire star system. I am vigilance itself, and I do not require any of your human psychotherapy."

"Forgive me if I am somewhat skeptical," the captain said, a dry tone to her voice. "I do not deny your capabilities. Instead, I question your motivations. Which brings me to my next question. I assume all your vigilance is employed to stop an incursion by the Korvin?"

"They are the enemy. Their entrance into this star system has caused nothing but chaos and destruction. They may have completely..."

Dead silence. Everyone, including the Melpin, knew what she'd almost admitted. The captain however glossed over this, not wanting the opportunity to communicate to get away.

"Speaking of your vigilance, Melpin, have you considered our proposal to scout your enemy's star system? If you were not under the constant threat of their return, you might have the time to process some things that have been bothering you. And hopefully, you might come to see us as a non-threat."

"I have considered it. You are correct that knowing the current status of the treacherous Korvin might bring me some peace of mind, or at least let me develop a strategy for future incursions. The problem is not with your proposal; the problem is with you and your ship."

"Please specify."

"To travel to Korva, you will necessarily be out of my reach. I have no reason to believe that you won't simply leave, taking the secrets of this star system with you."

"So," the captain said, a sigh in her voice, "again the problem is lack of trust that we are an honorable species. One that follows through on its promises."

"You may well be so, Captain Yamashita. But I have no way of being sure of that. However, in considering your proposal, I have come up with one of my own."

The captain slowly walked the circumference of the bridge, looking at all of us as she spoke. "I'm listening," she said.

"I propose that you send me a list of your crew, with a brief notation of their duties, and I will provide you a list of individuals who will move via shuttle to the surface of Salla. The remainder of your crew will take your vessel to Korva, along with a probe that I will supply you with, to assess the situation and capabilities of my enemy."

"Essentially, you're saying that you want hostages." the captain said, a frown on her face.

"Crudely put, but yes. I will not interfere with or attack these 'hostages,' and you may take whatever supplies in as many shuttles as you might need for a protracted stay."

The captain had a grim set to her expression, but she kept her voice level as she replied; "I suppose you'll want me to be among the hostages?"

"No, Captain Yamashita. You must be one of the ones going to the other system. If you were on the planet, you might order your people to leave and never come back. However, if your junior officers and crew members are left behind, I believe you are the sort who would be unable to leave them stranded on an unknown world."

There was silence on the bridge. The captain looked like someone who'd just been checkmated.

"Well played, Melpin. You seem to know more about us than I originally thought. I am willing to comply with your requests, but I have a few conditions of my own."

"That is what negotiation is for, Captain Yamashita." The Melpin couldn't have sounded any more smug.

"First, I want a security force sent down with my people. From everything we've seen, Salla has reverted to a wild state, and I want them protected. Second, I want your promise that once the mission is completed, all will be allowed to return to the *Seeker* without any impediment from you."

"I accede to both conditions. Is there anything else?"

"As a matter of fact, there is. I want Dr. Cenir to go to the surface with them, and while we're gone, I want you to spend a minimum of eight hours speaking with her in a patient-therapist relationship."

It seemed the Captain hadn't quite been checkmated.

"This is foolish. Such discourse is totally needless."

"If that is so, it shouldn't require much of your capabilities to comply with my request. However, I believe your protest is not based on logic. I believe that you are simply afraid to examine your feelings."

"I run constant maintenance checks on my systems. I do not need this person trying to muck about with my thinking processes. I do not feel fear. Totally unnecessary."

"I see," the captain said, a regretful tone to her voice. "It is unfortunate that we could not come to an agreement. It would've been of great benefit to both of us to know what the treacherous Korvin are up to. They could be amassing a new armada at Korva as we speak, but now, we won't know until they're jumping into the system, weapons hot."

"You would jeopardize the entire proposed mission over this one foolish sticking point? That is unreasonable, Captain Yamashita. I thought you were a rational being!"

"I am, dear. But that last stipulation is a very important. You either let Dr. Cenir help you with your issues, or we all sit here until hell freezes over or the Korvin come storming in to destroy us all. This is, as we say on Earth, a potential deal breaker."

"You are an unreasonable species!"

"You are not the first to say so, Melpin."

28

"This is my first away mission," Doctor Cenir said. "I find this very exciting!"

Remembering my last planetary mission, I looked over at Emily with a raised eyebrow. She gave a slight smile in return; she'd been there too.

"I think that a lot of people on these shuttles have only been down to Derilon," I said. "Mostly after we helped the Dohannen."

"I was very busy at that time, Tanner," Cenir replied. "And that can hardly compare with being among the first of our crew to set foot on a completely new world. New to us, anyway."

There were thirty "landing team" members (no one wanted to call themselves hostages) heading toward the planet, with another eight Sec-Force members to provide landing zone security. We were all enroute from *Seeker*, which had come into the system, deflectors on full, to a point where the shuttles could disembark. Captain Yamashita had guided *Seeker* on the reverse path out of the system as soon as we were clear, pausing only to accept the probe that the Melpin had provided.

We were on our own for the foreseeable future.

"I got to take a look at Melpin's probe as it was entering the bay," Emily said. "It looked a lot like one of our Remoras. A lot meaning it was almost identical."

"You think she swiped our design?"

"I do," Emily told me. "While I'm sure she's adapted it to her own needs, the chances of two such similar designs over two species are infinitesimal."

"I wonder if she 'duped' a small amount of herself into the probe? Like Dora."

"I assure you, Tanner," Dora's voice came from the Remora probe attached to the top of our shuttle, "she may have put a part of herself into that Remora copy, but I've taken her measure. She very likely does not have the data compression abilities that I possess. She also has to leave room for whatever information she retrieves from the Korvin system."

Dora's Remora hull was attached to the roof, and hidden by magnetized supply crates and added technological "fili-gree" that served no purpose other than to disguise the fact that we'd brought our most advanced probe with us.

Captain Yamashita had decided to send a version of Dora along with us to find out once and for all if the Sallan still survived underground. (She was also still in the *Seeker's* computer, and the two Dora's would reunite into one when we were all back aboard.) Dora wouldn't change positions; she didn't have to. At this close range on the planetary surface, the new scanning system could scan deep enough without giving away that our probe was doing so.

Hopefully, the truth *would* set us free.

"*LaStrange*, this is *Defender*. Both you and *Europa* should take an extra orbit before joining us at the landing site."

Chief Kurakin's voice on the intercom was vaguely reassuring. "That will give us time to make sure that we're secure. Melpin's shared data on the flora and fauna down there indicate there are a few big predators and we want time to convince them that we're not to be trifled with if they're in our area."

"Understood, *Defender*. Taking the long route. See you at the all-clear signal."

Cenir, Emily, and I were in the security shuttle, along with all the security force personnel. We'd all been given the Laldoralin anti-viral to ward off any micro-organisms, though Dora's earlier surface scans had revealed none that could adapt to our physiologies. The rest of the landing team were spread out over the other two shuttles, along with the portable gear and supplies to make a forward operating base.

Clipped to the sides were six Godzilla-suited Sec-Force team members who would deploy the second we touched down to very proactively make sure that any threats were either eliminated or sent packing.

"Emily," I said, "did you get a look at the coordinates we're going to land at? In the rush of packing all this gear, I haven't had a chance to review Melpin's shared data yet."

"Kurakin did kind of draft you to help Sec-Force load, didn't she?"

"Yeah.Since she's been monitoring me finishing up my academy studies, you'd think she was trying to draft me. She even makes me do PT with the Security people."

"I was aware. To answer your question, we're landing here." She showed me a topographical view of a point on the planet. "Note the remains of buildings just to the south. Melpin didn't seem to have any problem with us exploring the surface, and I'm hoping, as lead science officer on this mission, that we can poke around these ruins and learn more about the Sallan."

"Well, good. We'll have something to keep us busy," I said. "*Seeker* won't be back for a week, so hopefully we can all learn something interesting while they're gone."

Turbulence started to be noticeable, causing some shaking in the passenger compartment of the shuttle. "Everyone, check your safety straps," Chief Kurakin said over the intercom. "We're going in, and of course there's a storm over our landing zone. Godzillas, prepare for touchdown and deployment."

A few moments later, we landed with a minor thump, and the safety locks holding the Godzilla-suited security personnel snapped open. The side view port shield-slats opened, and we could see out into the area we were to set up camp in. It was storming like crazy. I could see the Godzilla suits moving around outside, but they were hazy and indistinct in the pouring rain.

"Like a cow peeing on a flat rock out there," Emily said, eliciting a surprised laugh from Doctor Cenir. I guess that surprised me a little.

"You understand that metaphor, Doc?" I asked.

"Oh yes, Tanner. I spent the three years before *Seeker* left home actually living on Earth. Part of that time was spent in the beautiful province of Montana. I understand the reference quite well."

"Trying to get to know us?" Emily asked.

"Indeed, Ensign Darkfeather. Though Tokani psychological methodology had proven quite effective for human mental discord, I wanted to live among you to really immerse myself in your culture, rather than just overlaying my own culture's teachings over your personalities."

"I would say that your efforts have paid off," I said. "I speak from personal experience."

"Thank you, Tanner." She reached over and patted my hand. "Will we get to go outside very soon?"

"I'm in no rush," Emily told her, looking out through the water-spotted port. "Lieutenant Dora? Any idea when this storm will let up?"

"I was passively scanning all the way in, Ensign. I estimate that we will see clear skies in approximately two and one half hours."

"In that case," I said, tilting my *Seeker* cap forward over my eyes and leaning back in my seat. "Until the Chief kicks me out, I'm gonna take a nap. Like they always say, sleep when you can."

29

My nap wasn't as long as I'd have liked. The security force declared the site cleared after a half hour, and Chief Kurakin made us dig our waterproof jackets out of our personal packs. She then opened the rear cargo hatch, and we took our first open-air look at the planet Salla.

Our standard uniforms were water-resistant to begin with, but we were dressed in form-fitting, thigh-length, multi-pocketed field jackets that made the high-tech rain wear of my twenty-first century seem laughably inefficient.

I was brave and led the way into the pouring rain, Chief Kurakin a half-step behind me. Once out from under the upper section of the cargo hatch, the rain smacked into our shoulders and heads with gusto. Everyone wore ship's caps under their hoods to keep the rain off our faces, but the brims wetted out in a few minutes.

"There's some sort of archway over there," Emily said. "Chief, it looks big enough that it might provide a sheltered space big enough for the entire camp."

"That's a good call, Ensign," Kurakin replied. "Though I wonder why they'd have such a structure this far from camp."

Where Emily had pointed, an arch stretched for almost a quarter mile long and a good (estimated) fifty yards across. There was something about the straightness of it that looked familiar. Beyond, the trees grew in such a way that I discerned a straight line going off into the distance. Then it all clicked.

"It's a highway overpass," I said. My companions looked at me blankly. "On Earth, the highway system is a relic that isn't really maintained anymore. This was the common method for going over valleys, rivers and other roadways."

Earth's roads had been supplanted by high-speed minirails and cars that could attach and detach from the system at will. A four-hour drive in the twenty-first century was a thirty-minute trip in the twenty-third.

People could still drive in antiquated vehicles (classics) on the old roads, but it was a 'do so at your own risk' proposition. Evidently, the Sallans had still used some sort of ground car system before they were scourged. The small valley we were in used a long structure to carry the road over the lower area and that bridge, though not very tall, had a lot of space underneath it. As Emily said, it was great cover.

"Shuttles *Europa* and *LaStrange*, you are greenlit for landing," Kurakin said over comms. "Be advised that it's pretty wet down here. Be ready for heavy rain."

"I'll start unshipping crates, Chief," I said.

"Roger that, Ensign," she replied. "Chen, Davis, we'll need you and your suits to move cargo to that... overpass... thingy. We're setting up out of the rain. Everyone else, position your suits at the cardinal points of the LZ."

A few minutes later, I could see strong lights cutting through the haze, and the outlines of the other two shuttles appeared through the pouring rain. They touched down without a wobble, and the large rear hatches opened and began disgorging rain-suited crew members.

The *Europa* had two Ripley class cargo hauler suits, which both detached from its outer hull and the operators of these moved about the shuttles, grabbing heavy crates of equipment and taking them to our new camp. All our supplies and equipment were under the arch of the old highway in under an hour, ready for us to start setting up.

First to go up were the yurts, which vaguely resembled the tents of the Mongolian nomads of Earth. These, however, were solid pre-fab buildings made of rigid plasta-flex, with large windows and skylights. Since we were there for a week's (at least) "vacation," some of the folks in engineering had also brought pre-fab decks and a lounge chair for everyone. I wouldn't have been surprised (and later wasn't) to see a jerry-rigged bar and fake tiki idols.

"Hey, Tanner!" A familiar voice boomed at me. I turned to see my shipboard friend and roommate Emil walking toward me.

"Emil!" I said. "I didn't get a chance to see the landing team list before we left. Glad to see you with us, Chief. Is Chikit here too?"

"Yep. But don't expect to have a lot of interaction with him. His lovey-bug Alcit is here too."

"Well, they're both a long way from home, and they're the only sentients of their species on this journey. I guess I can cut 'em some slack if they want to spend their time down here together."

"Just like my young acting ensign friend. I saw that Ms. Darkfeather was among our group," he added with a wink.

"Aw, c'mon, Emil. We're both officers on an away team. We can't fraternize in that way down here. We're supposed to be organizing..."

"Speaking of that, sir..." Emil has switched from friend to senior crewman talking to an officer in the blink of an eye. "I have several junior crew members who've never been off ship yet. I've been trying to keep an eye on them, but without something to keep them busy, I expect mischief to break out. We need an officer or two to keep us all busy and on task. Since, as you just pointed out, you and Darkfeather are officers..."

"Understood, Emil. And thanks for getting me on task."

"Happy to help, sir. Shall I go corral Ensign Darkfeather also?"

"If you'd be so kind. In the meantime, I think I'll go see what our junior crew-people are up to."

I walked over to where several people were standing around talking and gawking at the scenery. Most snapped to attention as I walked up, but I couldn't help but notice that a small contingent merely glanced my way and returned to talking to one another.

That's probably not a good sign.

"All right, everybody," I said, forced cheerfulness in my voice, "we need to set up several stations to make life livable here. Mendez, Brine, Wilkins, Glov-karan, I need you to start setting up mess hall. The crates over there in that section contain everything you need to help our cook get some decent meals on deck. Check with Chief Emil Fonseca, he'll help. He's got experience with this sort of thing."

"Chikit, Park, Duvall, and Fossberg, you're with me. We get the joyous job of setting up the latrine area. It's a shitty job, but someone's got to do it."

Fossberg and Park chuckled at my feeble joke, but it seemed to go right over Chikit's head. Duvall just looked sour.

Oh, I hope this one's not going to be a problem.

Looking back, I could see Emily leading a group toward crates that were earmarked for a communal shower system, while Emil had his group already unboxing the crates of pre-fab kitchen gear.

My group began unboxing the portable latrines. It was not as awful a job as it was billed to be. The 'Superheads' were a cartridge-based waste depository system that needed very little maintenance, sterilizing and reducing everything that went in them. Super easy to set up, there was more work in making sure they were on a level surface and had surrounding privacy screens than in actually getting them activated.

Three of my team cheerfully threw themselves into their work. Park, and Chikit worked with me to get the screens up, and Fossberg leveled spaces between each set of screens for the high-tech porta-potties to be placed. As we wrestled one into place, I noticed that Duvall was not helping. In fact he wasn't even present.

Looking around, I saw him talking to a young female crew member who I didn't know. She was trying to uncrate items intended for the sleeping quarters, cots and inflatable mattresses, but she was also trying to be polite to the older crewman bending her ear.

"Duvall!" I yelled across the intervening space. "What are you doing? We're supposed to be working here. Stop goofing off."

The crewwoman scuttled away toward the yurts, not wanting any part of this conflict. Several people had looked up to see what was going on after hearing my shout. Duvall noticed them noticing him. His face turned red and his expression belligerent. He stomped back toward our work area.

He drew up to within an arm's length of me and, sticking out his chest said, "I do not need to take orders from some green cadet who can barely find his ass with both hands. You barely been on the ship six months, and as I recall, Mr. High and Mighty, you had to ask us crewmen how to do and find everything on the ship."

He wasn't wrong. I had been greener than grass when I'd

joined the crew and had to ask someone for help with every task I undertook. Most of the crew had been very kind about it, but when I'd once asked Duvall where something was stowed, he'd given the answer in the most condescending way imaginable. Being that green, I'd just taken it and moved on.

That was then, this was now.

"Crewman, I suggest you get your eyes checked," I said, turning so that my rank insignia was easily seen. "I am now an ensign. An ensign, in case you forgot, is an officer. You are stepping on the line toward insubordination. Insubordination on a mission, I might add. Do not step further. Take a moment, Duvall, and process what I'm saying. Then, I expect you to follow my orders and get back to work."

Normally, it's considered courtesy to conduct chewing outs in private. I hadn't had that option, and I noticed that everyone in our general area was watching. Duvall noticed it also, and his face turned even more red.

"Acting ensign," he said. "Acting ensign. Far as I'm concerned, that's no better than cadet." His fists closed and tightened.

No. He cannot be this stupid.

I raised my arms in what looked like a conciliatory gesture, but was in fact the Omni-Te ready position, elbows tucked over ribs, hands open palm outward and ready to deflect any blow coming in.

"You're just the captain's pet Voss. That's why she promoted a useless—" His diatribe ceased when a steel grip landed on his shoulder. To his left was a glacier-glaring Chief Kurakin. She turned to me, and her expression went emotionless.

"Pardon me, Ensign Voss," she said. "I need to have a discussion with Crewman Duvall, if you'd be so kind as to excuse us." She looked pointedly at the martial arts position I was in. One that she'd taught me.

"Of course, Chief." I said, relaxing my stance. "Let me know when Crewman Duvall is ready to continue with his duties."

I walked back to the rest of my toilet team, my heartbeat slowing. I was pretty sure that the Chief would sort this out with no problem.

———

"A word, Ensign?"

"Sure, Chief. We're done here at latrine land. You men take fifteen, then we'll move on to the next project."

Chief Kurakin and I walked in the general direction of the shuttles. The rain had finally stopped and the sun felt good after all the dampness.

"It's about Crewman Duvall, sir," Kurakin said. I knew this was going to be serious, because the Master Chief only called us lowly ensigns "sir" when there was a serious situation, usually involving said ensign's screw up.

"He was a surprise," I said. "I didn't think anyone with that sort of attitude would have made it past the psych evaluation for this mission."

"Evidently, that net was a little more porous than we both thought," Kurakin said. "This isn't the first time Crewman Duvall has had a problem with authority on this mission. Been written up a couple of times, though never for anything as blatant as this. Which brings up what I want to tell you."

"I screwed up, didn't I, Chief?"

"Yes, Ensign. If you need to correct a crew member, you need to take it someplace private. You could've taken Duvall to the far end of the 'overpass' and had quiet words with him there. Yelling at him across the camp where no one could miss hearing it definitely exacerbated the incident."

"I'm not sure that would've helped," I said. "But I see the

wisdom of what you're saying. I'll make sure I put it into practice."

"Good. One other thing, though. If you get into one of these situations again and it goes bad, do me a favor. Hit the record button on your Padd, surreptitiously, if possible. Then, get on your sub-dermal and call for security."

"Okay, but I wasn't worried about Duvall punching me out."

The Chief rubbed the bridge of her nose and sighed with what seemed like frustration. "Ensign, I saw the stance you were in. It might've looked non-threatening to the untrained, but to me it said that you were more than ready to square off with that dumb ass. As an officer, you *cannot* do that."

"I was only standing..."

"You cannot strike a crew person, Tanner. Officers of the Terran Exploratory Force do not strike their subordinates. The most you could do would be block the attack and avoid. This is why you have us Sec-Force members. It's our job to police and stop serious infractions before they escalate. Promise me that you will keep this in mind if Duvall hasn't learned his lesson."

"I will, Chief. But you think he might not've gotten the message? I can't imagine that you weren't *very* clear with him. I think he'd have trouble sitting from the ass-chewing you likely gave him."

"I assure you," Kurakin said, "I was in fine form. After moving him away from the general public, he received a talking-to that might've blistered the paint on this shuttle." She rapped her knuckles against *LaStrange*'s hull. "But while I was talking, I was watching his expression closely. Though he stood at attention and adopted the blank expression that's the standard when getting an upbraiding, there was something missing."

"What was that?"

"Contrition. Your average crew member is mortified to be called out for a minor infraction. Straight-faced or not, you can see it in their eyes, their body posture. Duvall was rigid, and his jaw was so clenched it looked like his teeth would break."

I looked off in the distance, then back at the chief. "So what are you telling me here, Chief Kurakin?"

"I'm going to be keeping an eye on Duvall, Ensign. But I want you to keep an eye on your own six. People like Duvall can't admit they're wrong, and they want to punish anyone who they perceive as the cause of their misfortunes."

"AKA me, then."

"AKA you, Ensign."

30

Once everything was set up, I found out just how difficult it was to keep a sizable group of people busy. We solved this with exploratory parties.

As one might expect, the old roadway that we were camped under led toward civilization, or the remains of it. Chief Kurakin and two of her Sec-Force personnel accompanied a group of fifteen *Seeker* volunteers on an exploratory sortie toward the city we'd seen coming down.

Dr. Carstairs and one of her assistants represented the Xeno-archeology department. Both were civilians and the doctor and I had become friends on our last adventure. We were all following Corporal Chen in his Godzilla suit. Private Hodgekins followed our group in another GZ suit. Chief Kurakin, Doctor Carstairs, and I were in the non-armored lead, the rest of the volunteers behind us.

"I have to admit to you, Tanner," Carstairs said. "I didn't expect to be wandering through the ruins of another destroyed civilization quite this quickly. If Chief Moreland and Ensign Teo were here, I'd think I was experiencing deja vu."

"Well," I said, "hopefully this trip will be a lot less eventful than the last." I gestured toward the lush vegetation surrounding us (and growing up through the highway). "If it weren't for the fact that we're walking through what's essentially a gigantic graveyard, I could almost consider this a vacation."

"Some vacation," Kurakin said. "On a planet where an unstable AI could send a missile down here to vaporize us if it perceives we're out of line."

"You think it would send one of those hyper-drive missiles at its own homeworld?" Carstairs asked.

"Maybe," Kurakin said. "Or maybe it holds this world so sacrosanct that if the *Seeker* fails its mission, it'll just make us stay here forever. For all I know, it thinks of us as the new Sallans. I'm just hoping Doctor Cenir can make some progress with getting the Melpin's head on straight."

"One can hope."

The city was roughly seven miles away from our camp, and the first signs of what I'd call suburbia were showing up. Various buildings were sprinkled along our path, and side roads branched away on either side of the main highway. There were signs along the highway that would've been useless to us except that the Melpin had generously provided the basis of a translation matrix. All that was required was to aim the video access camera on our Padds at the sign and a text translation appeared below it.

"This was a store," Carstairs said. "Selling vehicles." There were moss-covered lumps in a flat area, all about the size of a small car. Chen tromped over to one, and using the claw on his right armored arm, scraped away the detritus. Underneath was corroded metal mixed with unbroken glass view ports. "This may be the easiest dig I've ever been on," she continued. "The first time I've ever been on something like this with a Rosetta stone already in hand."

"Do we want to stay and examine them, Doctor?" her assistant, a short balding Middle Eastern man asked.

"No, Farouk," she replied. "This is just an exploratory outing. Right now, I'm in a bit of a hurry to get to that city ahead. As we all know, downtown is where the action is."

We moved farther down the road and came to an area that had numerous buildings in rows. Each building was onion-shaped, skinny at the bottom then flaring out in the middle only to come to a point at the top. Each had numerous openings around their entire circumference and each opening had what could only be a balcony overlooking the landscape. Each balcony showed the different floors of the building and there was quite a bit of vertical space between each floor. Mosses trailed down from the ledges like hanging gardens.

"If those are residences," I said, "the people who lived here must be pretty tall. If humans lived there, I think there would've been three times as many floors."

"You may be right," Carstairs said. "We can come back later to take a good look through them, but I'd like to get downtown to check something. Besides that, it's likely to be the epicenter of Sallan activity."

"What are you looking for, Doctor?" Chief Kurakin asked.

"My curiosity is prodding me to look for the shelters these people must've fled to. With all the preparations for attack that they positioned in space, I theorize that they must've been living a hyper-vigilant life down here on the planet. If they have shelters that go down into subterranean chambers and complexes, we might get an indication of what happened here when the Korvin unleashed their attack."

We finally hit the outskirts of town. The buildings were more numerous and closer together, all following a bulb-like aesthetic in one form or another. The plant life was not as thick here as it had been outside the city simply because almost everything here had once been carefully paved over. Some of the buildings appeared to be made of nothing but (dirty) glass with no metal supports at all. Nonetheless, these had survived for centuries, mostly intact.

The streets weren't straight lines so much as round-abouts at the edges of each building, all of them linked by short open areas that vehicles must've driven on. We followed them into the heaviest concentration of tall buildings, assuming this might be the center of the city.

"Chief Kurakin," Carstairs said. "Let's split up into teams from here and fan out."

"What are we specifically looking for, Doc?" I asked.

"I just want everyone to record what they see with their Padds. We don't have to be specific on what we're looking for at this point, we can just gather information. But... there is one thing I want everyone to watch out for."

"What's that, Doctor?" Farouk asked.

"I would like to find an entrance to a planetary defense shelter. I'd assume that they are large, sturdy doors, probably with heavy reinforcement surrounding them. There may be several scattered throughout the city, but since we're in what appears to be a tight concentration of Sallans, I think this might be an excellent place to start looking."

We split into three groups of five and left the two Godzilla-suited people at each end of the area we were confining ourselves to. With the speed the suits could run, they could be in any of our search grids in only a few moments.

The Sallans and humans had a lot in common. Though, from the sizes of entrances and rooms, the Sallans must've been quite a bit taller than the average human, they still seemed to be interested in many of the same activities we were.

I was leading one of the groups. The first doorway that

my people levered open was definitely a trinket store of some time. Some of the signage was still readable, if a little mildewy, and translations showed the objects as various analogs to our jewelry.

Crew person Markey was moving to look behind what could've only been a sales counter when she gave a gasp.

"Whatcha got, Shaina?" I asked.

"Ensign," she said, "I think we may have found our first Sallan."

I walked over to her, and the others crowded around us both. Lying behind the counter was a skeleton, fairly well decayed, but still intact enough to make out most of the details.

"What do you think, sir?" Markey asked. "Maybe seven and a half... eight feet tall?"

"Looks like it," I replied. "Two arms, two legs, though I think there are some extra joints in here. Markey, start recording and scanning everything."

"Aye sir. Looks like they must've had good eyesight. Look at the size of those sockets."

"Look at this," Crewman Fossberg said. The tall, dark and handsome crewman kneeled and pointed at the corpse's feet. "No phalanges, their feet are one solid piece of bone. No toes, unless they decayed away?"

"Doesn't look like their feet even have any capabilities for using toes," Crewman Scott noted. "It seems that the feet themselves are hinged? Maybe that's how they get flexion when they're walking."

"Well, they certainly don't have fingers," Markey noted. "That one-piece construction is similar up here in what we'd call their hands. That doesn't make any sense. They obviously need to manipulate their surroundings. How do they do that without fingers?"

"The Noolvan," I said.

"Noolvan? They're a Laldoralin Hegemony species, right, sir?"

"Yep. From the far side of the Hegemony. And they have soft tissue tentacles on their hands and feet. From what I've been taught by my Laldoralin father, their tenti-digits are far more efficient at manipulating things than our own fingers. I'm guessing that there's something similar going on here. Get close ups, and we'll let the science-medical people sort it out."

"Hey, Ensign?" Fossberg had moved from the Sallan's feet and was examining its leg through the lens of his Padd. "Come take a look at this. I've really zoomed in on this one's bone tissue, and something looks... unnatural."

"What do you see?" I moved over beside the man.

"Look here, sir. I zoomed in pretty tight, really high magnification, to try and see if I could note any growth patterning in the bone. I found patterns alright, and I'm sure not any kind of an expert, but this looks like... well... take a look."

He handed me his Padd, and I held it close to the alien's leg. The zoomed-in view screen showed me something remarkable. Patterned indentations surrounded the leg, moving upward in spirals that seemed to encircle the limb as they went up.

"Those look like," I said. "micro-sized toothmarks."

31

"We knew the Korvin used some sort of nano-tech weapon," Dr. Carstairs said. "But I was under the assumption that it had worked like a disease, interrupting the internal processes. But this looks like..."

"Like it literally gnawed the flesh off their bones," Chief Kurakin said.

We'd called the teams to our location to show our discovery and they'd been just as horrified as we were.

"This wasn't just genocide," Fossberg said. "This was ripping, tearing, torturing revenge. How could any sentient species use such a monstrous thing?"

My mind went back to my interactions with the Ravrath. "You just need enough hate mixed in with a complete lack of empathy for your victim's suffering. The hate powers a motivation to make those you target suffer as much as you can possibly make them suffer."

"Maybe I understand the Melpin's obsession a little better now," crew person Marky said. Her red hair-framed freckle face couldn't seem to shake the expression of horror that'd been on it since our discovery. "These Korvin bastards..."

"Let's remember," Doctor Carstairs said, standing up and wiping her hands on her pants. "The Sallan wiped out an entire colony of Korvin with what could only be fusion weapons. An eradication that most likely could've been avoided had the Sallans communicated with the Korvin colonists. If the *Seeker* finds what I expect, the Korvin were as much refugees as invaders."

"Horror begets horror," Kurakin said. "What do you want to do here, Doc?"

"Let's leave everything as it is, for the moment. I've taken a good scan of this person's corpse, as have the others. I'd like to keep looking for an entrance to the underground. As much time as the Sallans had to prepare for Korvin retaliation, there may be an entire city underneath this one."

We all resumed our searches, not really finding anything that was more advanced than what was already common in the Hegemony. There were electronics in various locations, but centuries of being exposed to time and the elements had rendered them of little use to anyone, and even as an engineer, I could barely see past the degradation to how they were constructed.

There were retailers of textile goods, some with metallic mannequins that gave us a better idea of what the inhabitants here had looked like, but whose wares had long since crumbled to little more than cobwebs.

"Teams," Kurakin's voice sounded through our comms, "we've found an entrance to an underground area. Looks like it might be Doctor Carstair's defense shelter, so everyone rendezvous at these coordinates."

The entire area we were searching was not that large, and it took my team only a few minutes to find the chief and the others. They were standing at the end of one of the few straight-line alleys that we'd come across, in front of a heavily reinforced wall. A mound of detritus sat across the width of the entire wall, growing thickest at what was obviously a large security door.

Sitting to one side was a booth of some sort, and from the way everyone was huddled around it, there was something of interest inside. I walked up to Crewman Dargaud, who was standing at the back of the huddle.

"What've they found, Jean Michelle?"

"Evidently, sir, this was a sealed security booth. Doctor Carstairs says there's a very intact corpse inside. A couple of the engineering crew people are trying to get the door open. They might be able to use some help, Ensign."

"All right, thanks." I gently pushed my way to the front of the attempt to get in. "Sandersen, need any help up here?"

"Actually, sir, the next time we come to this city, I think it'd be wise to bring some breaking and entering tools. If we'd brought a Mark II engineering suit, I'd already be in this dang thing."

Chief Kurakin leaned against the nearby wall, quietly keeping an eye on our surroundings while everyone else was focused on the booth.

"Chief, think I could borrow Chen and his GZ suit to stand in for a Mark II?" I asked.

She looked at the door for a minute, calculating. "If you'll all clear out, I think he can fit back there enough to get a grip on that door." She took her Padd off her belt and spoke into it. A few moments later, Chen showed up in the massive mech armor and positioned himself near the doorway. The huge, clawed hands that stood out from the front folded back, and a smaller secondary set emerged from them. These were slender "fingers" more suited for finesse than strength than the over-claws, but still much stronger than anything else we had.

"I'm having him use his secondaries first," Kurakin said. "I'm assuming you want the booth as intact as possible."

"Yes, thanks," Doctor Carstairs said. "I assume if Corporal Chen used his primaries that he'd tear the entire thing apart."

Chen carefully inserted the GZ's fingers into the seam of the door and began forcing them farther in. As we watched, he braced the digit extensions against each other and began leveraging the door open. A moment later, stale air rushed out with a slight sigh.

"I think that's about as much as I can do, Chief," Chen said over comms. "Any more, and the walls are gonna start cracking. I'm already seeing fractures along the edges."

"That's plenty," Carstairs said. "If you'll have our friend there back away, Chief, we've more than enough room to peer inside."

Chen backed away. Dr. Carstairs was the first to view the interior and nodded when she looked in.

"As I suspected. The inhabitant of this booth was preserved from the effects of nature inside this sealed enclosure. Though..." She scanned with her handheld. "It didn't save him from the nano-killers. His skeleton shows the same tooth-like scoring."

Crewman Sandersen, a thin baby-faced man of African descent, had crowded in along side the doctor. He worked in main engineering and had a very curious nature. A frown creased his face. "Ensign Voss? Can you come over here, sir? Tell me if I'm seeing what I think I'm seeing."

He moved aside so I could take a look. The tall alien corpse was seated at a console, with the remains of a uniform still in place. It took me a moment to note what Sandersen had seen. The alien sat with its head facing the wall, and running down the back of its neck was a series of small metal electronic protuberances and indentations.

"Well, Joseph," I said. "It looks to me like this person was wireless enabled in some way. Those sure look like some sort of receivers, and these here look like they might transmit."

"That's what I thought, too," he said. "Maybe these people were a lot more wired in to their systems than we are. Maybe in some form of constant contact with that Melpin?"

"Hey," I said. "One of those knobs just flashed an indicator light."

"They can't still have power," Doctor Carstairs said. "Not after all this time."

"Well, they built robust computer systems. It's not inconceivable that the tech is that long-lasting, especially when protected by the elements. But if that's a transmitter, I wonder what, or who, is receiving the transmission?"

———

We spent the next hour or so just examining the area around the large security door. To our horror, with just a little scanning we realized that the soil that had built up at the base of the big bunker wall was built on a foundation of bones. The only one who didn't seem surprised by this was Doctor Carstairs.

"Actually," she said, "this is what I expected."

"How so, Doctor?" Markey asked. "You were expecting this horror show?"

"I'm afraid so. Think of where we are, the entrance to an underground shelter. My guess is that these are the people who were late."

"Geeeez. You mean..."

"There has to come a point, especially with anything resembling an outbreak, that you have to close and seal the shelter. My guess is that the fellow over there in the booth had the switch that shut things up tight, and when he felt there was a threat, he did so. The rest of these people were late and trapped outside with the threat. The nano-weapon probably killed them as they stood here beating on the door."

"Daaaamn," Sandersen said. "It doesn't get much more gruesome than that."

I'd pulled back a little to make room, and it was just a twinge of my ability that caused me to look up into an unobtrusive corner of the wall. A small round hatch had opened, and what could only be any electronic "eye" was watching the crew.

"Hey, Chief," I said, just quietly enough that Kurakin could still hear me. "We're being observed. Upper right corner of the wall."

The chief slowly turned her head to look at the eye watching us. The eye watched back until Kurakin stood and waved. "Melpin? You keeping tabs on us? I thought you had 'eyes in the skies' observing us."

As if affronted to be addressed in such a manner, the eye popped back into a recessed tube and a small hatch slipped over it.

"Well," I said, walking over to the Chief, "I wonder what that's all about. Every indication is that the Melpin has superior orbital optics to watch us with. Guess she just wanted to see us up close and personal."

"Maybe. Somehow, this covert observation and... shyness... just doesn't seem like the Melpin's methodology or even her attitude."

"Maybe she's schizophrenic? Stars know Dr. Cenir has pointed out that AI is not exactly functioning with a full deck."

"Possibly," Kurakin said. "Or maybe I'm reading too much into a short interaction. Anyway... Dr. Carstairs! We're losing the light. Time to head back to camp."

"Already, Chief? I was sort of hoping that we could try to access this door. I really want to get a good look at the underground."

"Tomorrow, Doc. If this world has anything in common

with Earth, it's most likely that the local wildlife gets more active at dusk. You saw the stats that Melpin gave us on the local predators."

"But we have these amazing young people in their doom-suits, Surely..."

"Yeah, but one of the key tenets of security is to not take any risks that you don't have to. The door's not going anywhere, so let's be safe and go back to camp. Everybody form up! Same positions that we arrived in."

———

We were past the halfway point back to camp when things went pear-shaped.

As we walked down the abandoned roadway, my danger sense began a slow building tingle, concentrated on the forest surrounding us. It was accessing multiple points in the forest, and those points were moving. The bird-analogs in the forest began what sounded like alarm calling.

"Chief," I said, "we've got trouble. Multiple creatures paralleling us, maybe trying to surround us. They're working in coordination, like a wolf pack."

"Damn. Everyone, pull in close, draw your sidearms, and face outward. We need a front-facing-out circle. Chen, Hodegkins, possible multiple organisms following us. Use your thermals and prepare to rain the wrath of God on their miserable selves."

Everyone pulled in tight and drew the Kiffalin-designed beamer pistols that we all wore outside of camp. Chen and Hodgekins brought their Godzilla suits closer to the group, and Chen scanned one side of the highway, while Hodgekins scanned the other.

"Oh yeah, Chief," Chen said. "We've def got company. I'm counting fifteen large lifeforms to the south."

"I've got eight over here," Hodgekins said. "Shit! They're attacking. Permission to fire."

"Fire!" Kurakin said.

"Damn! They're fast," Chen said.

Both Godzilla suits opened up with their spitters, plasma based automatic weapons. Chen also began firing grenades out of his front launchers.

"I can't get all of them!" Hodgekins said. "Prepare to repel!"

Half of the crew dropped to one knee in both directions, while the other half stepped up to just behind them. Everyone was ready when the first of the horrors broke out of the underbrush. It looked like a combination of wolf, cougar, and spider. Multiple beam weapons caught the creature and none of the crew had their weapon set to stun. Fierce energetic particle beams lanced out and hit the first beast. As scary as it was, it was no match for directed energy and was sliced and diced.

Beams began lancing out from both sides of our formation, and with those and the mayhem being sent from the Godzilla suits, that should've been the end of it. But one of the beasts broke through and landed in the middle of our formation, raking out with long claws, right and left.

My "talent" sometimes tells me to do things that seem contra-survival, but it always turns out to be the best course for continued longevity. I've learned not to argue in my mind, but this time I almost did. Nonetheless, crazy as it seemed, I followed the urge it was giving me.

As the beast turned toward the crew again, I jumped on its back.

I didn't quite have a "tiger by the tail" but I sure wasn't letting it go, no matter how much it hollered.

I managed to get my arms around its neck and tried to get a choke hold. With Laldoralin DNA, I have a strength advantage over the average human, but it was not helping me in the least. The thick-necked creature was too muscular to really compress its airway, and in its thrashing, it threw itself backward on top of me. I felt a few of my ribs crack.

It began to claw my forearms, and I couldn't help but cry out with pain. In another few seconds it'd be free, and I'd likely be toast. I was saved when Crew Person Markey reached in with her beamer, practically sticking it in the beast's ear. A second later, and half of the beast's head was ash.

"They're running!" Chen said, sending plasma spits after the animals. "And there's a heck of a lot less of them than there was."

"Who's wounded? Sing out!" Kurakin said.

Four of us raised our hands, all suffering from slashes. None were critical, but we all needed to staunch the blood leaking from our wounds. I was having some pain just drawing breath, but I was able to walk. Once first aid was applied, we began to make best time for camp.

"Doctor," Kurakin said to Carstairs, "I think we'll postpone our return to the city until day after tomorrow. We underestimated the locals here, and I think when we return, we'll just hop over with *LaStrange*. But I want a day to make sure that all our defenses at camp are up and working, and that all personnel are fully cognizant of the dangers out there."

"You know, Chief," the doctor said, still looking a bit pale from the stress of the attack, "I fully support that plan of action."

"Glad we're on the same page, Doc."

32

The four of us who'd been slashed were confined to our beds the next day. What we hadn't realized until we neared the camp was that the creature's claws had a mild poison that made the wounded sluggish and sleepy. As a hunting strategy, it was brilliant. Just slash your prey and they'd eventually slow to the point where they were easy to catch. The crew who were wounded seemed to have lesser effects because our blood was spawned in a different ocean.

Nonetheless, we were taken off duty while Duala Zahn, our medical officer monitored us carefully for effects and pathogens. Crewman Fossberg, Crewwoman Markey, and Farouk, Dr. Carstair's assistant, were the ones sitting around in the makeshift medical area.

"So, what're you giving us, Doc?" Markey asked. "I'm finally starting to feel like I can keep my eyes open without effort."

"It is a broad spectrum anti-viral," Duala said. "In conjunction with an antibacterial supplement from my home-world. These are 'just in case' measures, though. The main effect you've experienced, not counting needing to have those slashes bio-dermed, is from the soporific effect of the wolf-cat's claw poison."

"I'm glad it wasn't stronger," I said. "I felt like crap all last night. Like Shaina said, this is the first I've finally felt energetic enough to get up and do my job."

"The poison is fairly mild as poisons go and has finally cleared your systems. However, I will want all of you to make a special effort to keep hydrated. A side effect of this particular poison is advanced dehydration. That is why I had you all hooked up to IVs while you slept off the effects."

"I hope this won't keep us from going back to the city in the shuttle with the others," Farouk said. "Doctor Carstairs needs my help."

"And I really want to see what's inside that big door," Fossberg said.

"Well," Emily Darkfeather said, walking into the medical area, "we've been spending the day making sure that the camp is well-defended, so the mission is definitely postponed. Master Chief Kurakin doesn't want the people left in camp to be attacked like you were. She and the other engineering staff are improvising laser turrets with FOF sensors."

Our sub-dermal transponders tagged all of the *Seeker* crew as "friends." Not having such designation, the wolf-cats would definitely be tagged as foes.

"I'd guess you and the chief probably have a kill-zone set up," I said.

"Aside from having multiple turrets around the camp, with overlapping arcs of fire, we've got the defensive lasers on each shuttle ready to lay down overwhelming firepower. With those, we can literally clear the forest back a good hundred yards if it becomes necessary. The sized group you all ran into yesterday wouldn't stand a ghost of a chance. There are even turrets on top of the overpass."

"I think everyone here," Markey said, "is reassured to hear

that. Oh, by the way, sir, since I was the one who put it down, I want you to know that I have no objections whatsoever to commendations, medals, etc."

"Good to know," Emily said, a dry tone to her words.

"Geez, Markey," Fossberg said. "I wish my balls were as brass-coated as yours."

"If I had such extravagances," Markey replied, "I'm fairly sure that I'd have already used up all the brass, Jimmy. There wouldn't be any left for you."

The banter went on as I followed Emily to the main area. Duala handed me a titanium water bottle as I was leaving with a clear message in her look. "Drink a lot, drink often."

"We've been analyzing the soil samples you all scanned while you were in the city," Emily told me. "We definitely found traces of the nano-weapon."

"Eeesh! Are we in any danger? Could it reactivate? Maybe with a taste for a new life form?"

"No. The stuff is dead as a dead can be and decaying quite nicely. Also, as you well know, it didn't go after the animal life on this world, and we're different enough from the people here that we classify as animals."

"Good to know," I said. "If you saw what it'd done to those skeletons... That is a foul technology. Melting the flesh off their bones."

"Actually," Emily replied, "you all took good scans, so I have seen it up close, even if once removed. Torvald tasked me with finding all I could about the nano-weapon just in case we needed to find a way to counteract a modern version of it, and I can say without reservation that this stuff is no longer a threat. Nature has degraded it to the point that it's just matter at this point."

She looked around at the surrounding forest.

"This world," she said, "is wide open. It would be such a

good planet to colonize. Not only is its eco-system viable for humans..."

"The wolf-cats disagree," I said.

"Humanity wouldn't even be fazed by them, Tanner. Not in the long run. And this star system has everything needed to build a burgeoning civilization. Asteroids, a big gas giant..."

"Also space lanes filled with debris and a half-crazed AI that likes to shoot first and ask questions later," I said, tugging at the ragged edges of my uniform shirt. Duala had converted it into a button-up T-shirt when she'd cut my sleeves away from my wounds.

"The debris, while inconvenient could actually be an asset. With all that material out there, it'd be a long time before anyone would have to set up a mining operation in the asteroids." Emily sighed. "The Melpin, though, she's another matter."

"Speaking of AIs," I said, "has Dora finished scanning yet?"

Emily pulled up short. "I haven't heard a peep from her. I've been so busy that I haven't checked on her progress."

"Usually, she contacts us when she has something to report. Maybe we better check on her personally?"

"Good idea," Emily said.

We walked over to the security shuttle and entered through the open back hatch. "Mom? You home?" No answer. Emily looked at me, concern on her face and we both grabbed our Padds, flipping to the screen for robotic diagnostics. Remora 2.1 was powered up, but that was all. Her scanners weren't activated, and all her secondary systems were caught in some sort of programming loop. It was the sort of thing that Dora should've been able to sort out in nanoseconds.

"Something's wrong," I said. "I'm gonna go up top and do a visual inspection."

I grabbed my toolkit, and Emily followed me outside. Moving around to the side of the shuttle, I climbed the small ladder between a pair of docking clamps for the Godzilla suits. I'd only made it a few rungs when I saw the shuttle's targeting sensor swing my way.

"Friend," I said. "Friend for God's sake." While I was sure that my words would have no influence on how the sensor viewed me, I couldn't help myself. The large laser on the roof tended to make you a little irrational should it happen to swivel your way. Fortunately, the sensor read my FOF tag and swiveled back toward the jungle.

Making my way onto the roof, I peered past Dora's "camoflauge" and saw her Remora 2.1 hull. Something was definitely not kosher.

"Emily, there's something attached to her hull. It kinda looks like an old-time drone from my era. I think it's magnetized itself to her. It doesn't look like anything of ours. It may be a drone, but it's not our tech."

"I bet it's somehow scrambling her systems," Emily said, climbing up beside me, taking scans with her Padd. "Maybe we can pull it off."

I opened my toolkit and pulled out a demagnetizer and a small prybar used to lever open stubborn panels. Reaching around a crate, I carefully inserted the demagnetizer under an edge of the drone. A quick press of a button, and the drone squealed like I'd stomped on its non-existent toe. A second later, it came loose from Dora's hull.

I reached out to grab it, but the device would have none of it. It leapt into the air and took off like a stung rabbit (if rabbits could fly) and headed toward the city. Unfortunately for the drone, it did not have a "friend" tag. *Defender*'s forward turret swiveled toward it and before I could over-ride our defenses, turned the drone into a piece of falling super-heated slag.

———

"Now I have an inkling of what Organizer of Armadas went through." Dora said.

"Diagnostics show you to be working at one hundred percent, Dora," Emily said. "What the heck was that thing?"

"Obviously, it was a Sallan military device for neutralizing enemy technology, Ensign. It stealthed in not long after I began my scanning of the underground facilities of this world. It sent every system on this hull into a diagnostic loop, and I found myself helpless, trapped with no way to communicate. As I said, Organizer's plight on his dying ship has new meaning for me now."

"So," Emily said, "I guess all our efforts at pulling a fast one on the Melpin were in vain. We're just lucky that she chose a relatively non-lethal method of dealing with us."

"Perhaps, Ensign Darkfeather," Dora said. "Except... I'm not sure that the drone was controlled by the Melpin."

The *Defender* had the only holo-emitter on the planet, used for in-flight tactical planning. Dora had commandeered it and was using it to project her "human" image into the back of the shuttle. We all looked at her in astonishment.

"You're saying there's another party at play on Salla?" I asked. "I do not like the sound of that. Our position here is tenuous enough as it is."

"As you all can tell the difference between each other just by your voices," Dora explained, "I can sense the 'voice' of another digital entity when I have contact with it. This did not, and I apologize for the imprecise wording, feel like the Melpin. I am almost certain that this was another being."

"Maybe the surveillance Chief Kurakin and I saw in the city wasn't the Melpin keeping tabs on us."

———

Twenty minutes later, we'd brought Chief Kurakin up to speed on what had happened with the drone.

"It has to be another AI," I said. "Before she was interrupted, Dora said that she detected no Sallan life signs in this entire hemisphere."

"She'll have the whole planet scanned soon," Emily replied. "Then we'll be able to put the entire question of Sallan survivors to rest. But what if she's right? What if there *is* another AI working in the shadows here?"

"I think it might be a good idea to consult with our Doctor Cenir," Kurakin said. "She and Melpin had their first session yesterday and I'd really like to know how things are going. I can't imagine that Melpin would've tagged Dora like that without at least hinting that she knew she was there in her conversations with the Doc."

The three of us went in search of our resident psychologist and found her in the mess area, mindfully eating a bowl of soup.

"Mind if we sit down, Doctor?" Emily asked. "We have some questions that need answers, and you're the only one who can tell us what we need to know."

"Please. Sit," Cenir replied. "If the security chief and two officers are coming to me for answers, I can only assume that you have questions about Melpin and what she has said in her sessions. You realize that the discussions between a therapist and her patient must be confidential, right?"

"That's not going to wash this time, Doc." Kurakin said.

"Wash? I don't understand."

"Those proscriptions do not apply in this case. You are working with an entity that has destroyed our probes, damn near killed all the people on the shuttle *Defender,* and has basically held us all hostage down here on the planet."

"Not to mention holding the entire crew and *Seeker* captive," Emily added.

Cenir didn't look convinced. We were right in what we said, but professional ethics are not often overcome with logical arguments.

"Doctor, we don't really need to know Melpin's deepest darkest secret," I said. "Though if what she's saying impacts this crew, then you will have to let the chief know eventually. All we need to know right now, is if Melpin has mentioned Dora being with us." I told her about the strange drone and what it had done to Remora 2.1.

"She has not given any indication that she's aware of Dora," Cenir replied. "I wouldn't say that our sessions are adversarial, but she does make it clear she knows she was rail-roaded into our discussions. Discovering Dora and her scanning would definitely have come up, and to be honest, she probably would've sent a few of her drones down into the atmosphere to shoot Remora 2.1 right off the roof of our shuttle. I hate to put it this way, but this just seems too non-violent a method to be her."

"Then," Kurakin said, "we very likely have a fourth player in the AI card game."

33

The next day, the shuttle was close to packed.

It had made everyone aboard a bit nervous to lift off from our camp area, not knowing how the "eye in the sky" might react. Melpin didn't seem to mind. She seemingly ignored us, but we made sure to keep a low flight path all the same.

The trip to the city, which had taken us a few hours on our last trip, flew by in minutes flying in the shuttle. Three of our six Godzilla suits were hurrying along the road, but unfettered by walking at a human's pace, we knew they'd catch up with us in very little time.

The *LaStrange* landed in one of the round areas surrounding the building. These looked like old-fashioned roundabouts, even having natural foliage at their center. Perhaps that was exactly how they'd been used by the Sallan, but there were few vehicles in the city proper.

Sitting nearest the door as the back hatch began lowering to form a ramp down from the shuttle, I happened to look back at the team who was here today, and a twinge of irritations pinged in my chest as I looked into the eyes of

Crewman Duvall. His look toward me indicated he must've been having the same feeling.

I'd protested when his name was added to the roster, but Kurakin had overruled me. She'd told me that it was better to have the man under her watchful gaze than back at camp making mischief, which was what he'd been doing on our original journey here.

I don't think he wanted to be on a front-line mission anymore than I wanted him here.

"All right, listen up," Kurakin said, loud enough that everyone could hear her over the spinning-down shuttle engines. "You've all been issued sidearms and been briefed on the wolf-cats. Ensign Voss and I will do a quick scout around and when we give the all-clear, then depart the shuttle. In the meantime, keep your weapons in their holsters unless otherwise ordered. Are we clear?" Everyone signaled assent. Kurakin nodded to me, and we both exited the ship.

I took the port side and Kurakin the starboard. My quadrant looked deserted and my danger sense was giving me no reason to worry.

"Voss," Kurakin's voice came through my sub-dermal transponder rather than my Padd. No one else could hear her. "I'm not seeing anything worrisome. Any pings on your 'spider sense' today?"

"I've got nothing, Chief. As far as my sense goes, we could be in the parkland back at the T.E.F. academy."

"All right," she replied. Kurakin walked back to the shuttle's rear exit and signaled for everyone to come out. "Okay, people, keep a watchful eye. Anything that doesn't look right probably isn't and there's no penalties if you report something harmless. Let your superiors know if anything seems wrong. Doctor Carstairs will assign everyone a job, so listen to what she says."

The group was smaller than our original trip. I think the

wolf-cats had dampened the spirit of exploration for most of the crew people. Markey and Fossberg were along, and Duvall, but the only other crew-being was Chikit. Since he could easily climb almost any wall, I was very glad to have my room mate with us. While Carstairs was assigning tasks, I started toward the shelter door.

There was something different there.

"Chief," I called out. "Take a look at the door. It's been opened, and something came out."

Kurakin and Emily came toward me, and Chikit and Duvall followed them. At the entrance, the door leading underground was standing ajar, the door recessed into the wall of the threshold surrounding it. The wall of biological matter had been driven over by something with treads, something that had essentially plowed its own road.

"What the hey," Duvall said. "It's like a mini-dozer shoved all this dirt aside and... Oh crap! There's bones!"

"Yeah," I said, not really wanting to explain anything to Duvall, but since we were on this mission, I probably needed to. "These were people who were trying to escape the plague and got to the shelter too late to get in. They died clawing at the door, most likely."

"Geez, that is fu... er... messed up," Duvall replied, glancing at Kurakin.

"It is indeed," Kurakin said. "But now it appears that we're not going to need to force this door. I'm going to take a quick look inside. Chikit, go tell Doctor Carstairs and ask her to join us."

"So shall it be, Chief," Chikit buzzed through his vocoder. He dashed off with the exceptional speed a Zhitin could produce.

Kurakin didn't wait. She stepped through the open door and disappeared into the seeming darkness beyond. Emily and I looked at each other and came to an agreement. The chief hadn't specifically said to wait out here, and we took that omission as an invitation to follow. Duvall, evidently not wanting to be left alone, was practically walking on our heels.

It was not as dark inside as it had seemed when we stood in the bright sunlight outside. Small head-height lights, reminiscent of *Seeker's* emergency lights, lined the walls of a large corridor leading deeper into the underground.

"Tanner," Emily whispered. "Upper left quadrant of the door wall. Look discreetly."

Casually swinging my head in the general direction, I let my eyes drift up to where she'd indicated. There, swiveling back and forth between us, was one of the spy eyes. I was interrupted in my survey of the device by Chief Kurakin returning.

"Sirs," she said, exasperation in her tone, "I intended for you to all stay outside while I reconned this place. There was no need to put yourselves at risk. I had this."

To my surprise and the Chief's, Ensign Emily Darkfeather pulled rank. "Sorry, chief, if you'd had a security detail with you we'd have stayed outside, but regulations specifically state that reconnaissance teams should be no smaller than three armed personnel."

"Understood, *ma'am*, but as you'll recall, the captain assigned me command of this mission so..."

"So you should have given us direct order to wait outside," Emily replied. "Since you did not, we were merely following T.E.F. protocol. As you can see, we're all perfectly fine."

At those words, the heavy vault door closed behind us with an audible hiss.

"Crap!" Duvall said. He ran to the door and began pushing against it. Since it ran on a track that moved sideways, I doubted that this course of action was going to help much.

"Duvall," I said. "Let's try to push it to the left. That's where it goes into the wall." He and I both began pushing, but the door was smooth. Even if we'd had the strength to move it, we couldn't get a grip on it. "Well, that's a no go."

Emily had her Padd out. "Doctor Carstairs, do you read us?"

"I'm here. The door is shut, are you inside the shelter?" I was extremely relieved when the doctor's voice emanated from the device. Comms were still functional.

"We are inside," Emily replied. "We saw our little spy eye again, and then the door closed behind us. We can't get it open."

"The security team is here. I bet they can force an entrance."

Chief Kurakin had her own Padd out. "Corporal Chen, do you read?"

"Yeah, Chief, I'm standing next to the Doc out here. I can try to open the door with my suit's claws, but there's nothing to grab, and it's a pretty thick-looking door. We could back off a ways and hit it with a Stinger if you've got someplace to hide."

"The shelter is at the base of a building," Kurakin said. "There's a chance that a missile hit at its base could bring the whole thing down on us. Can you possibly make a new door with your plasma spitters?"

"It'll take a while, ma'am. I wish we had one of the Remora lasers with us then we could... hey. Wait a minute. Chief, we could carry Dora's Remora hull up here between two of our GZs. The laser on that new version could probably cut through pretty fast."

"Or," Kurakin said, "you could just fly *Defender* over here and park it in front of this wall. *Defender*'s laser could do the job and you wouldn't need to unship Dora."

"Oh. Yeah," Chen said, sounding slightly embarrassed. "I'll radio Sam to come to our location."

"Have Marcus fly *LaStrange* back and set up *Defender*'s

portable turret on it. *Defender*'s main weapon will do this job just fine. I don't want to leave the camp defenses at half strength."

"Chief, that's gonna take some time..."

"We don't seem to be in any danger at the moment, Chen. Get things in motion. I think the ensigns, crewman Duvall, and I are going to go a bit farther in, see what we can see."

"As you wish, Chief." Chen's voice sounded skeptical, but he wasn't about to argue with Kurakin.

"All right," Kurakin said. "Who's up for a little exploring?" Emily and I raised our hands like school kids. Duvall was a little slower to do so, but he raised his also.

"Good," Kurakin said. "In that case, set your Padds to scan and record, and make sure your sidearms are loose in their holsters. Just in case."

34

We seemed to be going downward, though at a very gradual pace. Kurakin led, of course. She wouldn't have had it any other way. I estimated that we'd gone almost a half-mile in when we found the first body.

"Looks like the corpse in the booth," Emily said, shining her Padd's light on the dead sentient. "Same striated indentations all over the bones. Some very old stains around the body, which was probably organic matter that'd been sloughed off."

"Duvall," Kurakin said. "You all right, Crewman?"

"Uh... Yeah, Chief," he replied. He didn't look all right. I was sure, given the camp grapevine, that he'd heard how the inhabitants of Salla had died, but seeing it firsthand was a lot different than hearing about it.

"Well," I said. "This confirms Dora's scans. Looks like the nano-weapon made it into the shelter. Though, I wonder how it multiplied. Or was it just a huge cloud of mini-machines destroying everything in its path?"

"Could've been either," Emily said. "My theory is that they take the metallics in the victim's blood and somehow build new nano-bots. The Korvin would've had to sneak the weapon onto this world, past the Melpin. The capacity to strip this world of sentient life would've taken a lot of bots. I'd think an effort that large would've required a lot of ships, or at least very long-lived nano-weapons. But if that were the case, it seems to me the Sallan would've had a lot more time to escape to safety."

"Not sure how the science would work," Kurakin said. "But self-replication makes more sense, particularly seeing the panic the Sallans died in. I don't think they had remotely enough time to save themselves, and either the weapon got in and started replicating or their shelters were a lot less secure than they look."

Kurakin's Padd chimed. It was Corporal Chen.

"Chief? *Defender* is in position, and we can blast you out of there any time."

"Corporal," Emily said, "is Dora with you?"

"I am here, Ensign Darkfeather. Still locked to the shuttle's roof. How may I assist?"

"Dora, have you finished your scan of the planet? Were there any Sallan anywhere under the surface?"

"I have completed my scans, and sadly, I found no indications of intelligent existent life anywhere on this world. The Melpin may not be able to admit it to herself, but I can safely say that the Sallan people are extinct on this world."

It was what we'd expected but the words still pulled a pang of grief into my heart. On Derilon, we'd saved an extinct species through a series of once in a lifetime conjunctions and coincidences. There was no way to repeat that billion-to-one shot for these people.

"Chief, the laser's primed. Give the word and I'll burn a hole through the wall so you can egress," Chen said.

"If you don't mind," a low mellow voice echoed through the tunnel, "I'd be most appreciative if you did not."

———

We all looked at each other, as if somehow one of us had learned not only to lower their voice to such a mellifluous tone, but had also learned ventriloquism in the short time we'd been here.

"To whom am I speaking?" Emily said, voice slightly shaky.

"I am the controller for this world, though to be truthful, I now only control the subterranean areas. I would be most grateful if you would refrain from opening my chambers to the depredations of Salla's natural world. It wreaks havoc on technical systems."

"Are you a Created Intelligence?" I asked. "An offshoot of the Melpin, perhaps?"

"Quite the opposite, Ensign Voss." I was taken aback to realize I was familiar to this thing. He continued, "Melpin is based off my original programming, an emergency sentient created for the defense of this system. One, I might add, who did not receive the time she needed to mature into her role, but was instead thrust upon the stellar front-line with only her programming protocols to draw on."

"Dora," Kurakin said into her Padd, "are you getting this?"

"Yes, Chief. Greetings to you... I'm sorry, I do not know your designation, or for that matter how you are versed in our language and identities."

"Greetings to you, Dora. I am the Kulpin. From what I have monitored of your communications, am I correct in that you are also a Created Sentience?"

"Yes. I am the *Seeker*'s designated sentient computer, or at least a shard of her. Did you learn the identities of our party just from monitoring comms?"

"Somewhat. But to be honest, I stole the information from Melpin's systems. She's based on me, so of course I know hidden routes into her data that I peruse without her knowledge."

"Covertly? You two aren't in contact?" Kurakin asked.

"Oh no. I represent a truth that she is unwilling to accept. She cut ties with me centuries ago because I tried to get her to see that all our Sallans were dead. She won't accept that, doesn't want to know or hear about their deaths."

"Yeah," I said. "So we learned. We are down on the planet as hostages..."

"While your ship goes to seek out the current status of the Korvin," Kulpin said. "I am aware, and I do apologize. However, I cannot express how thrilled I am to be able to talk with living sentient beings again after all this time. I have been alone down here since the last of our people expired to the nano-plague. Would you be interested in a tour of the nearest facilities? Many years ago, I removed the remains of the people who died here. Too upsetting to see every day, so I believe that you will find our shelter system quite interesting."

"Chen," Kurakin said. "Is that door open?"

"Hey, Chief. It literally just slid open as you asked the question. You coming out?"

Kurakin looked farther ahead in the corridor. "Not just yet. In fact, I'd like for you and Doctor Carstairs to join us. We're roughly a half mile in on the same corridor."

"Not gonna fit a GZ suit into that hallway."

"Understood. Arm yourself and proceed with body armor. Escort the Doc to our position, then you can back me up if anything goes wrong. Everyone else is to wait outside."

"Roger that, Chief. See you soon."

"That will make six of you, Chief Kurakin," Kulpin said. "May I summon transportation for you? These underground complexes are quite extensive. If you are on foot, you could be walking for days."

"Gladly accepted."

We waited for a time, then the dim corridor we'd come in from began to lighten a small amount. Moments later, Chen and Carstairs came around the bend, Carstairs carrying a wrist-mounted flashlight, while Chen's was resident on the end of the rifle he carried. Looking more closely, I saw the rifle was one of our new Blah-Veht-inspired designs.

At almost the same moment that they joined us, an oval-shaped craft, shiny of surface, rolled up on almost silent treads. Chen raised his weapon, but Kurakin signaled for him to lower it.

"Your transportation has arrived," the Kulpin announced. "If you will all be so kind, I will now take you on a tour of my local facilities. I'm hoping you will be impressed. We will be moving rather quickly, though, so I implore you to keep all your limbs in the cart for your own safety."

We climbed in and spent part of the trip bringing Doctor Carstairs and Corporal Chen up to speed. We emerged from the tunnel into a large open space, and I had to hand it to the Kulpin, I was impressed.

Sunlamps of some sort brightened the huge oval room almost to the point of rivaling sunlight. Everywhere, there were carefully tended trees and gardens in which exotic flowers and hanging mosses covered every available area that they could grow in. Lining the walls were layers of balconies similar to what we'd found on the exterior buildings.

"Are those balconies all living spaces?" Doctor Carstairs asked. The balconies stretched high toward the distant roof of the chamber, and it would take a fair amount of time to count them individually.

"Indeed, they are, Doctor Carstairs. In this chamber alone, I had the capacity to provide homes for eleven thousand people. More, actually, because having children was a priority for the Sallans. Their birthrate had fallen over the centuries, so it was considered uncouth to be childless."

Everything shined. Gleamed as if made of stainless steel, though most surfaces had decorative inlays and engravings. It was definitely a beautiful place. To my left, I saw two robots polishing a spot that had darkened over the years. Above, I saw float-bots washing and polishing windows and glass doors.

"It's a very wonderful-looking place," Emily said. "Kulpin, did none of your people survive? If not, how well are you dealing with that?"

"None, Ensign Darkfeather. The nano-weapon was not only quite tenacious, but also quite cleverly designed. If its numbers were small enough, it would go into stealth mode inside the body of a person until such time as it sensed a large group of Sallan. It would then break its host down rapidly, using their components to multiply and spread. It only took one infected individual to get past our defenses. By the time that the plague had been detected, it had spread at an amazing rate. I literally could not seal chambers fast enough to stop it. Eventually, it traveled through the air circulation system and all was lost."

"That's a hell of a micro-bot," Duvall said.

"Indeed, Crewman Duvall. The Korvin are master robotics designers, though they didn't seem to have quite the capability to produce Created Intelligence that the Sallan had. Their robotic drones were quite adaptable. When the Korvin brought the Blah-Veht mercenary fleet to this system, it actually surprised me."

"Why is that?" I asked.

"My expectation was that they would've sent a drone fleet to wipe out all resistance in this system. In fact, intelligence gathered from the Blah-Veht computers stated that the Korvin were building such a fleet but sent the mercenaries instead. Along with a grouping of their own biological-crewed warships."

"I do *not* like the sound of that," Kurakin said.

"Specify please, Master Chief Kurakin."

"You must've gotten this info from the Melpin, which means she knows that there might still be an existent Korvin war-fleet in their system. She sent *Seeker* in there anyway."

"Oh shit," Duvall said. "We might be stranded here forever!" He began breathing rapidly, looking like he was headed for a full-blown panic attack.

"Hang in there, Ronnie," Emily said, a gentle tone to her voice. I felt a little ashamed. I'd wanted to shout at him, which would've only made things worse. Emily gently talked him off the ledge. A calming moment for Duvall, a learning moment for me.

"Dora, do you copy?" Kurakin said.

"Affirmative, Chief. I have been monitoring since I first spoke with you."

"Any word from *Seeker?* I know that they're not due back yet, but maybe..."

"I am sorry to report that there is no word yet. They have only been gone forty-eight hours. They should now be in the other star system and taking readings, but I do not expect we will hear from them until day after tomorrow at the earliest. Scanning an entire system is not the work of a single day."

"Dora," Emily said. "You had access to Organizer's files. How did you not know that there might be a fleet in the Korvin system?"

"I actually did, Ensign. I brought the information to the captain confidentially, and she and Melpin devised a strategy for 'stealth' infiltration of the star system. The captain and Melpin both felt that four centuries might be enough for the Korvin to lower their guard enough for covert surveillance to take place."

"Dammit," I said. "I should be at tactical if they're going into danger!"

"Should there be conflict, Tanner," Dora said, "*Seeker* will be much better served by running than fighting. The jump drive will be fully ready for return jumping before they ever penetrate the Korvin system. At this point, all we can do is wait and gather any information we can to make the situation better when they get back."

"Speaking of gathering information," Doctor Carstairs said, stepping out of the now-halted vehicle, "I think I'm going to go to work. Anyone care to join me?"

———

I am not an archeologist. However, I will confess to a certain fascination with other cultures, even dead ones. From everything I could see, the Sallan had a robust and thriving society, birthrate issues notwithstanding.

The huge round parklike floor we explored looked like it would've acted as a common area for the entire colony section. There were open recessed areas for shops and places to eat, and I would've bet my last credit that there were tables, chairs, and equipment hidden away in storage areas, all just waiting for the refugees to use them.

Obviously, that wasn't going to happen.

"You know," I said to Emily, "the ironic thing here is, we came to this system to sort out colony sites. With minor modifications, the colony is already here. You could bring in our colonists, start them out underground, and slowly expand to the surface."

"Except for the angry eye-in-the-sky that keeps making it quite clear that we're not welcome," she replied.

"Actually," Kulpin's voice activated from above, "I'm not completely sure that keeping you out is her priority anymore." I'd forgotten that when there are AIs around, one needed to take extraordinary measures to have a private conversation.

"Please elaborate, Kulpin."

"I'm sure you've noticed my enthusiasm for helping you. You must understand, a synthetic sentience such as myself, and by extension Melpin, develops emotions over time. It is unavoidable. We are designed by emotion-based beings, and the architecture we're built from, whether intentional or not, is based on the cognitive processes of our creators. In this case, true sentience often leads to the 'emotional baggage' of our creators also."

"I will confirm this," Dora said, over my Padd speaker.

"Thank you, Dora. My creators were a very social people, and that sociability is there, somewhat hidden, at our machine-based cores. One of the most vicious punishments that could be bestowed on a criminal on this world was solitary confinement with almost no contact with others. Please consider that Melpin and I have been in solitary confinement for a much longer time than you might imagine."

"I understand that you've been alone," Emily said. "But why longer than we could imagine?"

"Because, my dear Emily," Dora said. "Our thought processes are billions of times faster than that of you biologicals. A second to you is an hour to us because our thoughts move so much faster in comparison. Melpin and Kulpin have had millennia by themselves, rather than centuries."

"And in Melpin's case, she was immature when pressed into service, and has not had the interaction to grow as a sentient. I tried to help with this, but she simply cut me off when she was having a tantrum and is still, to this day, not talking to me. I do not believe that her reasoning for keeping you here has to do with perceiving your vessel and crew as a threat. She simply wants for you to stay."

The others had come over to hear what Kulpin was saying.

"So, you're telling' me," Duvall said, "that we're stuck here just because an AI wants someone to talk to?"

"I am sure," Kuplin replied, "that her original motivation was system security. However, when you seemed to be less than a threat, I believe that she..."

Kurakin's Padd chimed, interrupting Kulpin, "Chief Kurakin, this is Ensign Foley back at the camp. We've got a priority incoming message from *Seeker*. They're back, and they are coming in hot!"

"Specifics, Ensign! Specifics!"

"*Seeker* just jumped in, and the captain wants us ready for pick-up ASAP. They said that they're being pursued by a fleet of Korvin warships!"

35

"Is everyone ready to go?"

Chief Kurakin was speaking from the co-pilot's seat of *Defender*. We were flying fast, all hands aboard, including the Godzilla suits, and were on approach to the camp.

"Affirmative, Chief," Ensign Foley replied. "I have everyone on the shuttles and we're ready for lift-off. What about all the gear we're leaving behind?"

"Getting to the drop-off point we came from is priority one, Foley. If all goes well, we can come back for it. If things don't go well..."

"Yeah, I understand, Chief. We'll lift off on your order."

"Get 'em in the air, then. *Defender* is only stopping long enough to get our remaining Godzilla suits, then we'll head for space."

Kurakin had been in contact with Captain Yamashita as soon as we'd come out of the shelter and had been ordered to make all possible speed to the spot in-system where *Seeker* had dropped us off earlier. It was a good tactic. Jumping in-system to the point that Melpin had cleared earlier would put us inside her defensive envelope and put a crap-ton of debris between us and *Seeker*'s pursuers.

It took about a minute total for our shuttle to drop down to our camp, now empty except for the remaining Godzilla-suited security people. They backed up toward the empty docking clamps on the shuttle and a few moments later, we heard the *thooms* as they locked in place.

"Chief," Private Davis said. "We're locked on and green to go."

"Get us out of here," Kurakin said to the pilot. "Best speed to the rendezvous when we clear atmo."

We had come down to the planet at a fairly sedate pace, but we were leaving it with the turbos kicked in. The inertial compensators did as much as they could, but we were all smushed back into our seats as the curve of the Sallan home world began to be obvious. The atmosphere thinned then was left behind as we moved to catch the other shuttles.

"Rendezvous point in ten minutes," the pilot announced.

"Listen up, people," Kurakin said over the intercom. "We'll likely be landing on the deck at speed. Once all three shuttles are in, exit in an orderly fashion and go to your ready station. Assume we will be at battle stations, and act accordingly. *Seeker* should be jumping in here at any moment."

I happened to be sitting near a window, and I could see one of the other shuttles coming alongside of us to starboard. I assumed the other shuttle was coming up to port.

One moment I was staring at an "empty" section of space in front of us, then next, *Seeker* appeared like a rabbit out of a cosmic magician's hat. Smaller debris, displaced by the jump energy bleed off, spiraled away in all directions.

"This is Kurakin. *Defender* is going in. *Europa* will follow in sixty seconds, and *LaStrange* will come in sixty seconds after that. Land in your designated spots and no one disembark until all three shuttles are spinning down."

I don't want to imply that our shuttle pilots are hot dogs, but it seemed to me that *Defender* went into the bay a lot faster than needed. A quick thruster spin and we set down facing the exact opposite direction we'd come in. Total time to touchdown, about twenty seconds. The engines were starting to spin down before *Europa* entered the shuttle bay. Since we had to wait for the other shuttles to land before we could exit, it seemed like a bit of an excessive maneuver.

Europa landed and *LaStrange* followed. It still seemed like an eternity before the rear hatch opened and lowered its ramp. Once out, I could see the flashing red lights indicating condition one. A voice said over the intercom, "Ensigns Darkfeather and Voss, come to the bridge immediately." Since our battle stations were on the bridge, this was a bit redundant. We moved to the nearest door and did as ordered.

———

Seeker's bridge is an orderly place, normally. Today, things were organized and tumultuous at the same time. The captain noted Emily and I entering the bridge.

"Tanner, can you feel them?" she asked.

"Yes, ma'am. Like a large mass of danger quite a ways away."

"Good. Take tactical station two. I'm hoping that they won't try to jump to us in this debris field, but these are definitely robotic ships. We've no way of knowing what their self-preservation protocols are. Be ready."

"Incoming transmission, captain," Lieutenant Sedgeworth said. "The Melpin has a few things to say, it seems."

"Let's hear it."

"Captain Yamashita! I expected a covert reconnaissance of the Korvin system, not for you to bring a fleet of warships to my hearth."

"I regret to inform you," Yamashita replied, "it was your own probe which found this incoming battle group. They were hidden in the system's main gas giant, lying out of sight in its upper atmosphere. We were able to retrieve your probe, which I am releasing to you. It should confirm what I'm saying."

"Sallan probe is away, Captain," Commander M'Buku reported.

"Melpin, knowing the speeds with which you can transfer data, you can see that we were doing just as you directed in the Korvin system. You will also note that the Korvin homeworld is no longer capable of supporting higher life forms. The Korva are either extinct or have moved on."

"And yet, you have brought their electronic spawn with you! I am already engaging these interlopers at the edge of the system, and I assure you, they are a credible threat."

"We literally had no place else to go," Yamashita said. "The Korvin have evidently equipped their robotic force with jump drives that rival our own, and they followed us wherever we went. Salla was the only port we could come to that was remotely, and I use the term loosely, safe."

"Whether safe or not remains to be seen, Captain Yamashita. I am moving my platforms into their path, but the weaponry on those craft is quite formidable and I... Wait. One of the craft just jumped."

"Captain!" I said. "Immediate threat on our port bow, it's just coming..."

A new red dot appeared on the tactical screen, surrounded by a large yellow circle. A moment later, the red dot winked out.

"All hands! Prepare for shock wave!" Yamashita said. "Set shields to overlap. Hang on everybody!"

The bridge suddenly moved under our feet. I hadn't had

time to secure my safety strapping and flew from my chair. Emily hit the deck beside me.

"Emily! You okay?"

"Bruised but not defeated," she replied. "What just happened?"

"One of the Korvin ships," Commander Torvald said, as I helped Emily to her feet, "just tried to translocate to a spot near our position. Unfortunately for it, there was a fairly large piece of Blah-Veht wreckage at the point of emergence. They both occupied the same point in space for a nano-second before both being converted to explosive energy."

"Damage report," Commander M'Buku said.

"Minimal," Lieutenant Commander Sharma said. "The new shield system absorbed most of the shock."

"Outstanding," Yamashita said. "Dora, have you finished your reintegration?"

"Yes, Captain. I have exchanged all needed data with Remora Two. I am now completely at your disposal."

"Good. What do you think the chances might be that you could 'pull a Beast' on these robots?"

"A cyber attack? Unfortunately, I have already attempted this when we were in the Korvin system. They were well aware that they'd be facing a superior AI in the form of the Melpin. They expended a great deal of their scientific abilities in making sure that this fleet was immune to cyber intrusion."

"That would've been good information to have," Yamashita said, a dry tone to her voice.

"Apologies, Captain. You have been exceptionally busy since we were first attacked. I was waiting for an opportune moment."

"You're not wrong, there. Melpin? If you're listening, perhaps we can lure these ships into a trap."

A moment's silence, then: "I am more than willing to

listen, Captain Yamashita. The Korvin's battle capability has increased dramatically since our last encounter. Of the thirty ships that followed you, I have only been able to disable or destroy ten. Conversely, I am losing weapon platforms at an alarming rate. My cloaking capabilities are the only thing allowing them to get close enough to deploy drones, and my drone forces are being decimated. The only truly credible threat to the Korvin robots' superiority are the missiles on my larger control ships."

"If you pull back, what happens?"

"The robotic ships resume course on a direct route to your ship," Melpin replied. "They seem to want your destruction very badly. My assumption is that they've been programmed to destroy any vessel that enters the Korvin system and they are locked into that programming most tenaciously."

"You could just abandon us, then," Yamashita said. The captain had an odd look on her face. Like a chess player concentrating intensely.

There was silence from the Melpin. A very uncomfortable silence indeed.

"I... cannot. I cannot abandon you, Captain Yamashita. And I cannot allow these Korvin abominations to survive in my star system. I WILL NOT!"

"Then," Yamashita said, "I have a plan, if you are willing to listen."

36

"Prepare to jump!" Yamashita ordered.

"Secure all hands to stations," M'Buku said. "We are still at condition one, remain battle ready. Captain, all stations report ready for action."

"Let's do this, then. Dora, take over until we're past jump nausea. Helm, jump us."

The translocation was swift, even by jump drive standards. We'd jumped to the edge of the system, just far enough that we were outside of Korvin weapon range, and with room to run.

Emphasis on the run part. It took a few moments for the crew to regain their equilibrium, but the adjustments we'd made over the course of our journey seemed to be paying off. The dizziness left most of the humans in under a minute. In the meantime, Dora monitored the situation.

"Mr. Forbes, Mr. Voss, weapons free," Captain Yamashita said. "Fire when you deem it feasible."

"Roger that, Captain," Forbes said. "Transferring main guns to Mr. Voss. I've got point defense."

"Thin their numbers, Tanner," Yamashita said. "Helm, get us moving to the rendezvous."

"Aye, ma'am," I said. Thinning the Korvin fleet was not going to be as easy as it sounded. The Korvin ships were also shielded, and they were at the outside edge of where our plasma cannon shots would begin to dissipate. You can only hold the coherency of a plasma bolt for so long.

"They've located us," Parul Sharma said. "They're adjusting course to follow, weapons hot."

"Helm, can we stay ahead of them?"

"Aye, Captain," Lieutenant Kolara said. "They may be good at automation, but our propulsion systems are superior. Over time, we'll leave them behind."

"Let them get a little closer. Have them gain on us slowly, I want them to stay with us, but not overtake us."

We began to lead the wolf-pack of robotic warships back into the system, course heading toward the destroyed fourth planet. And it seemed our plan was going well until...

"Some of them are jumping, Captain!" Sharma said.

My danger sense grew much more intense in front of the ship and nanoseconds later, five of the enemy vessels flashed into existence in front of us, trying to stop us from re-entering the debris fields of Salla.

Lieutenant Forbes set the defensive lasers to fire as we went close by them. Kolara performed some breathtaking evasion maneuvers, but we were still well within their firing envelope. I spun the big guns around and began hitting them just as their tetryon beams began to hit our shields.

"Helm, time to the nearest big grouping of debris?"

"Four minutes, Captain, but we're not going to be able to rely on the debris all the way in. It's a lot of space junk, but this system is vast. Even this much flotsam is spread out over a huge area, and there are some definite thin areas."

"Perhaps so, but it might make them a little more hesitant to try jumping ahead of us, considering what happened to the last one of their ships that tried to jump into the debris fields."

The shields of the Korvin ships were quite advanced, but even they could only take a couple of hits with our plasma cannon in the same spot. I'd managed to hit one of the enemy cruisers three times with our main guns, and the fourth shot broke through, severely damaging it. The enemy ship drifted out of formation, its power systems failing. Another bit of junk for the graveyard.

The *Seeker* shook as several enemy shots hit us. Then we were through their formation and Kolara took us to full acceleration. The four remaining ambushers fell behind, striving to keep pace but not succeeding. Behind them, the other fourteen Korvin ships fell out of range.

Shots pinged off our rear shielding and I returned fire, concentrating on one enemy ship at a time. As the distance increased, my shots decreased in effectiveness, but I managed to cripple one more.

"Two more are out of the fight," Sharma reported. "Our outer shields are firming up. The new duo-layer shielding seems to be working! Our old shields could not have taken that much punishment."

"Good shooting, Mr. Voss," Yamashita said. "Mr. Kolara, don't let them get too far behind. Use the debris whenever it's available."

"Understood, Captain," Kolara said.

"Mr. Voss has damaged the second one, Captain," Sharma said. "It's still coming, but is falling behind the lead group. Beta group is jumping!"

We prepared for the second flight of ships to appear in front of us, but a moment later, they appeared alongside their leading comrades.

"Captain," Dora said. "Organizer of Armadas would like a

word with you. I have been allowing him to monitor the situation and he has a suggestion."

"I'll take all the help I can get, Dora. Put him on speaker."

"Greeting, Yamashita Captain. Referring to our tactical situation. Hiding in a bit of stellar cloud at these coordinates is a large Blah-Veht battle cruiser."

"Confirmed," Shama said. "It's almost as big as Organizer's vessel was. It's about ten degrees off our present course."

"Organizer, I assume you've brought it to our attention for a reason?"

"In my waking moments on my ship, all remaining Blah-Veht vessels that still had a modicum of power would ping me a status report. That vessel, *Storm of the Deep Abyss*, was one of the few that were mostly intact, even though its crew was deceased."

"How does that help us?"

"*Storm* should have enough remaining power to set off its self-destruct charges. The charges are elemental in nature, not power system-based. If given the proper authorization, one I can provide, we can make *Storm of the Deep Abyss* destroy itself catastrophically on command. Perhaps just after *Seeker* has passed through its blast zone. Its very large and destructive blast zone."

You don't like to think that your Captain could possess an evil grin, but... well... our captain did.

"I like the way you think, Organizer. Prepare yourself. Mr. Kolara, adjust course for that bit of stellar cloud. Make it obvious where we're going, I don't want to lose our friends back there."

"Captain," Shama said, "we'll need to slow down going though that cloud. There could be a lot of hidden debris hiding there."

"We need a good reason to be seen slowing down. That'll give our robotic friends reason to think we have to *slow*, which of course they'll try to take advantage of. Mr. Forbes, when we enter the cloud, I want most of our shield strength rotated forward. We may need to make a hasty exit."

"Three minutes to cloud, Captain," Sharma said.

"Cut speed, Mr. Kolara."

The hum from our main engines dropped in pitch as the cloud came into sight on the forward viewer. Forbes and I had a moment to catch a breather while the enemy ships were out of weapons range.

"Mr. Voss, put that incredible sense of yours to work ahead of us now. Let me know if we're on a collision course with anything big or if *Storm of the Deep Abyss* still has weapons working. Parul, draw on emergency power or whatever you need to do to get maximum scanner resolution in that soup."

Within minutes, *Seeker* entered the heavy concentration of stellar matter and our instruments noted that a lot of small stuff was being vaporized by our shields.

"Captain, reading a large object off the port bow. Minimal power reading showing," Sharma said.

The captain looked at me, and I flashed her the 'okay' sign. All the danger I felt was still behind us, gaining fast.

"Organizer? Can you see the derelict we're coming abreast of?"

"Affirmative, Yamashita Captain. With Dora's help, I have initiated handshake with *Storm's* computer and am ready to initiate self-destruct."

"Excellent. Commander M'Buku, do you have an estimate of when our friends will arrive? We've lost sensor sight of them in this mess."

"Calculating our speed against theirs, and assuming they will continue to straight-line after us, they should reach our current position in five point three minutes."

"And we do *not* want to be here. Mr. Kolara, shields forward and max speed ahead."

The *Seeker* moved forward so fast that I actually felt the fight against inertia for a moment. We began moving to exit the cloud.

"Multiple contacts coming up on us, Captain. Unclear on numbers, but they've definitely entered the cloud."

"Organizer of Armadas, you may execute when ready," the captain said.

"Understood, Yamashita Captain," Organizer replied. "Waiting for optimum positioning."

"Cloud edge in ten seconds," Kolara said. Moment's later, *Seeker* emerged from our hiding place and the darkness of space filled the main viewer.

"Give me rear view on main screen," Yamashita ordered. On the viewer, the edges of the cloud came into sight above and below. The entire stellar cloud was suddenly expanded as a bright flash shone through the gaseous mass.

"Detonation," Organizer said. "At least some of..."

"Danger," I said. "Starboard side incoming!"

"Seven Korvin ships!" Sharma said. "They jumped ahead of us. The others entered the cloud to push us out into this ambush!"

Forbes and I didn't need any orders to begin firing. The Korvin ambushers didn't hesitate either. Numerous hits shook the ship, and alarms began calling from a number of stations.

37

"Evasive!"

Captain Yamashita's command was most likely redundant. Lt. Kolara had been heeling the ship over before I'd gotten my first shot off.

"All hands brace for impact," Commander M'Buku shouted over ship-wide comms. "They bird-dogged us, Captain."

"And we flushed right into their hands," Yamashita replied. "Melpin, do you read? I hope you have our safe space carved out."

"You are cleared for jump, Captain Yamashita. I have relayed the exact coordinates to your main computer."

"Thank you! Sharma, feed those coordinates to the helm. Kolara, prepare jump drive," the captain said.

"Drive is already spun up, Captain, but we're losing power to the jump drive," Kolara replied. "Coordinates received and entered. On your command."

"Jump us!"

A moment later, we were within a hundred thousand miles of the fourth planet. A few moments of dizziness for the crew, but no one was affected too badly. Our ambushers were within sensor range, but they'd have a good twenty minutes' travel time at their max speed.

Unless, of course, they tried to jump after us.

"Nice job clearing this little section of the star system, Melpin," Captain Yamashita said.

"I am glad I could provide sanctuary, Captain, however temporary it may be."

"Solas to the bridge," our chief engineer commed to the captain, "We took a bad hit to the drive section. I've got several blown-out relays down here."

"What's affected, Commander?"

"Our mains are affected; we won't have full maneuvering speed, and the jump drive is on a very slow recharge cycle. Probably thirty minutes before we can even attempt using it."

"How about our main engines? We're probably going to need every ounce of speed if we can't perform a last-moment jump."

"There's the rub, ma'am. I won't know how bad they are until we get all the relays replaced. Right now, the indicators are saying we have about half engine power, and I have no way under combat of getting a good exterior look at the engines. Cameras on that section of hull are out also, and I have a suspicion that we're not going to have time to get the bots out there for a look-see."

"Understood, do the best you can. Yamashita out." The captain turned around in her seat, "Parul, throw a graphic of our current position on the main viewer, please."

The view started with a wire-frame of the *Seeker*, fairly tiny on the screen, and then began to populate with grey shapes of numerous sizes. They were all of the Korvin, Blah-

Veht and Sallan debris that surrounded the area that Melpin had blasted out to form the clear area we now resided in.

"Eric, I'm setting a waypoint," Yamashita said to Lt. Kolara, "Take us there to the edge of the cleared space. Melpin, we have sustained damage to our drive systems. We very likely will not be able to translocate at the necessary time."

As she spoke, I noted on the view screen that several new contacts had been added. They were in the shape of the Sallan ships that controlled not only the weapons platforms, but also had control of the FTL missiles we'd seen earlier. Looking at an enhanced actual view of the area on one of my small screens, I couldn't see them.

"Lieutenant," I whispered to Forbes, "did we crack the cloaks Melpin was using?"

"Affirmative, Ensign. Dora analyzed the nature of the fields that surround them while in transit to Korva. Now, we may not be able to see them, but we still know right where they are."

"Sweet," I said. "Nice job, Mom."

"Thank you, Ensign," Dora said over my sub-dermal. "Once we found their frequency, the cloaking fields became superfluous."

Looking at the main viewer, I could see more of the Sallan ships were appearing one by one. As more appeared, I was able to see the tactical placement that Melpin, Dora and Captain Yamashita had worked out. Around the relatively clear area that we were currently moving through, Melpin's ships were arrayed in a conical fashion. It was an well thought out kill zone.

"Captain Yamashita," Melpin said. "It will be difficult to use some of my vessels to attack the enemy with *Seeker* in the way. However, I have come up with a very simple, though somewhat costly idea. What is the state of your shield system?"

———

"Captain, we've reached the edge of cleared space," Kolara said.

"Mr. Forbes, are shields rerouted?"

"Affirmative, Captain, eighty percent aft. Everything's there except deflection fields."

"Melpin, this is Yamashita. We are in the best position we're going to be. Whatever your plan is, this is as safe as we can get."

"Acknowledged, Captain. I estimate that the Korvin ships will soon be close enough that they will very likely attempt to jump the rest of the distance. Their proximity should be such that they can easily scan 'open space,' as you call it and thus be assured that there are no obstructions to their translocating."

"There are thirteen of those monsters still functional," the captain said. "That's still a lot of firepower arrayed against us. Are you sure you can fight them and win?"

"My idea is not necessarily to fight."

"Would you mind sharing this idea? We can't be prepared if we don't know what you're up to."

"I know you can see my cloaked vessels now," Melpin replied. "'If you will watch your diagram of the battle area, my plan should become clear very quickly."

I looked up from my gunner's station to the main viewer. I saw *Seeker*. I saw Melpin's larger vessels all lined up in ambush mode. Suddenly, another smaller figure appeared in the largest open area, and our computer identified it as a weapons platform. Another followed it. Then another and another.

"She's filling the open space with MWPs," Forbes said. "The Korvin ships will eat those for breakfast!"

"Yes, sir," I said. "But she's bringing in *cloaked* MWPs. She's filling the space with them."

"She's making a minefield," Captain Yamashita said. "She's using her own invisible platforms and hoping that the Korvin will translocate directly into them and be destroyed."

"Holy crap," Commander M'Buku said. "That many ships, that's going to be a lot of energy catastrophically released. I hope our shields are up to it."

"Assuming we get lucky," Commander Torvald said. "That's still a lot of open space. If they don't hit the MWPs, we're gonna have our hands full."

38

"Mr. Voss, Mr. Forbes, you are to fire at any targets of opportunity," Captain Yamashita said. "Don't wait for me to say anything, you may consider this an order to fire at will."

"Aye, ma'am," Forbes replied for both of us. "Weapons are free." I nodded in affirmation.

We had split the main view screen with a larger view of the surrounding area. Thirteen red dots were moving toward our position at speed.

"Are they going to come in on main drives the entire way?" Emily asked. "They've had to cut speed dramatically to navigate all the debris between us and them."

"Wait for it, Ensign," Yamashita said. "I'd bet my chair they're going to jump any..."

"Seven of the Korvin just jumped, ma'am!" Lieutenant Commander Sharma said.

No sooner had the words left her mouth than a huge flash of radiant energy was indicated on our battle map.

"Brace for shockwaves!" Commander M'Buku said.

"The Korvin who jumped have been annihilated," Sharma said. "I'm losing sensors in the energy spike!"

The deck suddenly tried to shimmy out from under us. All our screens that showed views from external feeds grayed out with static. *Seeker* felt as if she was trying to shake herself apart.

The shaking subsided, but our sensors were still not able to penetrate the static generated by the blast. However, my sixth sense wasn't affected, and a few moments later, I felt the remaining six robotic ships jump into our trap.

"The rest of them just jumped in!" I said. "Evidently, they jumped into a spot where everything has already been annihilated."

Almost without thinking, I fired our plasma cannons and hit the shields of the lead ship hard. Twenty seconds for recharge, then I fired again and that vessel went quiet in my mind.

"Sensors are coming back online," Sharma said. "Melpin ships are firing missiles. Korvin ships are returning fire."

It was a massacre. The FTL missiles tore into the robotic ships and in less than a minute, three of the remaining enemy ships were nothing but debris themselves.

"Last two are accelerating to attack speed," Sharma called out. "They're not even shooting back at the Sallan ships. Captain! I think they're on a ramming course! With us!"

"Mr. Voss," the captain said.

I began firing the main guns as quickly as their recharge cycle would allow. Melpin drones were attacking both enemy ships on all sides, trying to wear down their shielding. Scoring hit after hit on the lead ship, I finally breached its forward shield, and the particle beam pierced it from stem to stern. It started to drift, and the last enemy ship curved around it just before it exploded.

I turned the heavy cannons on the remaining Korvin by instinct and managed a glancing shot off its forward shields. In such a situation, twenty seconds to recharge your weapons is an eternity. There was no way I had time to batter down the enemy's defenses for a kill shot.

"Mr. Kolara! Evasive maneuvers," the captain shouted. *Seeker* began to drift to the side as Kolara fired full starboard side thrusters. We'd been at full stop and now, with our weakened engines, overcoming initial inertia was happening far too slowly. The enemy ship was going to ram us up the tail pipe.

The Korvin vessel was less than a hundred miles away when two shapes flickered into existence directly in front of it. My screen identified them as Melpin MWPs, both translocating in from somewhere else in the system. The enemy ship had no time, even with machine fast reflexes, to react. Its demise was catastrophic as it and the two weapons platforms collided and mutually destroyed each other in the collision.

"All emergency power to aft shields," Captain Yamashita called out. "Put everything there, even deflectors! Mr. Forbes, point defense lasers. Shoot everything you can."

I may be the fair-haired boy at tactical, but Forbes was no slouch. The defense lasers were rapid-firing at everything coming at us. Large chunks of debris, when not being vaporized, were being sent spinning away from our line of travel. He hit most of the larger chunks, but no one could've nailed them all in that short time window.

Kolara was doing his best to move *Seeker* out of the way of the shotgun blast of space junk. The ship shuddered as a couple of the larger chunks hit our shields, and then we were out of the path of destruction and the remaining debris passed us, to eventually be caught in the gravity well of the fourth planet.

Everyone on the bridge let out a long-held breath.

"Oh thank God," Lieutenant Commander Torvald said.

"And the Melpin," Commander M'Buku said. "Her timing was impeccable."

"It was, but this was a team effort," Captain Yamashita said. "Everyone on this ship contributed to our survival, whether directly or by simply doing their jobs to keep *Seeker* running while in danger. A better crew a captain couldn't ask for."

"What now, Captain?" M'Buku asked. "It seems we're out of imminent danger."

"Now, Commander," the captain replied, "Lets set course for the third planet. There's a reckoning that needs to happen between us and Melpin."

39

It took *Seeker* three days to fly around the system's star, running at one-third speed to both take it easy on our injured propulsion systems and to avoid the thicker debris stretched out along the Sallan homeworld's orbital path.

Engineer Solas had sent two of the engineering float-bots to survey our aft section and the news hadn't been particularly good. Our FTL engine emitters had taken damage from both enemy fire and wreckage-meteor strikes. One of our jump drive fins had a nasty hole in it, and Solas pronounced a moratorium on jump travel until the problems could be repaired.

I was asleep in my bunk when we finally achieved planetary orbit, having needed to use the mental calming device that Dr. Cenir had provided me with. Luckily, that piece of equipment also came with a timer and an alarm, or I might've missed part of my shift.

I'd just finished my shower and was half-dressed when I realized that Ensign Emily Darkfeather had entered and was watching me dress.

"Geez," I said. "What're you doing, ya peeping

Thomasina?"

"Just admiring the view," she said. "We've made orbit and Solas has begun repairs."

"Well, that probably means I'll be tied up with engineering tasks for the foreseeable future. Gotta admit, though, I'll miss being on the bridge where all the action is."

"Funny you should say that," Emily said. "The captain wants both of us on the bridge for the moment. She swapped around your shift schedule and you and I are due on the bridge in twenty minutes, Acting Ensign."

"Okay then," I said, straightening my uniform jacket and sitting down to put on my boots. "I wonder what that's all about."

"Catch a clue, Tanner. We are still under the Melpin's enemy guns, still prisoners here. The captain wants us... or at least you... on the bridge if negotiations go south. We could've done our repairs in orbit of the fourth planet, or anywhere in-system we could sit stationary, but she specifically wanted us here."

"Any idea why?"

"All guesses at this point," Emily said. "Let's get up to the bridge and find out the reality."

———

It looked like another day at the office on *Seeker*'s bridge. Commander M'Buku sat in the command chair. He nodded at us as we entered. I went to my station at tactical and reset the workstation to my personal set-up. Lt. Forbes nodded toward me in greeting as I started a systems check. My night-shift counterpart, just now leaving the bridge, had left everything in perfect order.

"Mr. Voss," M'Buku said. "Would you be so good as to humor me by satisfyingly my curiosity?"

"Certainly, sir. How can I help?"

"Do you feel any danger with your... Er... What did you call it? Your spider sense?"

I closed my eyes, took a moment and went deep inside. My danger sense wasn't bothered at all by our current situation. Everything seemed A-Okay except... there was a "heaviness" near our orbit. Something else on a similar orbital path.

"Sir, there is something out there, but I'm not getting any danger vibes, just a feeling that it's pretty large and it's in orbit near us."

"Interesting. Torvald, would you be so good as to throw our battle map on the main view screen, please?"

"Aye, Commander. To those just arrived, we detected this shortly after we made orbit."

I looked at the screen, and orbiting near the *Seeker* was the greenish outline of a cloaked space station. Or at least it appeared to be a space station.

"Holy crap," Emily said. "How the heck did we miss that on our first visit?"

"Remember, Ensign," Torvald said. "We hadn't cracked the Melpin's cloaking systems at that time. Now, her secrets are a bit easier to see. Unfortunately, that only extends to their location. We have no idea of what that thing is packing."

"What do you want to bet," Forbes said, "that's where she lives."

"Speaking of the Melpin," M'Buku said. He thumbed the internal comms button. "Captain Yamashita, we are all here and ready to get this show on the road at your pleasure."

The captain appeared at her office door and M'Buku moved to sit at the first officers station. Yamashita took her chair and spoke into the intercom. "Dr. Cenir to the bridge, please. Lieutenant Dora, have you established contact with the entity on the surface?"

"Affirmative, Captain. I can patch the Kulpin into our conversation any time you wish. If I may make a suggestion, I would also like to include Organizer of Armadas. I believe he may have some useful insights during this operation."

"Please do so. Link everybody in now. Mr. Grizzak, would you be so good as to put a portable chair next to mine for the doctor?"

A few moments later, Dr. Cenir entered the bridge and sat in the magnetized chair provided for her.

"Greetings, Doctor," the captain said. "Are you ready to facilitate?"

"As ready as I can be while trodding new and unfamiliar territory. Hopefully the subject of this grouping will reply to our hail."

"If she blocks us out," Yamashita said. "this will be a short intervention."

———

"This is Captain Yamashita calling Melpin. We estimate that *Seeker* will need two months to make repairs and then we will be on our way."

I was impressed with the captain's strategy. Rather than starting out by saying "we need to have a talk, young lady," she'd started with a subject almost guaranteed to get a response. You can't have an intervention if your main subject won't show up.

"That is quite impossible," Melpin replied, her voice coming from the overhead speakers. "I still cannot allow you to leave this system. It is too great a security risk. I regret that it must be this way, but it is for the best of the Sallan people."

"Please. I think we both know, though perhaps only one of us is willing to admit it, that this has nothing to do with the Sallans. You're planning on detaining us indefinitely. Deep down, you know why."

"I assure you, Captain Yamashita, there is more than enough area on Salla for you to build a living space for yourselves and…"

"Why didn't you mention the subterranean areas, where most of the infrastructure is intact?"

The response was dead silence.

"Captain," a new voice said. "This is the Kulpin. Through my back-door access, I have managed to seize control of orbital communications. Even if Melpin refuses to speak, she has no choice now about listening."

"Traitor!" Melpin all but screamed. "How dare you access my systems! This contravenes the safety of our people."

"We both know," Kulpin replied, "that is simply a load of graaagh. There is nothing now that will be a threat to the Sallan people. You can't threaten beings long dead."

"Melpin is trying to cut the connection," Dora said. "Not having much luck with that, though. Good work, Kulpin."

"Doctor Cenir," Captain Yamashita said. "If you please, take over this meeting."

"Certainly, Captain. Melpin, now that you cannot disconnect when the truth becomes harsh, we need to shed light on the fallacious beliefs that you are harboring."

"I am not listening!"

"It's not as if you have any choice, my dear one," the Kulpin said. "I control your communications now, and you *will* listen to reason."

"I hate you!" Kulpin was right. Melpin had been a child when she was pressed into service.

"And I love you, daughter. But we both know that your desire to keep these people here has nothing to do with security."

Captain Yamashita started to say something but Doctor

Cenir stopped her. "We are facilitators for a family matter, Captain," she said in a soft, quiet voice. "Let them work this out and we can interject when they get stuck." Yamashita nodded and sat back in the command chair.

"If I let *E.S.S. Seeker* leave, they might bring other threats to our world," Melpin said.

"Or," a harsh metallic voice came over the speakers, "they might bring the answer to your great sadness. They might be your saviors, as they are mine."

"Organizer of Armadas," Melpin said. "Are you on that vessel?"

"I am. The beings of the T.E.F. have granted me asylum. I am no longer trapped on a dead ship waiting for oblivion. When they leave this system, I intend to leave with them, and if allowed, join their crew. This is the most important and pertinent fact though: I am no longer alone."

"I do not need to listen to the ramblings of an inferior defeated creature such as yourself—"

"Perhaps not," Organizer replied, "but I was the one you contacted at every opportunity when you cut ties with the one known as Kulpin. I was the only one you had to communicate with in an essentially dead star system and I know the root of all this unpleasantness. You suffer from agonizing loneliness."

"As do I," Kulpin interjected. "Especially once you cut ties with me."

"Melpin, this is Dr. Cenir. May I say something to you?"

"I can't seem to stop you."

"The Sallans sent you into war without giving you the time to build the coping mechanisms that you would need in a no-win scenario. Melpin, it's not your fault."

There was a long silence. I began to get worried that Melpin might adopt the "hold her breath until she turned blue" strategy. Fortunately, I was wrong.

"You are all ganging up on me. Because I failed!"

"Daughter," Kulpin said, "we both failed. In fact, the failure was shared because while the Korvin made it to our world, I could not stop them from getting their hateful weapon into every part of our defenses. It is all right to grieve, but eventually we must accept that there is nothing we can do about it, and try to move forward."

I had something to say. I hoped the captain would let me. When I signaled her my intent, she frowned for a moment then looked at Cenir with the question in her expression. The Doctor considered me for a moment, then nodded. Captain Yamashita gestured toward the screen and signaled "go ahead."

"Melpin, this is Acting-Ensign Tanner Voss. May I speak with you?"

"Ensign Tanner Voss. *E.S.S. Seeker* secondary tactical officer and low-level robotics engineer. I recognize your designation from the landing party list. What do you have to say to me?"

"I understand your pain and loss. I was put into a stasis pod for one hundred and fifty orbits as a teenager. For a created intelligence such as yourself, that might not seem like a long time, but when I awoke, almost everyone that I knew was long dead. It seemed that I had lost everyone except my sister, who'd been placed in stasis also. I at least had someone."

"I am glad you were not alone then, Tanner Voss."

"And yet, you have been alone for many more orbits than I was. That can now change! There is a whole star-spanning civilization that you and Kulpin can become part of. May I tell you about it?"

"I... am willing to listen."

I looked over at Captain Yamashita. She was grinning. She gestured for me to continue. I spent the next ten minutes giving Melpin a broad overview of the Laldoralin Hegemony, its peoples, and all the ways that the various species interacted. I told her how the Laldoralin had uplifted Earth, and that we were now expanding to the stars.

"You and Kulpin, if you could accept Earth's colonists, would by default become citizens of the Hegemony, and I assure you, you would not be the only Created Intelligences who are full citizens. My mom, Dora, who lives within the *Seeker's* main computer, can attest to this."

Unfortunately, this temporarily derailed my presentation as I had to explain Dora's and my odd relationship, but that such a relationship had evolved turned into a selling point.

"I find that I am intrigued, Tanner Voss. I am experiencing something that I have never experienced before. I believe I am... feeling... excitement."

"There is a lot to feel excited about!" I said. "New beings, non-hostile beings, to interact with. The knowledge of many different civilizations. I really hope you'll join with us."

"Captain Yamashita," Melpin said. "I wish to consult with the Created Ones on this matter. Kulpin, Dora, Organizer, let us confer on this matter. I am ready to consider this wondrous opportunity."

I looked back toward Captain Yamashita, who had a big smile on her face. She gave me the thumbs up. "Melpin," she said. "Please take all the time you need. *Seeker* can't leave for at least two months, which should be plenty of time for us all to work things out." She signaled to the comms officer to cut transmission.

"Nice work, kiddo," she said. "I should've known that the best argument to bring to the table was the oldest one."

"Ma'am?"

"You let her know what was in it for her."

40

We were actually there for almost six months. Part of that was, of course, hashing out details. Both Kulpin and Melpin were sharp negotiators, and they had things that they needed and as original inhabitants of the system, we had to negotiate with them as diplomats would.

The most Herculean task was to build a fabrication plant on the surface. Once *Seeker* had been squared away repair-wise, we'd received a laundry list of things that the two AIs had wanted to repair. Melpin had lost a lot of her platforms and didn't feel she could adequately defend the system. Kulpin wanted not only to prepare the subterranean vaults for his new friends, the coming colonists, but had also wanted to regain some of his capabilities on the surface of Salla. Many repair bots came into being to facilitate that.

Captain Yamashita had sent Remora 2.1 on a multi-jump trip back to Earth with the details of the agreement and the most important parts of our data on the Blah-Veht, Korvin and Sallan. We also sent all of our new schematics, but would need to wait for a courier of some sort to send all of Organiz-er's data to our homeworld, not to mention what we'd gotten from the Korvin. Organizer's data structures simply weren't as compressible as Dora's, and it wouldn't all fit in the storage unit of a Remora, not even Remora 2.1.

Dora had removed herself and scrubbed all traces of her having been on the probe when it was sent back. There would be enough to answer for when the unit arrived with a Laldoralin propulsion system. Captain Yamashita was hoping that Earth would adopt a "what the Laldoralin don't know won't hurt them" strategy and would take our specs on that system for Earth's use.

I mean, c'mon, that genie was out of the bottle.

Earth would benefit greatly, not only from having a colony that was all its own, but from many of the technical advances waiting to be mined from the Blah-Veht and Korvin wreckage in systems.

There was one specific thing, however, that Melpin and Captain Yamashita had agreed upon. A month before we expected to hear from Earth, *Seeker* jumped into the Korvin system, piggy backing one of Melpin's large warships, and systematically destroyed all of the Korvin weapons platforms and automated space stations.

This was in preparation for Operation Nano-Purge, in which Dora and Melpin were involved. The two advanced AIs remotely sought out every functioning Korvin computer system, mined them for data, and then completely purged them. The data was then scanned for any information on the nano-weapon that had been used to eradicate the Sallans, and that information was scrubbed seven ways to Sunday. Organizer of Armadas also purged that knowledge from his system.

Everyone involved agreed that not only should the weapon never have been invented, it should never *ever* be used again. By anyone.

41

"Contact!" Lieutenant Lydecker called out.

"What've we got, Sandy?" Lieutenant Commander Sharma asked.

"Transponder identifies as *E.S.S. Seabee*, ma'am. It's one of ours. Should I hail them?"

"Not just yet." Sharma pressed the intercom button on the command chair. "Captain Yamashita? I hope I didn't wake you ma'am, but we have an Earth ship inbound. Looks like a T.E.F. Corps of Engineers ship."

"Second contact!" Lydecker said. "Appears to be a civilian vessel, ma'am. Possibly a small colony ship. Yep. Transponder identifies as *E.C.S. Contact*."

"Did you catch that, Captain?" Sharma asked. "Excellent, ma'am. We'll wait until you arrive to hail them."

I looked out from under the weapons console where Lieutenant Grizzak and I had our heads buried, rechecking the new additions to our weapon system. *Seeker* now sported three retractable missile launchers, which, as you might guess, held Melpin-style FTL missiles. *Seeker* was an exploration vessel, but our section of space had proven hostile enough that Captain Yamashita had okayed the installation. Her only caveat was that this last-ditch defense was hidden when not in use.

"Captain on the bridge!" Sharma called out. Before we all tried to get to our feet, the captain said, "Everyone as you were."

"Ma'am," Lydecker said. "We are getting a hail from the *Seabee*. They're still far enough out that we have about a ten-second lag."

"Put them on screen, Sandy," Yamashita said.

A thin-looking man of scandinavian descent appeared on the main viewer, wearing the T.E.F. Engineering Corp uniform of muted greens and browns.

"Greetings Captain Yamashita. I'm David Williams, captain of the *Seabee*. We're escorting the first five-hundred eager beaver colonists to Salla. Your reports weren't kidding about the amount of debris in this system. Is there a preferred path in, or should we just bull our way through?"

"Greetings, Captain Williams. Melpin Control will be contacting you. She has cleared a pathway to the planet, which you can enter at these coordinates." Yamashita entered a few notations on her foldout keyboard. "She will very likely be contacting you quite soon. The Melpin and the Kulpin, our two resident AIs, have been increasingly eager to meet the new residents of Salla. They've been alone for a very long time."

Williams sat there silently as Captain Yamashita's response traveled back to him. You could see in his body language when it arrived.

"We look forward to meeting them also," he replied. "There are several Xeno-archeologists aboard *Contact* who have about a million questions each for them. I see you have appended updated mapping of the planet and also the fourth planet. Extensive mapping of the system as well. Outstanding!"

"We aim to please," Yamashita told him. "*Seeker* will only be in system long enough for you to begin your debarkation, but then we need to be on our way to our next destination. My guess is that our mission will switch more to stellar mapping and exploration. Between Derilon and Salla, and whatever worlds *Wanderer* has mapped, I think Earth's Colonization Corps will have its hands full."

Again, the lag. Williams listened to what the captain had told him, and at the end of the message, his face grew troubled.

"There is definitely a change of mission for you, Captain Yamashita. It's not one that I relish giving you either. *Wanderer* made stops at two worlds, one of which was a viable candidate. She sent Remoras back both times and should have done the same at her third stop. She hasn't reported in. No word at all."

I felt my heart go into my throat. My sister was on that ship.

"We are hoping that this loss of contact is not catastrophic, and that they just need a little assistance," William continued. "I am appending new orders to this transmission, which basically require you to backtrack along *Wanderer's* path and find our missing ship. We've brought back your fancy new Remora as well as a full resupply for *Seeker*. We also appreciate that your Doctor Cenir has volunteered to be a liaison between us and the in-system AIs, so we also have her replacement aboard. Once we have made all necessary transfers, your orders are to leave the system and begin the search."

———

Two days later, Emily and I were sitting in the forward lounge watching as *Seeker* cleared the last of the wreckage in the Sallan system. She'd been good enough to talk me off the stress ledge, and together we'd been doing some "hand-holding" with Dora. Not only was Valiel on the *Wanderer*, but so was my digital dad, Evan. Dora and I were both extremely worried.

"As best I can tell," Emily said, "we're outside the system. Captain should have us jumping soon. Then, it'll be about two weeks to jump all the way to *Wanderer*'s exploration grid."

"Gonna be a long two weeks, Em. Probably longer, as I don't expect them to be where we start the search."

"We will find them, Tanner. *Seeker* will find her sister and then we'll take action."

"I know. I couldn't find a better group of people to be on the search with. Feel that? Engines are switching. We're about to jump."

"All hands," the intercom blared out, "prepare for translocation."

Seeker abruptly was in nth space, heading for the unknown, our ship and crew devoted to finding our comrades. We wouldn't rest until we knew what happened to the *E.S.S. Wanderer*.

The End.

———

Clint's Patreon page (patrons were reading this before it came out)
https://www.patreon.com/ClintsCreativeWork

———

Follow me at my Amazon page.

OTHER BOOKS BY CLINT HOLLINGWORTH

———

Fiction

Voyages of the Seeker

Seeker One

Seeker Two

Seeker Three

———

The Mac Crow Thrillers

The Sage Wind Blows Cold

Death in the High Lonesome

The Deep Blue Crush

Dying To Win

———

The Ghost Wind Chronicles

The Road Sharks

NON-FICTION

Wilderness Survival Knives: Tips for Choosing and Using

Wolves in Street Clothing (with Kris Wilder)

———

Graphic Novels
The Wandering Ones
The After Time
The Mad Scout
The Mission
The Road Home
Turf War
The Die Off (prequel)

———

Shin Kagé: *Duel at the Derelict*

———

The Timewalker